# Liberty's RUN 2

## TANKS FOR THE MEMORIES

### Walter G. Esselman

DARK MYTH

www.darkmythpublications.com/

Dark Myth Publications, a division of
The JayZoMon Dark Myth Company, LLC.
21050 Little Beaver Rd, Apple Valley, CA 92308

ISBN: 979-8-9863807-1-1

First Printing August 2022

Dark Myth Publications is a registered trademark of The JayZoMon Dark Myth Company, LLC.

10 9 8 7 6 5 4 3 2 1

# Dedications

Dedicated to Stephanie Bardy, whose love of "Liberty's Run" helped get me here.

And thanks again to all those who've helped make Uncle Danny sound more authentic.  But if I got anything wrong with his Mexican-Spanish, that's all on me.

Also, with all the military stuff.

# Forward

Hey!
Funny story!
…
…
I still don't like 'Forwards'….
~Nuff Said!

# Dramatis kinda Persona

- Liberty "Mija" Schonhauer
- Uncle Danny Ramirez
- Colin Boseman
- Dr. Miles "Tagg" McTaggert
- Tessy Ramirez, Danny's niece
- Brent Smalls, the Navy mechanic assigned to Liberty and Danny's ship.
- Diana Rivera, Danny's *Abuela* (Grandmother)

The USS Theodore Roosevelt (CVN-71):
- Rear Admiral Antony Cirilo
- Captain Deep Singh
- Lieutenant Washington the medic
- Sergeant Victoria Ruiz
- Private Collins
- Private Francis Percival Frankline
- Private Mullins
- Tricia Bath
- Private Locke *Deceased*
- Private Sondes *Deceased*


The Armory:
- Sergeant Wu of the LAPD
- Mrs. Khapor
- Simon, the tattoo artist
- Candace "Grandma" Rollins
- Giselle

- Stephen, the old entertainer

Dyson Science Building:
- Fred,  the unofficial leader of this group
- Renoir, The HairArtiste!
- Dr. Milton, Renoir's girlfriend
- Dr. Hauser
- Ted
- Raj, who arrived in a real suit of armor at Dyson
- Mr. Moyta
- Dakarai, nurse at Dyson of the LAPD

# Liberty's RUN 2

## TANKS FOR THE MEMORIES

## Volume Three - Continued
### *Chapter One*

*"¡QUÉ HORROR!* I can't go on any further," wailed Uncle Danny in utter despair. "You *must* go on without me."

Liberty Schonhauer went over to stand next to her friend.

Between wrought-iron bars, Danny's hand pressed against the front glass of a store, as if he could it open. She gently took his sleeve and pulled his hand away from the storefront.

"We need to keep moving," said Liberty softly, and she pointedly glanced at a zombie that was shambling as fast as it could towards them.

*"¡Neta!* I know," said Uncle Danny, and they resumed walking. "It's just that...what're the odds."

"It's stayed sealed this long," said Liberty soothingly.

They moved around a knot of zombies that wanted to follow. But the zoms could only move at a slow pace.

"*Inside!* Behind that sealed case in the front, I swear I saw a Domaine de la Romanee-Conti," said Uncle Danny. His voice soft, as if he were in church. "If that's out front, one can only imagine what is in back."

"True," said Liberty, who had no idea what he was talking about. But she played along. "One doesn't just keep Domaine de...Whatzits just out in the open."

"Uncle Danny blinked and said kindly. "It's expensive. Like, $19,000 per bottle expensive."

Liberty's eyes went wide. "Yikes! That's a little too rich for my blood."

"Me too," grinned Uncle Danny. "But now, we could give it a try. We would need to invite the Admiral over too. Something like that needs to be shared."

"Are we seriously talking about wine?" asked the third person, Private Frankline with petulant confusion.

Uncle Danny turned his weathered and lined face to the soldier. "¡*Oye!* I'm more than just a pretty face."

"Come on," said Liberty to Danny. "We need to memorize the nearest streets." She pointed forward; her arms covered with Japanese-inspired full-sleeve tattoos. "There. There're our cross streets."

The former Librarian with the dark red beret began to recite the street names out-loud, and Danny joined in.

"We got it," said Liberty as they dodged around more zoms. "Now we can find your wine shop again, once we're back on the Coast."

"Actually, that wine could be really useful for trading," said Uncle Danny seriously.

"Oh, that's true," said Liberty excitedly. "For trading and stuff."

"So...," began Private Frankline. "You guys like coming back to the Coast." His face scrunched up. "Like, even with all these zoms, and now those giant birds-things that want to eat us?"

"¡*Orale!* Those alien-birds have complicated things," admitted Uncle Danny, ignoring the descriptor 'things'.

Liberty gave a thoughtful grunt. "I wouldn't say '*like* coming back'. But, we have a Fleet full of people off the Coast that need medicine, and other supplies."

"They're counting on us," added Uncle Danny soberly.

Liberty continued. "Just like the people at the Armory and the Dyson Science building are counting on us to get them safely off the Coast now.

They were moving on foot towards the Old Armory, where they would meet an Abrams tank, which was towing a school bus, to begin the first rescue.

"And really the Coast is kinda easy to navigate," she added.

Frankline eyed the zoms who wanted to eat them. "You're shitting me?" He quickly added. "Sorry ma'am, but I mean..."

"It's okay," said Liberty kindly. They had gone over this in the mission briefing, but sometimes people needed it explained another way.

As if reading her thoughts, the Private said, in embarrassment. "I tried to pay attention this morning, but it was so early. And without coffee..."

"No worries," assured Liberty, quickly and honestly. "First thing to remember..."

"...Is not to get eaten," butted-in Uncle Danny jokingly.

## Chapter Two

Reflected in the barred window of the wine ship, a large alien-bird with a red tuft leaned forward. Rakduson smelled where Uncle Danny's hand had touched the window. The smell of the one that had shot her, shot the device in the back of her head. Which had produced a pain that had literally been blinding.

Pushing away several curious zoms with her wings, Rakduson kept low and continued after Uncle Danny and the other two humans.

# Chapter Three

Liberty, Uncle Danny, and Frankline dodged around knots of zoms as they got closer to the Old Armory.

"So...," began Frankline, thoughtfully. "When that device in the back of their heads is buzzing...

"Like angry bees," interjected Danny.

"Yeah," nodded the Private. "When that's happening, the alien-birds can only see you if you move too quick. And the zoms are pretty easy..."

"Just don't get boxed in by them," she said quickly.

"Yeah, yeah," replied the Private, and he thought for a moment. "So basically, we walk faster than a zom, but not too fast."

"That appears to be the butter zone," said Liberty. She almost made a joke about giving the Private a gold star, but she didn't know him that well.

"But...doesn't Mr. Danny have an immunity?" asked Frankline. "I mean, maybe I got one."

"Not exactly," injected Uncle Danny. "The virus just works really slowly on me. Luckily our Dr. Tagg managed to stop it pretty much for now."

"Lucky," said Frankline.

Uncle Danny chuckled. "In some ways...but, well, I can't date anyone because..." And he let it die there.

"Okay shit, that sucks," said Frankline sincerely. He almost bumped his fist against the Big Mexican's shoulder but decided against it. Uncle Danny might take it wrong.

To Danny, Liberty said. "At least you're still upright." His face had fallen, so she nudged him. "Hey! You okay?"

Jerked out of his thoughts, Uncle Danny said with some excitement in his voice. "I get to see Tessy soon."

"Yes you do," smiled Liberty. "She'll be so excited to see that you're okay."

The Big Mexican opened his mouth, but then he stopped, worried.

"What?" asked Liberty.

"Maybe...," said Uncle Danny.

"Maybe what?" asked Liberty with concern.

Danny's voice became weary, and his heart began to pound. "Or she might never want to speak to me again, 'cause I abandoned *Mi Mariposa Unicornio*."

The Librarian whipped around as they kept walking and caught him with a stern look.

"You *were* bitten!" insisted Liberty with her You-Cheesed-Off-The-Librarian voice. "You *thought* you were dying! Reasonably so."

"Still, I should've come back, or...something," mumbled Danny.

"And take her where?" asked Liberty.

Uncle Danny opened his mouth, but then closed it again.

"We've gone through scenario after scenario, even before we got our big boat," continued Liberty. "But even if we got that, then we had those damn birds. So, walking was only in case of a serious emergency. And thankfully, there hasn't been one of those."

"True," he admitted.

"If walking is out," asked Frankline. "Why are we doing it?"

"Ah! Walking with children is out," amended Liberty.

Frankline looked around furtively, and then he turned to Uncle Danny.

"Yeah! I gotta agree with that. You can't bring a kid out here in the open," said the Private. "She's right on that."

The Big Mexican chuckled. "Taking her side?"

"I'm taking the side, that I don't want no kid running away from one of those things and getting lost. Run-away...like I did," said Frankline. He looked down at his feet. "'Cause those things are scary close up."

"You're not wrong," admitted Danny with a chuckle.

"Yeah!" nodded Liberty. "And we firmly believe in running away to live another day."

8

"*¡Orale!* First time we ran into those birds....," said Uncle Danny.

"After they killed poor Bordereaux," said Liberty sadly.

"Yeah. We retreated to watch them at a safe distance," said Uncle Danny.

Frankline looked up in surprise and saw that they weren't joking. Nor were they making fun of him. His shoulders lifted, lightened by a burden that he did not know he had been carrying.

Liberty turned back to Uncle Danny and in her You-Cheesed-Off-The-Librarian voice. "And as for Tessy! We only just got a safe place to take her. Not that the medical ship wasn't safe, but our ship is a lot better.

"*¡Orale!*" nodded Uncle Danny. "We were really cramped on the medical ship."

"At least you didn't have to share a room with an 11 year old boy," said Liberty, half-joking. "I had to go to the bathroom to change clothes." Because she had flat-out refused to call a bathroom the 'head', even on a ship.

"Hey! It wasn't easy for me either," replied Uncle Danny in the same jovial tone. "Tagg's alarm goes off at 6 am, and he's doing 200 push-ups and then 200 sit-ups. Only in his shorts. And he mumbles as he counts."

Unconsciously, the Librarian purred. "Really?"

Uncle Danny realized what he said and glowered at her. "Keep your mind on the job young lady!"

Liberty let out a bark of laughter. "Yessss Uncle Danny! So anyhooooooo, getting back to Tessy, we've barely moved into the new boat." She gave a teasing smile. "We haven't even found the corkscrew yet."

The Big Mexican grinned. "Hah! That's true."

"And more importantly," continued Liberty with a gentle voice. "We should now have a safer way to get people off the Coast. I really think this is our best chance to get people out."

"I know. *¡Hijole!* You're right," sighed Danny. "Okay! But I still might be in a little bit of trouble."

Liberty bumped her shoulder against his arm. "It's gonna be alright. I got your back. I just wonder how Colin's going to feel. I mean having a baby sister around."

Uncle Danny's eyes went wide, but then he chuckled. "*¡Neta!* Oh, he's had it Made for a while."

"Um...I don't know about you two," said Frankline with concern. "But isn't that a lot of zoms in front of the Old Armory."

They had just turned a corner and now could see the Old Armory building rising up. They slowed, while moving occasionally to keep away from zoms.

"Um, *that is* a lot more zoms than we had before," muttered Liberty.

"Tank isn't here yet," murmured the Big Mexican.

"No *tank* you," said Frankline.

Liberty snorted and immediately put her hand to her face. "Sorry, I snorted." She glanced in embarrassment at the guys, but they were looking elsewhere. She followed their gaze.

Her eyes scanned over the mob of zoms in front of the Armory. Slowly, her smile faded, and her mind revved up.

The Librarian said thoughtfully. "That *IS* a lot of zoms."

Uncle Danny glanced at her; eyebrows furrowed. "Your voice has 'bad idea' written all over it."

Surprised, Liberty winced. "Really? I was kinda hoping that I was keeping it in."

"Okay.....so what is it?" sighed Uncle Danny heavily.

"You're not going to like it," said Liberty slowly.

"*¡Porque no!*" he nodded. "I assumed. But let's hear it anyway."

Liberty took a moment to get her ducks in a row and then said. "I'm worried that there're too many zoms. I think we need to draw some away."

"*Pollas en vinagre.* That *does* sound like a bad idea," nodded Uncle Danny.

"I know," replied Liberty. "But..."

"Wait?" asked Frankline, worriedly. "What do you mean, 'draw some away?'"

"We need to get some of the zoms out of that crowd," explained Uncle Danny. "Probably by having someone run past them, to get a bunch following."

Frankline's eyes went wide with fear.

"Not it," he blurted out.

"That's okay," said Liberty softly. "I wasn't thinking of you."

"Phew," said Frankline, and his chest deflated a bit. But then he blinked. "Sorry, I mean, I..."

"It's okay," said Liberty gently to the private. "I wouldn't just volunteer another person for possibly

11

dangerous duty."

"*¡No manches! Possibly?*" scoffed Uncle Danny.

"Okay, it's kinda dangerous duty," said Liberty, rolling her eyes with mock annoyance. "But, if it's done right, not *too* dangerous."

"But...I don't know about this," said Uncle Danny.

"The less zoms we have, the easier they'll be to deal with," said Liberty.

"Why don't we just shoot'em?" asked Frankline. "Or...we got the tank. Just, run over them."

"We would burn a lot of fuel, driving back and forth over them," said Uncle Danny.

"An' we definitely don't have that many bullets," added Liberty.

"No, no we don't," murmured Uncle Danny. "And if the tank is running over stuff, the bus has to follow."

Liberty looked at him questioningly.

The Big Mexican continued. "The mechanic was worried that, as the bus is dragged behind and is hindered, even by little things, that that might strain the cables, holding the two together. Like pulling too hard on a rubber band. Sure, the cable is strong, but..." His voice trailed off for a moment until he said. "*¡Mierda!* We do need to draw some off."

Frankline slapped Uncle Danny on the shoulder.

"Well, it's been nice knowing you," said Frankline, half-jokingly.

Danny looked at the Private with a furrowed brow. "I'm

not going."

Liberty handed her sniper rifle to the Big Mexican.

"You take care of her," she said earnestly.

"As if she were my own child," replied Uncle Danny solemnly.

"Wait!" asked Frankline. "She's going?"

Uncle Danny looked at the Private.

"Why do you think that I hated the idea," asked the Big Mexican, without any heat in his voice.

"But…," started Frankline.

"Even before I got this zom virus," said Uncle Danny. "I was not that fast."

"And I know the area," added Liberty.

Danny looked at her seriously. "Don't take any risks *Mija*."

"I won't," promised Liberty kindly. "I'm going to lead some away, and then lose them. No worries."

Uncle Danny grunted. "I worry!"

"Should we tell Captain Singh?" asked Frankline nervously.

"No," said Liberty and Danny in concert. Then they both smiled at each other with good humor. Liberty continued. "He'd just worry too."

"Bad enough that I have to worry," grumbled the Big Mexican.

"Now, stop that!" admonished Liberty. "This is a reasonable risk. *And* that is way too many zoms."

13

"I know," he said. "Just...be careful."

"Yes Uncle Danny," grinned Liberty, and the Big Mexican couldn't help but smile in return.

# Chapter Four

A young woman in blue jeans and big ol 'clodhopper boots stopped near the edge of the zom mob. She cocked a hip and reached down to pick up the bottom of an imaginary skirt to 'show a bit of leg'.

"Hey boys," she said with a sultry, breathy voice. "Anyone care for a bite to eat?" And then she blew them a big kiss.

"Ugnnnh," grunted one of the zoms in a cop's uniform. As they Lurched towards her, she started to lead them away.

"Come on!" cried Liberty. "There's more than enough for everyone!"

More zoms peeled away from the mob.

Since they weren't that fast, Liberty did not have to walk

very fast. But she found it difficult because some would start to stray away. Sometimes, she'd have to walk a little back quickly, to catch a stray's attention. And then she'd return back to the front.

As the Librarian reflected on her situation, a humorous thought came to her, and a bright, shiny grin appeared across her face.

Leading the zoms down a side street, she suddenly took off at a run. There was an inherent danger to doing this—because of those darn birds—but it was a reasonable risk. Unless Uncle Danny saw her do this, then she was dead meat. Ducking slowly around a corner at the end of the alley, she turned out onto the street. As the zombies lost sight of her, they slowed down, and then ground to a halt, moaning sadly.

Back on the street, the Librarian slowed her gait until she stopped before Uncle Danny, bouncing on her toes.

"I'm a sheepdog," she announced with a grin.

"What?" he asked in confusion.

"So, when I was leading the zoms away, there would be stragglers," she explained with breathless mirth. "An' I'd have to run around the main group to get that zom back interested in me again."

"What does...," started Uncle Danny uncertainly.

"Oh yeah!" chuckled Frankline. "A sheepdog usually is behind and gets the strays to rejoin. But she's in front."

"Just like a sheepdog," chuckled Liberty.

"I'll have to take your word for it *Mija*," said Uncle Danny unhappily.

16

Liberty looked at Frankline.

"He must not have seen *Babe*," she suggested.

The Librarian straightened her beret.

"Okay, break's over!" she grinned. "Back to work."

Uncle Danny's stomach clenched, but he trusted her to stay as safe as possible.

After Liberty pulled another batch of zoms away, she herded them further along the street. It didn't make sense to just add one mob to the other mob. When they were far enough away, she saw just what she needed.

Coaxing the mob of zoms to follow her, Liberty went down another alley. In it, there were several abandoned cars packed in tight. She hopped up onto the first one and jumped from car to car as the zoms tried to follow.

At the last car, she jumped a little ways past the front bumper, in case there were any ankle-biters. She blew a kiss to the zoms on the other side of the gridlock and made a gentle pirouette.

One of the alien birds suddenly appeared around the corner.

Liberty froze. This bird had a Magenta tuft and cuts on her face. And she looked really pissed. Or maybe, wondered Liberty, I'm just anthropomorphizing, though if what Danny believes is right, and she had no reason to doubt it, then...

Bursting into view, an alien-bird with an orange tuft could not stop in time. He bumped into Magenta's backside, who snapped at his face. Orange Tuft nearly lost an eye, before he rapidly scrambled back, and bolted away.

However, Magenta Tuft followed in irritation, pecking at Orange's rump.

With that, Liberty moved carefully around the corner. No danger was in sight; just boring ol 'zoms. So, she took off a regular pace to swerve around the knots of zombies.

After a moment, she did glance back and saw that Orange Tuft was now returning with a Green Tufted bird. They both looked determined. And definitely more scared of what was behind them, than what was in front. To her dismay, they were walking in the same direction as her.

"Seriously guys?" grumbled Liberty under her breath. "The City of Angels has lots of places to see. The Chinese Theatre. Universal Studios. You could get a map to the star's homes. That's always fun. Why go this way?"

Apparently uninterested in touristy-type stuff, Green and Orange Tufts patrolled behind her. The devices in their head gave its angry buzz. Focusing ahead, Liberty strained but could not see Uncle Danny yet.

Darn it, she swore inside. She didn't dare call. These things might not be able to see her moving, but they probably will come and investigate a weird noise or talking.

Liberty's stomach was oiling so she took several slow, deep breaths and kept moving around the knots of zoms. Some started to follow, but nothing dangerous. In fact, as she neared the next knot of zoms, she got an idea. The Liberian veered a little closer but stayed just outside their reach.

"Hey cutie!" she whispered huskily to a zom, who was admittedly a bit of a Daddy.

The Daddy zom and a couple other zoms peeled away as

18

she turned her attention forward.

Still, Liberty did not have eyes on Uncle Danny. But a careful glance behind showed that she had acquired over a half dozen admirers, including a girl who was actually kind of cute, despite her zommie appearance.

Oddly, she found that she was having fun and gave a soft swish of her hips. High-School-Liberty would be hard-pressed to recognize her now. And best yet, her lovely admirers were between her and the alien-birds.

Thinking of her admirers made her think of Tagg, and her heart gave a little happy bounce.

"Sorry dear," she whispered to herself. "I couldn't help myself. I was flirting with all these gorgeous zoms today, including this *hot* girl zom. Will you ever forgive me?" She chuckled without any sound. "Hoooooow can I *EVVVVER* make it up to you?"

But step by step, Liberty really did wish that she had not gone so far away. That began to put a damper on her good cheer.

Moving carefully around a knot of zoms, she spotted Danny and Frankline on a roof near the Old Armory. Carefully, she put her arm up to slowly wave at them. But they were looking down the street that she had left by.

Liberty did not dare to do more. Even a gunshot might attract the bird's attention. And those two aliens were probably more scared of that Magenta bird than a Librarian, even an armed Librarian.

The Librarian tried to wave again when Frankline suddenly pointed towards her. Danny whipped around and saw her. She could not see his grin from here, but she

19

knew it was there.

Relief washed over her. She only had to get to their building, and Danny and Frankline could help take care of her stalking birds.

Captain Singh called out over their earpieces, and it sounded like a bullhorn on the quiet street. "This is the tank! We're almost to the Armory. What's your situation?"

In the Poop, thought Liberty.

"*Hiet doe!*" screeched Green Tuft and he nodded his sharp beak in Liberty's direction.

"Frankline? Liberty? Danny?" called out Singh.

The alien-birds sprinted in her direction. They moved so fast. But, they had to get through her zom admirers first.

Liberty ran towards the guys.

The alien-birds muscled their way through her zom admirers, but it did slow them down.

"*Guk fowe,*" ordered Green Tuft, and Orange went wide.

Directly ahead, a knot of zoms loitered directly behind a Honda. Normally, she'd run around them.

Hunching forward, she pulled in her arms and dove in amongst them. Hands grabbed at her, swiping at her head and shoulders. As she reached the car, she hop-slid up onto the trunk. Rolling to the side of the car, she dropped off the side. The car and zoms were now between her the Green tuft. And Orange was somewhere on the other side. She stood slowly and began to walk towards the guys.

Now, she could see Orange, but he had slowed just past the car. Looking around in frustration.

In the distance, Liberty saw Danny and Frankline run out of a building just ahead, but then they stopped when they saw her stalling. They were still kinda far away, but she'd get there soon enough.

Suddenly, the Librarian stilled. Her head was cold. Reaching up, she only found brown hair in a messy bun.

Eyes widening, she began to turn with a white-hot rage. Orange Tuft was still not close, so she looked behind her. Green Tuft had gotten tangled in the zoms by the car.

And there, in one of the zom's hands, was her beret.

Liberty saw red.

Instantly, the Librarian sprinted back. Orange slowed, trying to figure out what was going on. Meanwhile Green was still distracted by zoms that encircled him, hoping that he was edible.

Behind her, Liberty distantly heard Uncle Danny calling out.

But she was waaaay too furious.

Up onto the sidewalk beside the car, she reached the circle of zoms with the alien-bird inside.

Drawing her Glock, she shot two zoms in the back of the head to make some room. As they fell forward, she zeroed in on the zom with her dark red beret.

Green Tuft turned to look at her and began to open his mouth.

With barely a glance, Liberty emptied her clip. She squeezed the trigger so fast, that the bullets nearly came out of the barrel one on top of the other. The alien-bird tilted back with a surprised noise.

21

As the Librarian was firing, she bared down on the zom with her beret. Later, she would remember the zom's eyes growing wide, almost like it was surprised.

Liberty hit the zom in the jaw with the top of the gun, and it staggered back, out of the knot. Grabbing her beret, she tried to run, but the zom held onto it firmly. The move almost yanked her off her feet.

The zoms turned to reach for her. She needed to move away now! Out of the corner of her eye, she saw Orange Tuft bearing down on her. She twisted with her gun, but it clicked empty.

Darn, she swore inside.

"LIBERTY!!" cried a voice.

Uncle Danny appeared on the hood of the Honda. He fired at Orange, who staggered a little but would not stop.

"Get out!" cried Danny as he kept firing.

A zom nearly snagged her arm.

Danny fired again at Orange, and the alien was nearly upon her. The Big Mexican was shouting something.

Liberty's focus returned. Orange's beak opened, but at the last second, she dove aside. The alien whistled right past her and slammed hard, right into the zom. The impact made the creature let go of her beret. Bird and zom crashed to the ground. The alien was not moving. Sliding in a fresh magazine, she fired three times into the back of Orange's head, just to be certain.

Swiftly, she turned to go, and almost collided with two more zoms, who had gotten curious. Awkwardly stumbling aside at first, she quickly regained her footing and launched herself towards Uncle Danny. He was just sitting down on the hood of the car.

"Hurry," she said as she put on her beret.

"You go!" he ordered.

"Not without you," insisted Liberty as she ran over

Uncle Danny hopped down onto the pavement. "Hey, I can't just jump off cars that easily anymore. I'm an old man."

"Bullsh..stuff," grinned Liberty.

They walked quicker than normal towards Frankline. The Private was waiting with his sidearm.

"It's true," insisted Uncle Danny as then went. "You get to be 50, and you're not as limber as before. Getting old, *muy difícil.*"

Suddenly, Frankline ran towards them. He barged between the two, shoved them - almost violently - aside. Stumbling, Liberty was trying to figure out what was happening when she heard shots.

"WHAT THE….," growled Uncle Danny. He found his footing and swiveled around; teeth bared.

There was a thud, and they saw Green Tuft on top of the Private.

"Shit!" cried Liberty. She sprinted over. "Oh No, No, No! I thought I got it!"

But Green Tuft was not moving. She saw it leaking a blue liquid, like blood.

Liberty began to call out to the soldier, but she couldn't remember his name. Why couldn't she remember his name, she thought harshly to herself.

"Frankline?" called out Uncle Danny.

That's his name, thought Liberty. But is he…

Below the bird came a tiny voice, muffled by feathers. "A Little Help!"

Liberty jumped forward and she and Uncle Danny levered the alien off the Private. Getting down on one knee beside Frankline, Liberty looked over the soldier swiftly.

"What do we have?" she asked breathlessly.

"I'm good…I think," replied Frankline.

"Sorry," said Liberty. "I thought I had 'em."

"It was dead bird walking. Really!" replied Frankline with a wan smile. "I'm not even sure I hit it. Just slowed its momentum enough to remind it that it really was dead."

Liberty helped the Private up as Uncle Danny stood guard.

Frankline said quickly. "Oh! I'm sorry that I pushed you two. It was running really fast, an' I didn't have time."

"It's okay," said Uncle Danny. "Good eye."

"Really good eye," added Liberty.

"Just…," started Frankline, who looked a little embarrassed by it all.

"We better move before any feathered reinforcements arrive," said Uncle Danny.

There was a rumble down the street.

"Help has arrived," said Liberty in relief.

Uncle Danny looked at the Private. "Take a moment and

reload." Then he turned to Liberty and growled. "Did you really go back for your hat?"

The Librarian almost reached for her beret but then she managed to stop herself. She took a breath. "I had a moment. That zom grabbed it, and I'm Sorry."

Relaxing a little, Uncle Danny gave a smile. "You just scared me, that's all." He looked at her hat. "That's the one that you got from Mr. Jamie, right?"

"Mr. Jamie?" asked Frankline curiously.

Liberty glanced at the Private. "Mr. Jamie saved me at the start of the outbreak. He's the reason that I survived this long. And when I saw this hat in that zom's hand…"

The tank/bus reached them and came to a stop.

"It's okay *Mija*," said Uncle Danny, and then he waved to the tank. "Really!"

Captain Singh stood up, out of the tank. "You're alive. Even the Private."

"The Private was a big help," insisted Liberty emphatically.

Singh raised an eyebrow and Ruiz, who was near the front of the tank navigating, looked over in surprise.

"He almost became bird food saving us," nodded Uncle Danny.

The Captain looked at the Private. "That true?"

"Um well, a bird-thing was trying to sneak up from behind…," replied Frankline, and then his voice trailed off.

"Good job," said Singh, and then he looked at the Old Armory. "Hey, not as many zoms as I feared."

25

Liberty smiled and suggested with an airy voice. "Maybe they got bored with the siege."

Frankline looked confused.

Uncle Danny whispered to her. "Sure. Keep your badass secrets to yourself, *Mija*."

Looking ahead, Liberty just gave a little smile and whispered back. "If I tell them the beginning, then I might have to tell'em how the plan almost went tits-up."

Chuckling, the Big Mexican nodded. "*¡Neta!* Well, we're all still alive." He smiled again at Frankline.

"Thank God," whispered Liberty with relief.

Dropping next to them, Captain Singh looked from the Old Armory to them.

"I just tried the Old Armory on the Sat Phone again," said Singh. "But still no answer."

"That's not good," said Uncle Danny worriedly.

"Actually! It's probably just that the Sat Phone lost its charge," said Liberty quickly. "We were having to use a thing to charge it, which was dying when I was last there."

"But, what if the zoms got in?" asked Uncle Danny.

"There's really only one entrance and two fire exits," said Liberty soothingly. "And we had those pretty well blocked up. Besides, these zoms would not be standing out there if a door was open."

"True," nodded Danny with relief.

"So, how did you get people into the Armory?" asked Singh.

"Liberty'd repel down the side like Spiderman, strap

them to her, and then haul 'em them back up," explained Uncle Danny.

"Actually, Sergeant Wu helped bring me up," interjected Liberty, sheepishly.

Uncle Danny continued. "Anyhow, that's how she took my niece up." His brow furrowed and he looked at Old Armory.

Liberty patted his arm. "It's going to be okay. Tessy is in really good hands."

"I just can't stop worrying ," admitted Uncle Danny.

"I know," said Liberty and she bumped her shoulder against his arm. "She's going to be happy to see you again."

"You're niece, right?" asked Singh.

"Okay folks," said Liberty with a clap of her hands. "We need to move forward, so that I can talk to the Armory."

The Librarian then noticed Private Collins, who was standing in the doorway of the bus, but did not step out. His eyes were darting about though.

"Um...," started Collins.

But Singh did not hear the soldier behind him. "We'll roll up in front of the Armory and go from there."

Collins' almost stepped out, but then froze. Instead, he called out louder. "Sir? I see a problem."

Singh turned around curiously. "What's wrong?"

"Well sir," said Collins. "The tank with the bus is not that maneuverable."

"Go on," nodded Singh.

"Well, we need to get everyone in the bus, but the door

is on the front right-hand side," said Collins. "The way we're coming in, we'd have that door sticking out, right into the mob of zoms."

"Who would jump right on board," nodded Singh.

"I mean, ideally we'd cut a hole in the roof, but I don't know how to do that," said Collins.

"I could," said Frankline.

Singh looked at the Private. "You could?"

"Yes sir. But...I'd need the right tools," nodded Frankline, but then he frowned. "Not sure where to find those around here."

"So, maybe we table that idea for right now," suggested Liberty. "There's two abandoned pickup trucks right next to the building. Why don't we drive the bus beside those? Oh, but we still need to have the door facing them."

"And we do need to manage our fuel consumption," said Singh, but then he hastily added. "Right now, we're okay, but if we run into problems."

"And what little gas we had left, is with the pickup," nodded Uncle Danny.

"That's okay. We're pressed for room on top of the tank as is, what with my people and the spare cable," said Singh, and the Big Mexican felt a little better. He didn't realize that that had been bothering him too.

"Actually," said Collins, a little loudly. "I was thinking about the windows. If we bust out a window or two, we could bring in people that way."

"Damn good idea," smiled Singh. "Collins, Frankline, Liberty, and Danny, can you make an opening in one of the windows?  You'll have to do it on the move."

"Absolutely," replied Liberty.

"Okay then people," called out Singh.  "We're burning daylight. Let's go."

As Singh got back on the tank, Collins jumped fully back into the safety of the bus as the rest climbed inside.

Collins turned to Frankline.  "Hey?  Can you keep the bus behind the tank?"

"And let you get all the fun," grinned Frankline.

"It was my idea," said Collins, not getting the humor.

Frankline rolled his eyes good-naturedly as he got behind the wheel.

Liberty was already examining the windows on the left side.

"The glass is going to be the easy part," said Collins. "Do you mind?"

"Be my guest," said Liberty gallantly.

Collins grinned.  "I always wanted to do this in school." As the tank lurched forward,  he took out his sidearm.

Uncle Danny said.  "We better hurry.  We don't want any glass in the bed of a pickup, where the kids are going to be."

Without answering, Collins hit the window with the butt of his Sig Sauer.  It cracked but didn't break.

"Oh, come on," growled Collins under his breath.  But the next hit took out the upper window.  He quickly took out the bottom window with one hit.

While he finished knocking out all the glass, Liberty

looked at the other windows.

"Should we knock out more?" she wondered.

"Maybe we should wait and see," replied Uncle Danny thoughtfully.

"Um, we also don't want too many other ways for those bird-things to come in," suggested Collins nervously, and then he added quickly. "Ma'am."

"Very true," agreed Liberty, who wasn't sure how to take being called 'Ma'am'.

Collins—not noticing this—kept talking, pointing to the pieces of metal, smack-dab in the middle of the window. "The problem is these bars in-between. Not everyone's gonna to fit through that."

"I wonder if we can cut it out," mused Liberty. "I know we had some tools at the Old Armory."

"If you can get me that far," said Frankline from the driver's seat. "I can probably get rid of those." He almost called her 'Ma'am' because Collins had, but wisely decided not to.

"Luckily, and I guess it's luckily, most people have slimmed down," mused Uncle Danny.

Singh came over the earpieces. "Okay, the tank has reached the edge of the zoms. Hold on."

Through the degenerated window, they could immediately hear the crunch and squish of the tank's progress.

Liberty's face twisted up.

"I agree *Mija*," said Uncle Danny sympathetically.

"Those poor people," said Liberty softly.

The tank driver, Bath, called out over the earpieces. "I'm maneuvering right next to the building. Just tell me when you want me to stop."

"Copy that," replied Collins, who had his M4 Carbine trained on the window.

The tank slowed as it ground over the mob of zoms.

Uncle Danny was looking upward. "I really wish we hadn't taken out the window until we had stopped."

"The sound?" asked Liberty.

"I like being on foot," said Uncle Danny.

Liberty patted his shoulder kindly.

"Stop. Stop!" called out Collins and the tank/bus came to a halt. Leaning out the empty window, Collins looked for a moment. Then he moved back and turned at Liberty. "See what you think Ma'am."

Liberty—still ignoring the ma'am—looked out the window. They were flush against the first truck. She leaned back to try and put her sniper rifle down, which Uncle Danny took up.

"Thank you," she said to him. With the glass all knocked out, she easily slithered through the upper part of the window. Dropping onto the bed of the pickup, she looked back at Uncle Danny.

"Hey! This was where I first met you," said Liberty, and then she added with cheeky dryness. "Worst day of my life."

To Uncle Danny's surprise, he let out a little bark of laughter. "For me too. *Que horror.*"

31

Liberty was grinning at him when Singh jumped onto the second pickup and climbed over to her.

"This is where you go up, right?" asked the Captain.

"Yep," said Liberty as she looked up. "Last time I repelled down here was to get Uncle Danny's niece. It feels like a hundred years ago now."

"Hey sir?" called out Frankline from inside the open bus window. When the Captain looked at him, the Private continued. "If I can get the right tools, I can take out this metal." He tapped the metal in the middle of the window.

"For big *hombres* like me," added Uncle Danny.

Singh nodded to the Private. "Come on."

Frankline went through the window and dropped next to the Captain when there was an astonished cry from above.

"Liberty!!" cried a voice. "Holy Sh..., I mean Wow! Is that you?"

Looking up, the Librarian saw Sergeant Wu above, and her heart nearly cheered out loud with joyous relief.

"Hey! Sorry to drop by unannounced. We were in the neighborhood and thought we'd just dropped by," she said. "Hope it's alright?"

"Damn right it is!!" cried Wu. "And where've you been? And who's that with you?"

"My name is Captain Singh. I serve aboard the aircraft carrier, the *Theodore Roosevelt*. We're here to help."

"No shit!" exclaimed Wu. "The Fleet is real!"

"It's true!" cried Liberty. "A real honest-to-goodness

aircraft carrier."

"*Mija!*" came Uncle Danny's voice from behind her.

"Oh! And you remember that little girl that I brought up last time," said Liberty.

"Tessy?" smiled Wu. "Yeah. She's doing pretty good, all things considered."

The Big Mexican called out from inside the bus. "What's all things considered?"

Hearing him, Liberty sent the question up.

"Oh!" said Wu. "It just means considering she can't go to school with her friends, or even to the park."

Uncle Danny let out a sigh of relief from behind her. "*Gracias a Dios.*" She looked back quickly to smile.

"Can we come up?" asked Singh.

"Permission to come onboard?" blurted out Frankline.

Singh looked at the Private for a moment, who gave a little wince. But then the Captain smiled and looked up. "Permission to come onboard, Sir?"

"Sure! Sure!" replied Wu enthusiastically. Then he smirked teasingly. "If Liberty hasn't lost her touch."

"Just send down that rope," growled Liberty with mock annoyance. She turned to Uncle Danny. "Come on."

The Big Mexican shook his head and came over to the other side of the window. He just put his wide shoulders against the bottom half of the window.

"Oh no," winced Liberty. "It's going to be a hard fit."

Uncle Danny stepped back. "Maybe if they can remove the metal in the middle. But in the meantime,…"

Liberty quickly nodded. "When I see her, I'll tell her that you came back for her. Better yet, I'll bring her to you myself."

Nervously, Uncle Danny nodded.

"It's going to be okay," smiled Liberty gently.

## Chapter Five

Once they were on the roof, Liberty turned and gave Wu a gigantic bear hug. He was still grinning when she stepped back.

"I can't believe that you're actually here," said Wu excitedly. "Everyone is going to freak, especially Candace."

Mind whirling, Liberty was having trouble placing 'Candace'. It was like a popcorn kernel stuck in her gums.

"Sergeant," said the Captain. "We can take everyone here to safety. There's an empty boat waiting for them."

"I....I didn't even dare hope," said Wu. Tears were brimming in his eyes.

"We tried to call," said Liberty with her You-Cheesed-Off-The-Librarian. "Some of us were worried."

Uncle Danny joined from the bus. "Some of us may

have cried. Manly tears, but still..."

"Oh! Our SAT phone finally died," shrugged Wu, a little apologetically.

Liberty and Uncle Danny grinned to show that they were mostly teasing.

"That's okay," she assured. "I'm just happy that you're in one piece."

"We should be able to bring most everyone with us," said Singh. "Um, how many do you have?"

"26 souls," replied Wu.

Singh's brow furrowed.

Liberty looked at the Captain. "Sergeant Wu's mom was an air traffic controller, so she..."

"It's okay," said Singh as he turned to her. "How many do you think the bus can hold?"

"Actually, not everyone is going," said Wu.

In unison, Liberty and Singh looked back at him in surprise.

Wu replied to the look with mock indignation. "And leave my town unguarded? I'm staying here."

"But....," started Liberty. "Are you sure?"

"I'm not ready to retire from the force yet," nodded Wu. "And until I do, I can help people shelter here. And this will make our food last longer."

"*And*, if this works, maybe we can come back," said Liberty brightly.

"Just get my people to safety," said Wu earnestly. "Then, we'll see."

Once down in the Armory, there was a sudden crush of people, all talking excitedly at once. After a moment, the Captain called them to order and explained that they were from the Fleet.

An older man, Stephen, moaned. "Oh, and I get so seasick."

"Hopefully you'll get used to it quickly," suggested Singh, and then he introduced himself, Frankline, and Liberty.

"We know Liberty!" cried a tattooed man. "Before she made it big in the city. Now she's back to rub elbows with the little people, the hoi polloi."

"Hi Simon," she chuckled with an enthusiastic wave. "And Stop That. I had to keep going or put you all in danger. Long story."

"That's okay, we still love you," said the tattooed man, and he peered at her arms. "You didn't mess up any of my work, did you?"

Liberty smiled and lifted her arms to show that her tattoo sleeves were still seamless.

"Whew," said Simon. "I put a lot of work into those."

"Okay," said the Captain, like a schoolteacher with a rambunctious class. "We'll have more time to talk later on, but right now, we're burning gas." He quickly explained the basics of their plan.

Frankline turned to Singh. "And Sir, I still need to see if they got any tools to cut through the metal in those windows."

"Should. Let me show you what we got," said Wu.

As they left, Singh went deeper into the plan.

"Well, what're we waiting for?" cried one of the men, Ted. "I'm ready to get outta here."

"First, get whatever you need," said Singh. "And check twice! We don't know when we'll get back."

"Hopefully Never!" grinned Simon as the tattooed man ran off.

The majority of the crowd left rapidly, and the Librarian turned to Singh. "In fact, I should check my bedroll. When I had left, I only planned to be gone for the day."

"Everything is right where you left it," said a matronly voice.

Liberty pirouetted to see an older woman.

"Grandma Rollins!" squealed the Librarian. She leapt over to the woman and hugged her so tightly. There was a scent of peppermint from the woman, and to Liberty it smelled like safety and home.

"Careful, careful," moaned the older woman happily. "I break easy."

"Nonsense," said Liberty as she leaned back, but she did not let Grandma Rollins go. "You're one of the toughest people I've ever met."

"Pfft," replied Grandma Rollins. "Well, now that you got me nicely buttered up, let's check your bedroll."

"And then we need to get your stuff too!" said Liberty as she let her go. She needed to check with Uncle Danny, but they could invite the older woman to join their crew on the yacht. "I can help you carry anything."

Grandma Rollins smiled sweetly, almost apologetically.

"Honey, I'm not going to go off, galivanting around the Coast."

Liberty started in surprise and, worriedly, her face fell. "But...,"

"I'm not dying either," said Grandma Rollins quickly. "But Russell and I have discussed this. You know, how we'd talk about 'If the military finally came to rescue us' talk. But, after everyone had fallen asleep, we talked about it For Real."

"You could be safe," murmured Liberty weakly.

"I am safe sweetie," said Grandma Rollins with a warm smile. "And important to boot. Because survivors are going to keep filtering through. And some will have children that need my help."

"About that," said Liberty. "The last person I brought in was a little girl. And I brought her uncle with me."

"*MI TIO?*" cried a little voice from around the corner.

Liberty immediately recognized the girl who ran up. But the little girl saw the Librarian, gave a squeak, and instantly dove behind Grandma Rollins. The older woman smiled.

"Tessy, you remember Liberty, don't you?" she asked gently. "She carried you up."

"The one who isn't afraid of heights," mumbled a small, hidden voice.

The Librarian squatted down and the little girl, Tessy, peered out.

"My name is Liberty Schonhauer," she said. "And I'm here to take you to safety."

39

"Safer than this?" blinked Tessy.

Liberty nodded. "With your Uncle Danny, who misses you so much."

"So...he really did make it?" asked Tessy, and her voice faltered.

"Turns out that your Uncle Danny is different," explained Liberty.

"How different," asked Tessy.

Liberty opened her mouth and then closed it. Finally, she said. "I don't know. Or...really I don't understand. But he's *really* down there right now, and he *really* missed you. We wanted to come sooner, but we didn't have a good place, and then it was too dangerous. *But finally*, we can take you to a big boat, out in the sea."

"No more growling people?" asked Tessy.

Before Liberty could ask, Grandma Rollins stepped a little aside to reveal more of the little girl and explained. "Tessy calls those poor people outside the 'growling people'."

"Oh!" said Liberty with a smile. "Growling people. I like that. And no, the growling people can't swim. At least, all I've ever seen them do is sink. So, out on the water is safe."

With a mischievous grin, the Librarian looked sideways at Grandma Rollins.

"Actually," said Liberty. "It's a yacht. Like a really big yacht."

"Wait, what?" asked Grandma Rollins.

"It even has working showers," said Liberty with a

conspiratory whisper.

Tessy looked up at Grandma Rollins.

"Is she telling the truth?" asked the little girl.

Grandma Rollins sniffed. "She wouldn't dare lie to me. And she's trying to tempt me."

"Is it workin'?" asked Liberty with a sly, hopeful smile.

"A little," admitted Grandma Rollins. "But…."

Liberty's smile dropped but did not go away. With a resigned sigh, she said. "You're needed here."

Grandma Rollins patted Liberty's arm and then squatted next to her. But it took her a while longer. "My old bones. I might need help up."

"No problem," said Liberty in an aside.

To the little girl, Grandma Rollins gave the sweetest smile. "Now, you need to go with Ms. Liberty."

"Aren't you coming?" asked Tessy.

"I need to stay here in case more children come through," said Grandma Rollins.

"So...you can help them, like you helped me?" asked Tessy.

The older woman nodded.

Tessy's little lower lip quivered, but she did not cry. She just nodded.

"There's a boy on our ship too," said Liberty with some forced excitement. "His name is Colin. Maybe the two of you will be friends."

"Maybe," said Tessy uncertainly.

41

Grandma Rollins looked over at Liberty.

"Why don't you see if there's anything you need from your bedroll," suggested the older woman.

"You good?" asked Liberty as she stood.

Without looking up, Grandma Rollins just nodded, but she reached out to pat Liberty's knee.

The Librarian started to step away when she stilled. Turning quickly, she smiled at the little girl.

"Can I tell you a secret?" asked Liberty.

Tessy's eyes grew wide, and she replied with a curious whisper. "What?"

"You have to promise not to let your Uncle Danny know," said Liberty. "This is a tall person's secret. Can you do that?"

Nodding emphatically, Tessy took a step closer.

Liberty crouched down so that she was eye level with the little girl.

"Do you know what time of year it is?" asked the Librarian.

Tessy shook her head. "Um, I think it's after Halloween, but we don't have a calendar here."

"It's almost Thanksgiving, and that means...after that...," led Liberty.

"Christmas!" squealed Tessy.

Liberty put her finger to her lips, and Tessy put her hand over her mouth, but her eyes overflowed with delight.

"Me and your Uncle Danny talked about Christmas," said Liberty. "And I shouldn't share this without his permission, but he was so worried about you—here!—all alone."

Tessy frowned, puzzled.

"Christmas is a time for family," said Liberty. "And your Uncle Danny thought of his wonderful niece, whom he desperately wanted back."

"For Christmas?" whispered Tessy in wonder.

"Having you on the yacht on Christmas morning, would be all the presents that Uncle Danny needs ever," nodded Liberty.

"Really?" asked Tessy with wonder.

Liberty just nodded as she stood again.

Tessy whipped her head towards Grandma Rollins.

"I'm so sorry," said the little girl.

Grandma Rollins looked puzzled. "Whatever for?"

"I need to leave, because I think my Uncle Danny needs me," said Tessy.

"That's quite all right," chuckled Grandma Rollins warmly. "I need to be here…"

"To help other kids, right?" nodded Tessy solemnly.

"Exactly," smiled Grandma Rollins.

Tessy suddenly threw herself to hug the older woman around the neck.

"Whoa," said Grandma Rollins with a chuckle and she started to teeter.

Liberty placed a leg right behind the older woman to brace her. While Grandma Rollins hugged Tessy, she also looked up at the Librarian with a happy smile.

It was a smile that Liberty had missed, and she was so sad that the older woman was not coming too. Everyone needs a Grandma Rollins now and then, she decided.

Once Tessy was good, Liberty went to her bedroll. It was half of a sleeping bag. She remembered when that had been a luxury. Shaking her head, she reminded herself that they needed to go quickly.

Soon, Liberty was back on the roof with the three books that she had saved. Her worldly possessions now condensed to a half-full Dora the Explorer backpack.

"Kids first," suggested Sergeant Wu.

"Definitely," nodded Liberty.

Having worked together for a while, the two fell into a familiar groove. Once lowered down onto the truck bed, Liberty would unharness each kid, and then hand them through the window to Uncle Danny. No one had many belongings. Belongings slowed people down.

In between passing the kids through the window, Frankline was working with some tools to get the whole window open.

Suddenly, the Private let out a big whoop. Liberty turned, just as Frankline tossed the metal from the window into some zoms. She saw something sticking out though.

"There's that one...," started Liberty.

"Way ahead of you," smiled Frankline. He pulled out some duct tape and put it over the very sharp bit. "As safe as I can get it." He tested it by climbing through and then by giving the duct tape a little punch. "All good."

Satisfied, Liberty went back up onto the rooftop. The last child was Tessy, who had insisted that the others went first, just in case. A move that made Liberty like the little girl all the more, though she suspected that there was more to it.

"Here we go again," said Liberty gently. "But now it's down."

Tessy instantly stiffened and gestured for Liberty to get closer.

"You okay?" asked the Librarian, concerned.

"I'm still scared of heights," said Tessy, embarrassed. "Sorry."

"You have nothing to be sorry about," whispered Liberty.

"I mean, I figured that the other kids should go first, just in case," said Tessy. "But now that it's my turn…"

Liberty bent down to look in her eyes. "It's okay to be scared."

"You're not scared," replied Tessy.

Liberty gave a happy little chuckle. "Sure I am. Not of heights, but of a lots of other things. Like making sure I get you safely back to our ship."

"Really?" asked Tessy.

"And I won't stop being, at least a little scared, until I have you onboard," said Liberty.

Tessy straightened. "Oh! We should go then."

Liberty did not want to say that she was also scared that Tessy would be upset with Uncle Danny. She hoped that

that would be okay.

However, she had to concentrate on getting the girl down safely. Guiding Tessy towards the edge, she smiled reassuringly to her.

"First, we need to put a harness around you," began Liberty, and then she explained what they needed to do to keep safe. However, she noticed that Tessy's attention had wandered. She was looking out over the zoms in front of the Old Armory.

"Sometimes," said the girl slowly. "I'd sneak up here, and just look out. Just to see if I could see my uncle again. I know it's stupid..."

"Not stupid," replied Liberty quickly. "It's understandable. But he's down there, right now."

"And he's going to stay there?" asked Tessy, her voice raw.

"He really thought that he was going to die," said Liberty, earnestly. "And then, he would have been a danger to you. He needed to get you somewhere safe before that ..."

"Can we get a move on," grumbled Ted loudly. "I *need* to get away from this God -forsaken place."

Liberty gave him a sharp look, but it was Wu who spoke up.

"You'll get your turn soon enough," said Sergeant Wu with authority.

"Hello?" called out a voice, which had a big heap of worry in it. "Everything okay up there."

Liberty looked over the edge and saw Uncle Danny on

the bed of the pickup.

"Hey!" called out Liberty. "We're coming down."

"Oh...okay," replied Uncle Danny.

While the Sergeant stared Ted down, Liberty turned to the little girl who was now harnessed to her.

"Hold on," said the Librarian.

Tessy nodded nervously.

Carefully, they stepped over the edge as the little girl began to breathe faster. As they descended, Liberty whispered calming words to Tessy. Shortly, they touched down and Uncle Danny was right there.

"Tessy!" he said brightly.

However, the little girl focused on unbuckling herself from the harness. The moment that she was free, she stepped away from everyone and looked up at Liberty.

"You should hurry back up," said Tessy. "We should get going as fast as possible."

"Okay," nodded Liberty. "As long as you both are good."

"I should get in the bus," said Tessy. Her voice was a little stilted.

Uncle Danny looked puzzled, and he was about to move forward, but Liberty touched his forearm. He looked at her.

"Maybe you could lift her into the bus and then spot me," suggested Liberty softly.

The Big Mexican was about to say more, but then he just nodded. "Maybe that would be for the best."

As Liberty went back up, Uncle Danny looked at Tessy.

He took a deep breath and then said. "Let me help you inside."

After passing Tessy through to Collins in the bus, he turned back.

Getting the adults down was quicker, except for Stephen, who had a bit of an anxiety attack. After Sergeant Wu and Grandma Rollins had gotten him past that, Liberty took him down.

But every time she came down with someone, she related to Uncle Danny a little more about her conversations with her. She told him everything, but gently, because of Rule #1, no lying.

Finally, Stephen was down and in the bus.

Liberty looked up at Uncle Danny with concern. "You good?"

Uncle Danny just nodded.

"Okay, I got your back," said Liberty.

"I'd rather walk across town again," chuckled Uncle Danny with very little humor.

"It's going to be okay," assured Liberty.

"Okay *Mija*," nodded Uncle Danny, and he at least attempted a smile.

"Is everyone in?" asked Singh from the tank.

"We're almost ready," called out Liberty and, as Uncle Danny went back into the bus, she swiftly went back up.

The moment she reached the top, Grandma Rollins said. "Go. We'll be fine."

"But...," started Liberty.

"Really, we'll be okay," assured Wu. "As much as I'd like to ride on a tank…"

"It is fun," wheedled Liberty.

"I bet. But *really!* We're going to be okay," said Wu.

Liberty wanted to say more, but she could not find the words. Instead, she jumped forward and hugged them fiercely.

"Thank you," said the Librarian to both of them. "For all your help. For keeping me sane."

"I'm just glad that you're doing well," said Wu.

"He was pretty worried when you left," said Grandma Rollins.

"I know," said the Librarian softly. "I guess I was…"

"Liberty?" came Singh's voice over her earpiece. He was not upset.

"I'm coming," said the Librarian through the earpiece, and then she looked back up.

"Go!" said Wu with mock sternness.

"Don't be a stranger," said Grandma Rollins.

"Okay, but I'll be back," said Liberty earnestly, her mind roiling. She wanted to say more, so much more. She finally blurted. "And I'll bring back good beer."

"Hey! Don't even tease about that," said Wu.

"And not too much," said Grandma Rollins primly.

"Oh please!" said Wu to her. "You like it just as much as I do."

Grandma Rollins sniffed at that, but she was definitely

hiding a smile.

"Liberty!" was all that Singh said.

"Sorry!" she called over her earpiece.

"Shoo! Shoo!" said Grandma Rollins.

Liberty was almost all the down when Wu leaned over the edge.

"Hey! Keep an eye out for some wannabe-military-Gravy-Seals-type dudes," he warned.

"Good guys, or...?"

"Don't know," said Wu. "And, maybe they've moved on, but they asked to come in shortly after you left with the boy."

"What stopped you?" asked Liberty.

"I...Besides all the AR-15s that they were carrying, and the mismatched military gear," started Wu. "They just...I don't know."

"Your Spidey sense went off?" asked Liberty as she reached the bed of the pickup.

"Something like that," shrugged Wu. "So, I asked — well, maybe begged them — for any food, because we were starving."

Liberty chuckled. "That must've made them leave quick?"

"Like their pants were on fire," grinned Wu, but then his smile faded. "Their Boss-man had a trimmed white beard and eyes that made me nervous. Like he was on a mission. So, I couldn't let them in. Not with the kids, and Candace, here."

# Chapter Six

As they left the Armory, Liberty attempted to casually wipe away a tear.

Silently, Uncle Danny bumped his arm against her shoulder companionably and smiled. She tried, but she just couldn't muster one.

"They're going to be okay," he whispered.

"I know," replied Liberty softly. "When all this started. Sergeant Wu had commandeered a big ol' grocery truck. So, they do have enough canned goods to last them for a few more years. At least until the expiration dates started hitting."

The Librarian blinked hard. Wait, had Wu and Grandma Rollins been holding hands when she came back up? They were a little different in age, but still. Her breath hitched. Then she realized that the 'Candace' that Wu had mentioned was Grandma Rollins.

"You're smiling," said Uncle Danny beside her. They stood towards the front of the bus while Collins covered the open window, the barrel of his rifle trained on the hole.

Liberty looked at him, but she didn't want to say that Grandma Rollins was a cougar, not in front of a bus that knew her.

"I'll tell you later," promised Liberty.

Comically, Uncle Danny harrumphed. "You better!" However, the smile slid from his face. He started to glance back but then stopped himself.

"It'll be okay," whispered Liberty.

"I...I just feel bad," said Danny.

Near the back, Tessy was talking animatedly with the other kids from the Old Armory. No one had taken the rear most seats, once they realized that that was a body wrapped in blue tarp.

To distract her friend, Liberty said. "Last time we were going this way, we were on foot. Now! We're moving up in the world."

Despite himself, Uncle Danny smiled a bit. "True. We'll be fat as butter if we're not careful."

"Having too much food to eat," said Liberty wistfully. "That would be kind of wonderful."

That got a bigger smile from him.

"True," agreed Danny.

The tank was making good time towards the Dyson Science building at a sedate pace, but suddenly they began to slow, and then stop.

Liberty and Uncle Danny looked forward, trying to see out the front of the bus and past the big ol' tank.

"What's...?" began Frankline in the bus driver's seat when a voice came over their earpieces.

"Liberty?" asked Singh with quiet calm. "Can you get on top of the bus? We have something odd, and I need eyes up there."

"I can," replied the Librarian quickly. She moved over to the open window as Collins exited the seat beside it.

"Not many zoms," reported Collins, who looked relieved to not be going.

"Thanks. I'll take it slow," replied Liberty and she went to the window.

"I'll hand out your rifle," suggested Uncle Danny. "Just don't fall on your butt."

Climbing out, Liberty used the window as a step and awkwardly climbed up on top of the bus. Turning around —still on her stomach—she took her rifle from Uncle Danny.

"I'm coming up too," he said and handed up his shotgun.

Liberty gave a little smile as she took it. "Just don't fall on your butt."

"I just need to...," started Uncle Danny when he glanced at the back of the bus.

People were still trying to figure out what was going on, but in the back was Tessy. The little girl was standing on her seat with an ashen look and Danny's heart lurched.

"I'm just going to go up onto the roof," he began, but it was too noisy with people speculating. Eyes narrowing, he bellowed. *Disculpe!* I need a moment." Everyone went quiet, mostly out of surprise. However, Uncle Danny was only focused on one person.

"I'm just going to go up to the roof, to make sure that Aunt Liberty is safe," said Uncle Danny. "Just up to the roof."

Tessy's shoulders deflated.

"If you need me," said Uncle Danny. "You call out this window and I'll be right there."

Tessy nodded and said 'okay', but he could not hear it.

"I'll be back," said Uncle Danny, and after a moment Tessy nodded with more assurance.

"Liberty?" called out Singh over the earpieces. "You in place."

"We're almost ready," replied Liberty.

"We?" asked Singh.

Sure, that his niece was okay, the Big Mexican climbed out and up onto the roof. There, he lay down beside Liberty.

"I'll watch low," she said.

Danny nodded. "And I'll watch the friendly skies."

Moving now like a well-oiled machine, they slid to the front of the bus. As Liberty peered forward, Uncle Danny looked everywhere else.

"In place," said Liberty over her earpiece.

Singh was not that far away, but she was reluctant to

make too much noise.

Uncle Danny glanced forward for a second, and then did a double take.

"That wasn't there before," he commented. However, he forced himself to look around and keep an eye out for trouble.

"No, it wasn't," agreed Liberty with thoughtful concern. She looked through her sniper scope.

Out here, she could hear the rifle shots and watched a zombie go down.

Glancing up from her scope, she saw Singh looking through his binoculars.

Over the earpieces, Singh spoke with a calm, meticulous voice. "I got two people so far on some kind of scrap barricade."

"It's like the wall of a castle," added Liberty.

"A broke-ass castle," grumbled the Captain.

As they spoke, more zoms were gunned down.

"That pile of zoms in front is going to be a barrier soon enough," added Uncle Danny as he gave it a quick glance.

"Which brings a danger all in itself," said Singh.

"Oh!" said Liberty, a little excitedly. "That's right. Because all those bodies are going to bring disease. Like when they used to fling corpses over the walls during a medieval siege."

"Maybe it'll be alright," mused Singh. "But I wouldn't want to live next to that many dead bodies."

"Hope they also have an unlimited supply of ammo

too," muttered Ruiz.

Singh called out. "Bath, can you look at this gate they have?"

"Sure thing," said the tank mechanic who poked her head out of the tank. The Captain handed her a pair of binoculars. After a moment, she reported. "Looks like a wall made out of a bunch of sheet metal. Not sure how sturdy."

"The gate?" asked Singh. "Is it big enough to drive through?"

"Looks big enough," said Bath after a moment.

"I wonder if it's worth it," pondered Singh. He felt the vibration of the engine and he knew that every second wasted more gas. He turned and looked back at Liberty.

Without being asked, the Librarian said. "The best route around—that isn't jam-packed with cars—goes through a bad neighborhood, which is jam-packed with zoms."

"Plus, we should see if they need us to take anyone," said Uncle Danny. "Children and people like that."

"Agreed," said Singh. "Do you two want to come with?"

"I will," said Liberty.

"I can, but I need to tell Tessy where I'm going," said Uncle Danny.

"Definitely," agreed Liberty seriously.

Soon, Liberty and Danny walked away from the bus. But the Big Mexican did wave back to Tessy, who was at the front window, watching nervously.

In the Frankline turned to the little girl and appeared to

speak soothingly.

On the street, Liberty said softly. "We're going to be okay."

"I'm more worried about her," said Uncle Danny. He turned to look forward and tried to put his game face on.

"If you want to wait...," offered Liberty gently, as they stopped beside the tank.

Uncle Danny thought about it a moment and then smiled at her. "Thank you."

"For what?" asked the Librarian in confusion.

"For being a good *amiga,*" said Danny. "For letting me stay, if I really needed to."

Liberty grinned. "Of course...wait, *amiga* is 'friend', right?"

"Definitely!" nodded Danny.

"Then I got your back, amiga," grinned Liberty.

Uncle Danny was about to say more, but then he just smiled. "Ditto."

However, he did wave back at Tessy once more.

On the tank, Singh turned to Sergeant Ruiz.

"If something happens, I need you to get out of here. Head straight for the coast if need be," ordered Singh. "Get these people safe."

"Yes sir," replied Ruiz.

"And Bath," said Singh to the tank mechanic. "Keep the motor running."

"Will do," replied Bath, and this time she did salute.

The Captain returned it and then led Liberty and Uncle Danny towards the metal wall. The barrier had been built across the street. It looked haphazard to Liberty, but then her eyes were pulled to the right of the big door. Someone had written on it with fluorescent orange spray paint.

"Careful with the zoms," muttered Uncle Danny as he drew out his cleaver.

"What?" asked Singh as they got closer. There was a ragged line of fallen zoms across the street.

"Think I saw movement from that pile of zoms," said Uncle Danny.

"Ankle-biters," said Singh with distaste. "I hate ankle-biters."

"And, we don't have time to check each one," said Liberty with annoyance.

"I see a little path through," said Uncle Danny. "I'll go first."

"Hello?" called out one of the men from the wall as the other one disappeared.

Singh waved, a little distractedly. "One moment please."

Uncle Danny suddenly brought his cleaver down. There was a horrible cracking noise and the zom was laid to rest. Moving cautiously, they weaved through the line of dead zoms.

It wasn't until they were all the way through that Singh realized that Liberty and Danny had put him in the middle. He wasn't sure if he should be touched, or annoyed. Probably both, he decided. But they had work to do, and he looked up at the guard on the wall.

"Hi! My name is Captain Deep Singh of the United States military. Out of the aircraft carrier, the *Theodore Roosevelt*," he said. "Can I talk to whomever is in charge?"

"There is no carrier," said the first guard, Zeke with a suspicious glance at them and then he looked past them. "Is that a tank?"

"It is," replied Singh.

Liberty's eyes went wide with delight. "Ooooh, the Bill of Rights."

The Librarian went along the wall, to where something was written.

"Liberty?" called out Singh, wondering where she was going.

"She's okay," said Uncle Danny. "She just can't resist the written word." Besides, he already confirmed that she was far enough away from the pile of ex-zoms.

The second guard, Mark, reappeared. "What's up?"

"They say they're from the Carrier," sneered the first guard, Zeke.

"HA!" said Mark, and then he looked down at them, both literally and figuratively. "You don't expect us to believe that."

Singh furrowed his brow. "I live there."

"Sure," said Mark. "Where there aren't any zoms? Can we go to the moon next? There isn't such a place."

Pressing the conversation forward, the Captain said. "We're heading for the Dyson Science Building to rescue some people there."

"Where's that?" asked Mark.

"On the City of Angels campus," said Singh.

"Why?" asked Mark suspiciously.

"There's a pregnant woman there," said Singh. "We want to get her somewhere a little safer."

"And you're doing all this one for one pregnant lady?" asked Mark.

"To begin with," said Singh. "But the most direct path to them is this way." He motioned through their compound.

"So? You're going to go through us?" asked Mark defensively.

Singh shook his head. "No. But we were wondering if it was possible to get passage through."

"What do you mean?" asked Mark.

"If you have another big gate at the other end," said Singh. "We can drive straight through. No stopping. And then we'd be gone. We don't want any trouble."

"And yet you're heavily armed," said Mark.

"There're zoms out here," shrugged Singh. "And, if you have anyone who isn't suited for life out here, like little children, or older people. We can take them somewhere safe too."

"The mythical Carrier," scoffed Mark.

Liberty returned from the writing on the wall with a pensive look.

"Sergeant!" called out a voice on the other side of the wall. Soon, another man appeared. Like the other men, this fellow was dressed in mismatched *faux-tacticool*

60

military gear.

"What've we got?" asked the new man.

"Lieutenant Carl, these people want to pass through U.S. territory," said Mark to the new man with an amateur salute.

"Immigrants?" asked the Lieutenant, Carl.

"No sir," said Singh.

At the Captain's back, Liberty urgently whispered to him. "We need to go."

Lieutenant Carl squinted hard at them. "What do you want then?"

"They say they want to pass through us, on the way to the university," said Mark.

"Is that a tank *and* a school bus?" asked Carl.

"We're transporting some people to safety," said Singh.

"They *say* they're from the Carrier," said Mark. "And you know how Larry spent a whole afternoon looking up and down the coast for it."

"To be fair to Larry," chimed in Singh helpfully. "We're out farther than he could probably see, even with binoculars."

"That's convenient," said the Lieutenant. "And you just want to pass through? Like some *Goddamned Trojan horse?"*

"A what?" asked Sergeant Mark.

"NOW," hissed Liberty behind the captain. "We're going to need to find another way around."

Singh did not look back at her, but to the men on the wall he said. "Okay! Well, thank you for your time. We'll find another way around."

"Damn straight," snarled Lieutenant, and his eyes went from Singh to Danny. "And don't let me see your kind around here again."

Uncle Danny started to stiffen, but Liberty murmured. "Let's go!"

Taking the lead, the Librarian led them through the line of zoms. One of the creatures gave a wiggle, but Uncle Danny decided to let it be. It wasn't going to harm them. Clear of the zoms, the temptation to run was really strong.

"Don't run," said Singh softly. "Walk calmly."

"Never run from predators," added Liberty. "Even marshmallow ones."

"I'm feeling exposed," grumbled Uncle Danny.

"Hopefully they'll be happy to see us go," said Singh, and then he glanced at Liberty. "And what made you so nervous?"

"It's like 'Animal Farm'," said Liberty.

"The book?" asked Singh, confused.

"Yeah. They had...well, some kind of Bill of Rights," said Liberty.

"Some kind?" asked Singh.

"HEY YOU! STOP," came a voice from the wall, and they heard the sound of metal on metal.

Liberty, Danny, and Singh stopped and turned back.

"This is troubling," murmured the Captain.

"Kind of far to run," commented Uncle Danny as several men—carrying AR-15's—came barreling out of the metal gate.

"Back up slowly," murmured the Captain.

They started to move back as the men from the compound moved through the line of zoms and leveled their guns.

"Team," said the Captain over the earpieces. "If they fire, get out of here."

"But…," started Ruiz.

"That's an order," replied Singh immediately with authority. "Protect the civilians at all costs. Do you copy?"

There was only a brief pause, but Ruiz said. "Yes sir."

Stopping just past the line of mostly-dead zoms, the men from the compound glowered at them. Liberty saw the guard from the wall, Mark, and the Lieutenant in the mix.

"They're bunching up nicely," muttered Liberty.

"Not real military," replied Singh with the barest of nods.

"Gravy Seals," sniffed Uncle Danny. "Best description ever."

At the front was a neatly-dressed man with an immaculate white beard. He was almost impeccable, reminding Liberty of such words as 'dandy' or 'fop'. But his eyes made her nervous: as cold and dark as stones on the ocean floor.

"Now, what do we have here?" asked the man in front.

"I'm Captain Singh, serving aboard the Theodore Roosevelt carrier. And these are my companions, Liberty, and Danny. And you are?"

"General Edward Soleton," said the man with perfect diction in a Midwestern accent. "Leader of the United States."

"Oh?" said Singh, without any change to his voice.

"I see you put up the Bill of Rights," chimed in Liberty.

"Wrote them myself," said General Soleton, puffing out his chest.

"I like in the First Amendment where it says, 'Congress shall make no law prohibiting the free exercise thereof Christianity," said Liberty, with honey in her words.

Singh's brow almost furrowed.

"It *is* very good, isn't it," smiled General Soleton, proudly.

"Finally got the wording right," smiled Liberty.

"Exactly," nodded the General with enthusiasm.

"We're totally supportive, but we do need to keep going," said Liberty. "We're taking some civilians to a safe place."

"No, you're not," said the General.

"What?" asked Liberty.

"You're taking them on some kind of trip," said the General, and his voice became hard. "But there's no fleet out there to rescue us. What are you really going to do with those people?"

Liberty gave a light laugh. "You got us. We say that because the truth is harder to explain."

"And...what is the truth?" asked the General.

"We do have a refuge," said Liberty. "It's high up, great

water supply. And the zoms have to go up a winding path to get there. Heck, half of 'em fall to their death or whatever before they even get to the gate. Just because they wander too close to the edge."

"So, you lie to them," asked the General, softening.

"Well, look at how long it took to explain that" said Liberty. "Versus saying 'Fleet'. We found pretty quick that it was dangerous to explain out here. Better to explain at the foot of the mountain."

"And where is this mountain?" asked the General.

"This is really dangerous, standing out here like this," said Liberty. "I mean, your pile of zoms aren't exactly all dead.

"Really, I just saw one move," added Uncle Danny. "Be careful going back."

Lieutenant Carl snapped at the Big Mexican. "You shut up."

"Yeah. So, we really need to go," finished Liberty. She started backing up again, and the guys followed her lead.

"But now that we have a safe way to travel on the coast, we can help you resupply," said Liberty.

"By travel, you mean with the tank," said the General.

"But, we'll be back soon," said Liberty.

The General drew his revolver, and the others lifted their AR-15's to point at the three.

"You mean, Our Tank," said the General.

"We don't have to resort to this," said Liberty, slowly and patiently. "There aren't a lot of people left, and we're all facing the same things, zoms and those giant birds."

"What giant birds?" asked the General.

"See!" cried Mark the guard. "I told you I saw big birds yesterday. And everyone said I was crazy."

"Stupid is more like it," sneered Lieutenant Carl.

"Hey! She's saying that I'm right," said Mark.

Without looking at them, the General snapped. "Shut up you two." Then he gave a hard look at the Liberty, Danny, and Singh. "I'm going to need you to tell your men to exit my tank."

"We need that tank to pull the school bus," said Liberty.

The General pulled back the hammer on his revolver. "I'm not asking."

"Ruiz, you have your orders," said Singh in a calm voice.

"Yes sir," replied Ruiz over the earpiece.

"What orders?" asked the General.

The tank began to move slowly forward and turned towards the side street.

"Tell them to stop!" demanded the general. "Right now!"

Suddenly, the tank did stop, now fully visible to the General and his men. Singh's soldiers were moving across the surface.

Singh glanced over his shoulder.

The general grinned. "That's better,"

The turret suddenly turned.

Over the earpieces Bath said. "Y'all need Jesus."

"Wha...?" started Singh.

Uncle Danny's eyes widened, and he hissed. "Kneel." He grabbed Singh's shoulder and dragged him down, while Liberty followed her friend's lead.

"What're you...?" started the General.

The mechanic, Bath, suddenly popped out of the tank and let out a furious howl.

"All right you ball-lickers! This is Major Bath! Put those Goddamn guns down , or I'm going to put a 120mm shell right between your baby blues. Hell, it'll probably go straight into your compound. Because I will huff and puff and *blow your shit apart!*"

"Wait? Major Bath?" asked the General snottily.

"As in Bloodbath sweetie," snapped the mechanic. Without turning, she called out. "Ready to fire?"

Ruiz popped her head out of the tank. "Ready to fire Ma'am!"

"On my mark and be ready with that next shell!" ordered Bath.

"We got 6 more," replied Ruiz.

"Plenty to bring their lame ass compound down!" snarled Bath. "Okay. Ready!"

The General straightened even more to make himself taller. As if Bath wasn't standing up in an 8 foot tall tank.

"You're bluffing!" bellowed the General, but there was a waiver of uncertainty. "If you shoot us, it's liable to kill your people too!"

"Oh! You mean the Captain?" asked Bath. "He's a pain

in the ass anyway." Without looking at Ruiz, she called. "Ready! Aim!"

"Wait! Wait!" cried the General. Slowly, he put down the hammer of his Colt and lowered it. "You leave, and you don't come back. Ever! Do you understand? You are now an Enemy of the United States now."

"Honey, I'm a black woman in 'Merica. I've been treated as one my whole life," sniffed Bath. "Now Singh, get your ass back in here!"

Singh, Liberty, and Danny kept low and away from the cannon. As the Captain reached the tank, he scrambled up.

Liberty and Uncle Danny went inside the bus, and Frankline closed the bus door.

"Uncle!" cried Tessy and he immediately pulled her to his side.

Tapping her earpiece, Liberty said. "One moment, I'm going up onto the roof. In case anyone tries to follow." She practically had to climb over Collins, sitting by the open window.

"What?" asked Collins.

"Sorry! Can you hold this?" asked Liberty. She handed him her rifle and was at the window.

*"Mija?"* called out Uncle Danny.

"I'm good," smiled Liberty. "Really!"

Shortly, she reported over the earpieces. "I'm up on top of the roof, ready in case anyone tries to follow."

Atop the tank, Singh gave a little wave to her. "Thank you." He climbed over to Bath. "Take us outta here."

"Yes sir," replied Bath nervously.

Starting slowly, the mechanic kept turning towards a side street.

"Can we go any faster?" asked Singh with a neutral tone.

"I need to ramp up slowly sir," said Bath. "If the tank goes too fast, the towing cables might snap."

"And we don't want that," agreed Singh quickly. "Okay. As fast as you can."

The sniper rifle went off.

"We okay Liberty?" asked Singh over the earpiece.

"Warning shot," replied the Librarian. "They looked like they were tempted to rush us, so I skipped a bullet in front of them."

"Everyone be ready," warned Singh.

"Oh no!" called out Liberty.

*"Mija?"* came Uncle Danny over the earpiece.

"That general guy was trying to march across the dead zoms and tripped," said Liberty. "I think...oh shoot. Yep, his hand is bleeding."

"Did something...?" began Singh.

Gunshots came from near the compound.

"Whelp," said Liberty. "Looks like we're down one general."

Uncle Danny grumbled unhappily. *"¿Neta? ¡No manches!* We tried to warn them! Something was bound to go wrong."

Slowly speeding up, they left the view of the compound

69

behind. Liberty crawled to the back of the bus roof to keep watch.

"For that matter *Mija,*" asked Uncle Danny over the earpieces. "Where did you learn to bullsh..." His eyes darted down to little Tessy. "Bull-talk like that?"

"What?" asked the Librarian in confusion.

Singh added. "You were working over that general-guy, pretty good."

"I...I don't know," said Liberty suddenly. Her voice filled with a nervous embarrassment. "I was just trying not to throw up. But, um....I figured that anyone that called themself 'general', might be subject to flattery. Especially if they're the pigs from 'Animal Farm'."

"You mentioned that before," said Singh curiously. "But it's been forever since I read it."

"Oh! In the book, the pigs write rules for everyone, but later, they add in exceptions for themselves," said Liberty. "Congress cannot establish any religion above another, period. There's no mention of any religion."

"So, they were—what?—making up their own thing?" asked Uncle Danny.

"Rewriting the Bill of Rights to suit them," sniffed Singh.

"Jerks," grumbled Frankline over the line. "I hate people like that."

"Well, there're not our problem anymore," said Singh. He turned to look at Bath. "And speaking of acting outside orders."

Bath made a small peep but kept driving.

Ruiz popped her head up from inside the tank, speaking

quickly. "Sir! To be fair, you gave me the order. An' she had a viable option for de-escalating the situation. An' she should not be in trouble because she's a civilian, but *IF* someone needs to be held accountable, then it should be me."

Face like iron, Singh looked up at the Sergeant. "I'm thinking of doing just that."

Ruiz's back stiffened, but she did not move.

Looking back down, Singh asked. "Bath? What is—I mean 'was'—your rank when you were in the Army?"

"Um...M1 Abrams Tank System Maintainer 91A, Specialist/SPC (E-4) / Corporal/CPL (E-4)" rattled off Bath quickly. "Honorably Discharged. Sir."

"And if our main gun had gone off?" asked the Captain.

"Um...about a 50\50 chance that it would explode in the cannon," said Bath. "I need to look into it. It's making funny noises."

"Funny noises?" asked Singh.

Bath scrunched up her face. "Yeah. Well, you might not hear it, but it's loud and clear to..." She stopped, saying quickly. "Never mind...er, Sir. Just trying to help."

"Okay," said Singh. "You did good Sergeant Bath."

The mechanic blinked. "Um, I was a corporal, sir."

"You were," smiled Singh. *"Sergeant Bath."*

Bath' smile grew wide as the Captain turned to Ruiz, who was still at attention, standing ramrod straight in the moving tank.

"And Diana Ruiz is now my Staff Sergeant," said the

71

captain.

"Sir, yes sir!" called out Ruiz.

The captain noticed that she was trying to keep the smile off her face.

"Staff Sergeant Ruiz," barked the Captain with mock gruffness. "I don't know how it was where you were, but I'm okay with a smile, even a grin at a time such as this." She gave a big smile. "Unless you're being sarcastic. Then keep that shit to yourself."

"I'll try Sir!" grinned Staff Sergeant Ruiz. "But no promises."

This time it was Captain Singh's turn to smile. "I'll take it."

"Um, Captain, where're we going?" asked Bath.

"No idea," said Singh over the earpiece. "Liberty? A little help?"

"Coming," said Liberty.

Looking back, the Captain saw her tottering carefully along the top of the bus. He almost wanted to tell her to be careful, but immediately stopped himself. Don't Mother Hen, as his wife had always said. And he smiled a little at the thought, hearing it in her little Minnesota accent.

Laying down on the front of the roof, Liberty said.

"Before my friend, Mr. Jamie, and I found the Old Armory, there was a refuge here for a short time," said Liberty. "Almost all the streets are crammed with cars, except one. However, there might still be a problem."

Bath murmured as they reached the first street cross-street. "Oooh, that is definitely a lot of cars. And how'd that one end up on its side?"

"Godzilla?" suggested Frankline.

A laugh burst out of Ruiz, but then she said. "Stop that! No joking."

In the bus, Frankline ducked his head a little bit in mock chagrin. "Yes Staff Sergeant."

"Don't you 'Staff Sergeant' me," snipped Ruiz, and Liberty couldn't tell if she was miffed or not. She wondered if Ruiz knew.

"Okay, that's enough," said Singh with a level voice. "Bath, keep moving."

"If I'm right, it's not the next street, but the one after that," said Liberty, still over the earpiece.

As they slowed to a halt, Bath called out. "You mean the one with tons and tons of zombies in it?"

"Yep," said Liberty softly. "Those idiots behind took the only safe street to cross and put a damn wall through it."

"And the other direction?" asked Singh.

"Worse," said Liberty. "Unless we want to go miles and miles out of our way…"

"No. Not with our fuel consumption. We're going to need to chance it," said Singh. "Sergeant, do you think the tank will get through there?"

"Sergeant Bath?" asked the captain.

"What? Oh Yes! That's me now," said Bath quickly.

There was a good-natured titter from the team.

Singh ignored it. "Sergeant Bath, can the tank get through that many, and maybe more zoms?"

73

"Oh yeah," said Bath as she slowed down to a crawl. "Tank treads will be fine, and the bus's tires are already flat. I am a little worried about the people on top of the tank though. They're going to need to stay away from the edge or get grabbed."

"What about the bus, and the cable?" asked the captain.

"I think it should hold," said Bath. "I do have a spare, but..."

"Understood," said Singh. He thought for a moment, and there were only tank and zombie noises. "Okay. Team, we are going to drive down that street. Everyone on the tank, pull into the middle. I don't want any shooting unless there is a *real* and present danger."

"And the bus?" asked Frankline over the earpiece. "What should we tell everyone?"

Before the captain could answer, Uncle Danny spoke up. "Let me."

"Okay," said Singh, grateful for the assist. "Thank you."

However, in the bus, Uncle Danny still had Tessy wound around him. He looked down at her.

"Okay, we need to turn towards the rest of the people," he said gently.

Tessy did not let go, but she shuffled around with him, so that they faced the people in the bus.

"What's going on?" asked Ted with an angry prelude to panic.

"We need to get to that Dyson building still, but the best route is through the street up ahead," said Uncle Danny. "Unfortunately, it's covered in zoms. So, we're going to have to drive through them."

"Can't you get them out of the way?" asked Giselle with a frost in her voice.

"Not safely," admitted Uncle Danny. "If they walk out of the way...that would be good, but...they tend not to. No, we're probably going to have to drive over some..a lot of them. This is going to make some terrible noises."

"Are you *trying* to scare the children?" sniffed Giselle with disgust.

"Just letting the kids know what's going to happen...all of you," said Uncle Danny. "I'm not going to sugar coat it. I don't want to hear these noises either, but...we're going to be okay."

"How can you be so sure?" asked Simon, the tattoo artist.

"Because we're in a big old bus, so we're pretty safe in here," replied Uncle Danny calmly.

"Maybe a song," suggested the old man, Stephen, as he stood up. "I remember all my old camp songs."

Uncle Danny smiled gratefully. "That's a great idea!"

## Chapter Seven

"I'm going to have to turn in a wide arc so that we're facing the zoms," called out Bath over the earpieces. And her voice turned thoughtful. "It looks like a block party gone wrong."

"Don't take the Brown Acid," murmured Singh.

"What?" asked Bath.

"Never mind," said the Captain. "We're pulled into the middle back here."

"Okay then," whispered Bath unhappily. "Hold onto your lunches."

The tank went through a dozen zoms, but still the monster vehicle pressed on. Zoms did not even try to get out of the way, and they were taken under the treads with merciless efficiency. Some zoms on the sides tried to reach over the edge of the tank, but the soldiers were out of reach.

"How much farther Liberty?" asked Singh over the earpiece.

"This is a pretty long block," said Liberty. "And we're not even halfway."

Bath saw there were more cars on the left side of the street. Adjusting her course, she cut closer to the buildings on the right side. Unbeknownst to her, under the bus, bodies had started to collect.

"I think I'm a vegetarian now," said Bath. "Just sayin'."

"I think that's a reasonable response," replied Singh with a soft paternal tone.

## Chapter Eight

In the bus, Giselle grumbled. "This is horrible."

However, she had been quickly shouted down by the adults who had understood what the old man, Stephen, was doing. Still, she continued to mutter.

"Teaching such songs to children," continued Giselle.

The old man called out a little loudly over the noise of the mashed bodies.

"What should we sing next?" he asked.

"Great Green Gobs!" cried the kids.

Stephen put his fists on his hips, with a theatrical flair.

"Againnnnnnnnn?" he asked with mock disapproval.

"Yaaayy!" called out the kids, and more than a few of the adults, including Private Frankline.

Uncle Danny sang along softly because he didn't like his singing voice. Tessy on the hand, while still attached to him, belted out the song with Feeling.

"Great green gobs of greasy, grimy gopher guts, mutilated monkey meat, chopped up parakeet, french-fried eyeballs floating in a pool of mud, and I forgot my straw."

"Oh no!" cried Stephen with mock concern. "We forgot the straw, what're we going to do?"

And the singers all replied. "But I got my spoooooooooooon!"

Stephen clapped joyfully. "Yes! And that song was actually sung to the tune of "The Old Gray Mare'." Because the old man liked to sneak in some learning when he could. "And that song goes like this!"

"Danny...what am I hearing?" asked Singh with casual horror.

"I think this fellow was an entertainer at some point," explained Uncle Danny softly.

"Was...that song really about...gopher guts?" asked the Captain.

"And chopped up parakeet, Sir," offered Frankline cheerily.

"And don't forget the French fried eyeballs, Sir," added Ruiz over the earpieces with mock earnestness.

"I...I don't know what to say," said Singh.

Uncle Danny said. "I'd say it's just the distraction the kids needed."

The Captain chuckled. "That's good then."

"Past halfway," called out Liberty over the earpieces.

Snap!

The tank suddenly lurched ahead and almost spilled Mullins off. Ruiz just managed to grab her.

Singh twisted to look back at the bus.

Frankline muttered in the driver's seat. "Oh, oh." Out of reflex he pressed the gas pedal, which of course did not do anything.

The bus was quickly slowing to a halt.

Giselle cried out in alarm. "What's going on?"

"It's okay!" called out Uncle Danny loudly. "It's going to be okay! Everyone, just hang tight." He called over his earpiece. *"Mija?"*

"I'm okay," she replied immediately from the roof. "But the cable snapped."

"Okay," said Uncle Danny with some relief. He started to move towards the front, but Tessy was still attached. He looked down. "We need to go forward."

Too frightened to talk, the little girl just nodded, so Uncle Danny took a moment to hug tighter.

"We got this," he said softly.

"But...but this is a lot of zoms," whispered Tessy softly, urgently.

"What about when the barricade at the airport went?" asked Uncle Danny. "Were there more or less zoms there?"

Tessy blinked. "Um. I...think that was more."

"'There were more," said Danny. "Not 'was more'."

80

The little girl rolled her eyes at that. "Fine. There Were more."

"¡Orale! And we made it out of there," said her uncle.

Tessy nodded quickly. "An' we can make it outta here."

"We will," agreed Uncle Danny with assurance. "But we need to move forward."

Meanwhile, the old man, Stephen, began to talk soothingly to everyone.

Uncle Danny moved to the front of the bus with Tessy.

Beyond the window, he saw the snapped cable on the ground amongst mashed-up zoms. Some of the poor creatives were still moving. He pulled Tessy a little closer, so that her face was pressed against his old coat.

"Looks like someone is getting up on the tank. Bath isn't it?" said Liberty over the earpieces.

Scrambling across the top of the tank, the newly minted Sergeant, Bath, stepped past everyone to look back. The right side of the bus was actually pretty close to the storefronts. There was really only room for one zom at a time.

"Good thing I decided to hug the wall," she said out loud.

"Sergeant," said Singh. And then he added. "Bath. What's our situation?"

"Working on that now," said Bath. And then she remembered to add. "Sir." It had been a few years since she left, so she was a little rusty. But she pulled her attention back to the problem.

Looking around, Bath saw a few abandoned cars further

up the two lane street with sidewalks. A street packed with hungry carnivores.

"We've got to do something," said Ruiz urgently. She shouldered her rifle, eying the zoms coming closer to the edge.

"Give her a moment," said Singh softly.

Ruiz just nodded and went to confirm that everyone was okay, usually with a reassuring smile, but sometimes with mock gruffness.

'Don't tell me that these things worry you!!" demanded Ruiz. "Did becoming Navy make you soft?"

And that produced a healthy little chuckle, even from the one she had asked.

Singh watched. The Staff Sergeant just unerringly knew what their people needed. Amused, the Captain decided that it was a form of magic and was not going to interfere.

At the rear of the tank, Bath turned to the Captain.

"Sir, permission to plan out loud?" she asked.

"Permission granted," nodded Singh curiously.

"It's going to get icky sir," said Bath.

"'Icky?" asked Ruiz, catching her attention.

"Icky real fast," said Bath as she got on the earpieces. Quickly, she outlined her plan, and then she added uncertainly. "Any thoughts?"

Everyone looked from the young African American woman to the Captain. Singh gave a little smile.

"Well, you heard her," said Singh. "We got a plan. Let's MOVE, we're burning daylight."

"Wait!" said Uncle Danny. "We need to distract the kids in the bus. *Los niños* don't need to see this. We might need something bigger than even the 'gopher' song."

Tessy suddenly straightened and beamed up at her uncle. Letting go of him, she turned to the back of the bus.

"Did I ever tell you how *Mi Tio*...Uncle saved me from an Army Of Zombies with only a meat cleaver?"

"It wasn't an army," grumbled Uncle Danny, getting embarrassed.

Tessy stepped forward. "Come here. Everyone." She waved the kids forward and then they all sat in the aisle. Luckily being smaller, they managed it.

Giselle leaned toward the little girl.

"Are you sure you want to talk about this?" fretted Giselle.

But Tessy ignored her and. with animated hand gestures, spoke quickly.

"We were at a Chinese restaurant for my grandpa's birthday, because he likes Szechuan, which is okay, I guess. But Grandpa got to choose because it's his birthday, and then Uncle Danny had to go pee. Well, he didn't say that, but he was moving kinda quick. And then these zoms burst through the front door. And everyone was panicking. And this old zom lady was coming right at me..."

"Isn't this a little too scary for children?" insisted Giselle.

As if she hadn't heard the woman, Tessy kept going. "An' I threw an egg roll at the lady, but of course it didn't do anything. But then Uncle Danny was suddenly there with this *biiiiiig* cleaver. The same one at his hip."

Everyone leaned closer, even some of the adults, and were caught up in the story.

Uncle Danny called out over the earpieces. "We got our distraction, but I don't know for how much longer."

"Then let's go now!" ordered Singh.

Bath sent the tank forward, immediately crushing a half dozen zoms. But her work had only started. Moving further down the street, she did a 180 a little too quickly.

"Slow down Sergeant," said Singh. "You almost flipped a few of us off."

Grimacing with embarrassment, she whispered. "Sorry."

Driving forward, a little more cautiously, she reached an abandoned car and started to push it down the street towards the bus. Two zoms were unfortunately pinned between the car and tank and Bath felt terrible, even if they were mindless beasts.

"Sorry," she muttered.

# Chapter Nine

In the bus, people heard the tank moving cars and several kids started to stand. In a second, they would see the carnage outside, as the tank rolled over zoms.

"Whack!" cried Tessy.

That got the kids attention again and they sank back down to listen.

"And Whack again!" she continued swiftly. "Dad and Grandpa were....so anyway, Uncle Danny took my arm, and we were able to escape out the back door. But! We were in the middle of the City of Angels, and Uncle Danny didn't have the car keys. He actually didn't even have a driver's license because he was here on a Veez-something."

"Visa?" asked Giselle, with an oily voice.

"Yeah. Because my father hurt his back, An' without Uncle Danny, my father's company would have died."

Giselle looked like she wanted to say something pointed about that.

But Tessy talked faster "But we didn't have any way to drive so…"

## Chapter Ten

Bath fervently wished that she was in the bus right now. Or even on that ugly, cramped ship that she lived on. If you can call it living,  sharing a tiny room with four other women. Only on Pornhub does that go well. She dragged her attention back to her maneuvering.

Soon, she had placed two cars—sideways—across the street from the bus to the opposite storefront. This created a barrier. However, the area before the bus still had a large number of zoms, shambling about. She needed to make some breathing room.

First though, she had to call over the earpieces. "Okay, can someone make sure that I can crawl under the bus? You know...without getting eaten, please and thank you."

"Because it's not Saturday night," said Ruiz in an aside, which got a small laugh.

Bath's eyes widened and she gave a mock growl.

"You stop," chided Bath.

However, Ruiz grinned unrepentantly while Singh away and tried to not notice.

"I can check under the bus," said Frankline.

Singh hid his surprise, managing to cover it with a quick. "Thank you."

Frankline reached to open the bus door.

"Oh!!," said Bath urgently. "And don't forget that the corridor between the bus and the storefront is still open. I couldn't close that. Sorry."

"Don't worry about it," said Uncle Danny. "I'll take the corridor."

"And me," said Liberty over the earpieces.

"Go ahead," said Singh.

Frankline opened the door and a zom was there. He kicked it in the face and the creature went down hard. At the bottom step, he raised his M4 Carbine to shoot it.

Uncle Danny suddenly called out. "I got it."

Frankline began to look back in annoyance, but then he noticed all the civilians behind the Big Mexican. He gave a little nod. "Okay. I got my work cut out for me anyways."

As the Private jumped in front of the bus, Uncle Danny went to the door. The zom was just trying to get up. The Big Mexican saw the worry in Tessy's face, as well as some others.

"I'll be right here," reassured Uncle Danny. "I'm not taking *any* chances."

"Okay," nodded Tessy with a small voice.

"Walk in the park for me and your Aunt Liberty," shrugged Danny. "Besides, you have your audience waiting."

Tessy nodded and turned back. "Where was I?"

Uncle Danny drew his cleaver and descended upon the creature.

"Whack, whack," said one of the kids in awe.

Giselle stood and looked out the front window. "Is the tank just driving around out there?"

Tessy spoke up, a little loudly. "Do you know that Uncle Danny once threw a zom through a window? Like a big store window?"

"What?" asked another kid. "No!"

Excitedly, Tessy leaned forward. "IT'S TRUE!" She raised her voice because there were gunshots from all around the bus. "Uncle Danny and I were trapped in this store, an' we were gonna get eaten. But then, he just picks up this big zom…"

## Chapter Eleven

Liberty smirked as she walked across the roof. "You're going to have a fan club." She fired at a zom who was trying to get between the wall and bus. Thankfully, there was not a lot of room.

"She shouldn't make such a big deal outta it," grumbled Uncle Danny with embarrassment.

"She's proud of her uncle," insisted Liberty. "It's cute."

Grumbling, Uncle Danny shot the next zom trying to get through the hole. "We're going to fill this up fast."

"Front is clear!" called out Frankline over the earpieces.

"Coming," cried Bath. After she ran over two more zoms, she started to back the tank towards the bus.

As she maneuvered the behemoth, Frankline peered closer to the lower half.

"Jesus," muttered Frankline.

"What is it?" asked Bath with concern, and she immediately stopped the tank.

"Oh. Sorry!" said the Private swiftly. "No! You're okay. It's just that the bottom half of the tank is...well, you don't want to see it."

"I'm sure," replied Singh soberly.

As she finished positioning the tank, Bath added with a sad sigh. "Poor things."

Frankline looked down at his own uniform covered in blood from laying under the bus. It was bad, like when his Daddy came home from the slaughterhouse bad. However, he suddenly looked up and at Bath. She was climbing across the tank. The newly minted sergeant wasn't even wearing a uniform, just civilian clothes.

"Hold on!" he told her. "For real this time."

Bath froze in confusion while Frankline jumped back into the bus. He wasn't even sure he'd find anything.

From his open window, Collins' head whipped around looking where zoms futility pawed at the frame, but could not climb in.

"What's wrong?" he asked, with a hint of panic.

Tessy's storytelling began to slow.

"Nothing man! Everything's good," said Frankline quickly with a jovial tone. But he made sure to face forward, so that no one saw that his front was covered in blood.

Swiftly rooting around the driver's seat, the Private found a likely candidate. He jumped out of the bus and tore open the package.

Frankline looked up at Bath. "Good to come down now."

Despite being puzzled, Bath nodded, and Singh came over to help her down!

"You know, I can get down from the tank safely," said Bath a little archly.

"Sorry," said Singh, backing off. "I'm fussing. But I also didn't want anyone spraining an ankle right now, jumping off a tank."

"He does that," called out Ruiz as she came over.

As Singh gave the Staff Sergeant a mock dirty look, Bath climbed down very carefully. Mostly because she didn't want to hurt herself, especially saying that she would be fine. Singh handed down the last of the metal cable. Then, Ruiz handed down the mechanic's tools in its 'PBS' tote bag.

As she was fixing the last of the cable to the tank Bath now saw the underside of the tank. "Yikes."

She heard the Staff Sergeant call out.

"What'chu doing under the bus Private?" asked Ruiz.

"Huh?" came Frankline. "Oh! I'm just trying to get things ready, Ma'am."

"Is that a raincoat?" asked Ruiz.

"Yes Ma'am," replied Frankline dutifully.

Raincoat? wondered Bath, but she did not have time to look back.

Once the cable was fixed, she went quickly to the bus and found Frankline already laying down. There wasn't a lot of room underneath the bus, what with all the bodies that had churned up underneath it. But there were still some paths. Frankline had them covered though.

And right where the cable would be attached to the bus, the ground had been cleared and an old plastic raincoat lay on the bloody pavement.

"Thank you," said Bath.

"Well, let's see if it works first," said Frankline, low-key.

Having done this once before, Bath quickly attached the new cable and gave an experimental tug on it.

"I hope this one holds," she said worriedly.

"It'll be good," said Frankline optimistically, and Bath gave him a smile.

The tank mechanic and the Private stood up, and she saw his bloody uniform.

Immediately, Bath looked down at herself, first tugging at her hand-me-down Snoopy shirt . Then she inspected her pants. which were a little too big, but still fit with a belt. They were the only clothes she had in the whole world, and they only had one or two spots of blood on them.

The mechanic gave a radiant smile to the Private.

"Thank you again," she said.

A little embarrassed, Frankline looked down and mumbled. "Let's just get everyone home safe."

"Okay everyone!" called Singh from back on the tank. "Let's try this...Danny? Hey Danny? What're you doing?"

Frankline and Bath looked around the edge. There was a barrier of dead zoms by the back of the bus now, which

Liberty was covering. However, Uncle Danny was pulling dead zoms out from underneath the bus. He stepped away from his pile and spoke over the earpieces.

"Dragging bodies underneath the bus is straining the cable," said Uncle Danny. "Ideally, we'd get all these bodies out first."

"Which is too dangerous," said Liberty worriedly from above.

"Which is why we can't do that *Mija*," replied Uncle Danny, with a warm, patient tone. He walked back over to the bus door and glanced down at the ex-zom. "Hey, I think that's a real Rolex."

" I call dibs!" grinned Frankline as he jumped towards it.

"No!" said Uncle Danny swiftly, and a little too sharply.

Frankline froze.

"It's bad luck to rob the dead," said the Big Mexican stridently. "I mean if you really need it. You know, being a pirate is one thing, but grave robbing...you could end up in Hell for that."

The Private took a cautious step back from the Rolex, and then they both noticed that Liberty was looking over the roof of the bus, looking in surprise at the Big Mexican.

Suddenly worried, Uncle Danny asked. "Did that come out bad?" But, without her needing to answer, he just nodded and looked at the Private. "*¡Disculpe!* Sorry, I didn't mean to snap."

Frankline raised a hand. "It's cool Sir." He chuckled as he held up his wrist, showing that he already had a watch. "I mean, you're not wrong."

94

"Still...," said Uncle Danny apologetically.

"Okay! Grave Robbing later. Everyone back to their positions," said the Captain. "I don't want to finish this Op in the dark."

"Amen," added Uncle Danny.

Bath started to run to the tank but stopped to look back at Frankline. "Thanks again for your help."

The mechanic climbed up and was soon safely inside the tank, once again. And Staff Sergeant Ruiz immediately looked calmer.

While Liberty settled down onto the roof once again, Frankline and Uncle Danny got into the bus.

"Everyone set?" asked Singh. "Okay then, head 'em up and move 'em out."

Cautiously, the tank moved forward, and the cable pulled taut. Slowly, Bath gave it a modicum of speed. The bus began to move once again.

Everyone gave a cheer.

Tessy ran to Uncle Danny at the front of the bus and hugged him close. He smiled down at her, but then looked up. People were staring at him with something akin to awe.

A little embarrassed, the Big Mexican looked down and focused on his wonderful niece.

"Oh no," he muttered softly. "What tall-tales have you been telling?"

Tessy looked up in concern. "But. I thought you needed to distract people while you worked?"

The Big Mexican beamed a proud smile. "And you did

wonderfully, *Mi Mariposa Unicornio!*"

Over the earpieces, Bath called out. "Coming up to the next mob of zoms. Hang on tight everyone. I'm going to go a little slower this time, so as not to tax the cable."

"Thank you, sergeant," said Singh atop the tank. "Everyone good in the bus?"

Frankline turned around in the driver's seat and looked back.

"We're good Sir!" he reported.

"Oh!" exclaimed the old man, Stephen, as he turned to the people on the bus. "Time to sing again!"

"Oh God no," muttered Giselle.

"Great green gobs of greasy, grimy gopher guts," they began.

It was slow going.

However, they soon broke out onto a larger street, and the zoms thinned out immeasurably. Over the earpieces, Singh heard a cheer from the bus.

Hearing those cheers, he added softly. "I agree."

The Captain turned to the Librarian on top of the bus.

"How much farther Ms. Liberty?" he asked.

"We're not far," she replied. "But...I don't know how far those weirdos with the guns went though. We might want to take a couple of side streets to avoid them."

"Damn straight," muttered Bath.

"Sergeant Bloodbath," said Singh in a warning tone.

Chastened, Bath whispered. "Sorry Sir."

"Liberty, what is the quickest route," asked the Captain. "I don't want to waste any more time."

"Straight ahead," replied the Librarian without hesitation.

"Okay then, we'll just have to keep an eye out for those men," said Singh.

The tank/bus headed straight for the City of Angels University. Atop the bus, Liberty watched the streets and rooftops ahead.

But Singh kept everyone on their toes.

"Keep your head on a swivel," he ordered. "Just in case."

Thankfully, the zoms were less dense here so Bath did not have to run over as many.

Liberty reared up.

"Captain Singh?" she called out over her earpiece.

"I'm listening," he replied immediately.

"I think I just saw someone on the rooftops," reported Liberty. She scanned again. "Don't see 'em now, but I'm sure that someone was there."

"A lookout?" asked Singh.

"Maybe," she replied.

Singh sighed. "Can I just say that I wish this thing went a little faster."

"If we didn't have the bus, we could do a cool 45 miles per hour," replied Bath, however she added quickly. "But...at least she moves."

"Very true," agreed Singh.

"And walking even a few people out of town can easily be suicide," added Liberty, with her 2 cents.

"Okay. Everyone pay attention," said Singh.

They kept lumbering along.

Like a sick turtle, grumbled the Captain to himself. However, as much as Singh itched to go faster, they could not risk breaking their last cable. Pushing the bus with the tank did not seem like a good idea.

Glancing through her scope, Liberty called over the earpiece. "We got fortifications coming up on our right."

Singh looked through his binoculars. "I see 'em. Might be old. But this is almost the area where those pseudo-soldiers were."

"Gravy seals," smirked Private Mullins.

Atop the bus, Liberty called out. "I got someone. What do you say? A contact? Maybe someone holding someone."

"Bath, stop the tank. Okay everyone! Stay away from the edges of the tank and stay in the bus!" said Singh over the earpieces.

Behind him, Uncle Danny, he heard Collins softly whisper. "Gladly."

Singh, ready with his own M4 Carbine, continued. "Hold your fire until I give the order. Liberty, keep an eye on those rooftops." And then he remembered that she was not one of his enlisted and added. "Please."

"Got it," replied Liberty, and she shifted her focus to the rooftops on either side.

Inside the tank, Bath slid out of her chair, but she stayed

inside.

Atop the tank, Singh began with gruff authority. "Identify yours..." But he stopped when he realized that the person might be holding a baby. His voice immediately grew calm and helpful. "Hello? Can we help you?"

"He's got a weapon," murmured Mullins swiftly. "Slung across his back."

"But his hands are full of baby...let's see how this plays out," replied Singh softly.

"In Vietnam, they'd booby-trap baby-type-stuff to ambush our people," murmured Mullins.

"*Very* good point," replied Singh. Lifting his rifle, he aimed it at the approaching man's feet and called out. "Hold it right there."

The man with the shaggy beard froze and clutched the bundle to his chest more tightly.

"Please," cried the man. "Take my son!"

"Can you open the bundle a little?" asked Singh.

"What?" asked the man in confusion.

"Please," said Singh. "We have to be careful."

"Oh...sure," said the man, who still didn't seem to get it. But he opened the blankets to show a little pink face blinking at the bright sun. "His name's Francis, an' I know it's a crappy name, but his Mom really wanted him to be named after her grandfather, an' she was dying, so I couldn't just say 'no', but if you'll..."

A shout rose up from the fortifications. It was too hard to hear, but someone sounded really pissed. And Singh glanced at the big metal wall, further down the street.

99

The man looked back in concern. "Shit, I figured I'd have a minute more."

Singh waved the man closer. "Hurry!"

The man ran up to the edge of the tank. "Please! I don't know if you really do have some kind of refuge, or if there really is a Fleet out there, or not. But I...I can't have my son live out here. I don't want him to...not after losing his mother, right after he was born. Please! If you can't take me, I understand, but please take my son."

"Vincent!" shrieked a male voice. "Why aren't you watching the Goddamn back door?"

"Go to the bus," ordered Singh urgently.

The man, Vincent, ran towards the bus. The Captain turned as well. He waved to Uncle Danny through the front window and gave a thumbs up.

Inside the bus, the Big Mexican nodded and said. "Open the door."

As Frankline did so, Uncle Danny pried Tessy from him. "I need you to get back and get low."

"But...," started Tessy.

"*Por favor, Mi Mariposa Unicornio,*" whispered Uncle Danny urgently.

"Come on Tessy," said Stephen, with a kind voice. "Let's let 'em do their work."

The little girl allowed the old entertainer to steer her further back into the bus. Stephen was trying to get all the kids to crouch down low in the aisle.

At the door, the father stopped when he saw the Big Mexican. But he steeled himself.

"Please," said Vincent. "I don't want my son to die out here."

Before Uncle Danny could reply, there were more shouts from the militia compound.

A voice by the metal wall, in a near panic screamed. "HEY! HEY! THE TANK'S BACK!"

"Shit," hissed Vincent. He shifted his son to one arm and tried to get at his rifle.

Uncle Danny stepped aside to leave the stairs free. "Hurry! In."

"Vincent? SHIT! VINCE'S DOWN WITH THE TANK!" cried one of the militia by the compound.

Vincent looked up in surprise.

More men and a woman with mis-matched military gear boiled out behind Lieutenant Carl, leading the pack. Set outside the metal wall were three foot concrete barriers and the pseudo-soldiers crouched behind them.

Lieutenant Carl kept standing and called out to the tank/bus. "Don't you take anyone with you! As the newly appointed leader of the United States of America, I order you to Stand Down and surrender."

"My name is Captain Deep Singh of the United States Military, and I serve under Rear Admiral Cirilo of the aircraft carrier, USS *Theodore Roosevelt*. And I say, 'No, thank you'," replied Singh politely but firmly. "If someone asks for safe passage, I will not deny them."

"You don't have that kind of authority, because I didn't give it to you!" screamed Carl, his face growing red.

"Be ready," whispered Singh to the soldiers around him.

They readied their own M4 Carbines. Mullins lay on top of the tank, aiming her rifle. The Captain called over the earpieces. "Liberty, do you know where that side street up ahead goes?"

"Should be to the university," replied the Librarian on the roof of the bus.

"But how quick? Bath?" asked Singh.

Over the earpiece, it sounded like Bath was working on something inside the tank, but she replied. "Ramping up will be slow Sir. And I can't push that cable too hard...."

"Yeah. We need it to last until we reach the coast," finished Singh with a resigned tone.

"Sorry. I've got to get back to work Sir," said Bath. "Let me know if you need me to drive us outta here."

At the bus, Vincent jumped onto the steps and held out his son.

"Please?" he asked, eyes wide with fear but not because of the Big Mexican.

Uncle Danny took the child, a little awkwardly.

Vincent jumped back down the stairs and ran back to the tank. "Wait! Wait!"

"Get the hell over here!" demanded Carl. "And where's your boy?"

"Listen," tried Vincent as he moved in front of the tank. "I can stay. But let them pass."

"Are you going weak on me?" asked Carl.

"Hell No!" replied Vincent hotly.

"Then where's your boy?"

"Francis' not coming back," said Vincent.

"Like hell!" snapped Carl. "That's It! I will be obeyed! Aim for the bus and kill his boy."

Singh bellowed. "That bus is full of civilians *and other children*. We will fight to protect it."

"We don't have to do this!" cried Vincent. "This is stupid! We don't..."

A shot rang out and hit Vincent. He staggered a little but did not fall. Singh could not see where the man was hit, but Carl turned to see who had fired.

Vincent suddenly roared. "You assholes!" He started to shoot his rifle even as he staggered forward. "This is the thanks I get! After Sacramento. Pismo Beach!!"

As one of the militia collapsed, the rest started shooting.

Carl threw a bouncy temper tantrum, trying to say something, but no one was listening over the roar of gunfire.

Vincent was peppered with shots. He slowly sunk to his knees, still shooting though.

But the militia turned its attention to the bus. A bullet hit the right side mirror.

Uncle Danny was still a little stunned that he was holding a baby. The child looked very, very fragile in his gigantic, scarred hands.

Frankline jumped up and pulled Uncle Danny, and the child, down.

Outside, Singh ordered. "Fire at will!"

Opening up, the U.S. soldiers peppered the front of the

metal wall. But the concrete barriers gave them some protection. And two more militia, one still buckling his pants, ran out to join the fight.

In the space between, the unlucky zoms, who happened to be wandering there, got torn to pieces.

The front right window of the bus exploded as more bullets hit it.

Liberty was itching to help, but she kept an eye on the rooftops, and she was glad she did.

Two pseudo-soldiers appeared atop the roof, just behind the tank. They had been trying to flank Singh's people and were surprised to see her. The pseudo-soldiers started to fire at her, wildly.

Twisting, Liberty fired and immediately hit one. She fired again but missed the second pseudo-soldier as he dove behind a big metal air conditioning unit.

"Darn," swore Liberty.

The pseudo-soldier jumped out though. "Ha ha! You missed! You shoot like a girl," he crowed, aiming his rifle at Liberty.

But he was standing so still.

So, the Librarian took the shot.

The pseudo-soldier blinked in confusion and slowly tumbled back.

"Idiot!" she snapped softly. Why couldn't you have just run? She asked herself bitterly, and then she remembered the 'shoot like a girl' remark. "Jerk."

Trying to shake it off, Liberty kept an eye on the rooftops. It was only when she was sure that they were clear, that she saw something on the tank.

Mullins shuddered and slumped down. Singh saw this and tried to move towards her, but he was pinned behind the turret.

Over the earpieces, Ruiz suddenly called out from inside the tank.

"Odds?" asked the Staff Sergeant.

Puzzled, Singh was about to answer, when the mechanic piped up.

"Um, 80/20," said Bath, and then she added. "Ma'am."

"Well, it'll have to do," said Ruiz. "We ready?"

"As ready as we'll ever be," replied Bath, a little uncertainly.

"Mother Mary, watch over us," said Ruiz.

"What she said," added Bath.

Ruiz called out. "Everyone off the tank, right now!"

"What?" said the medic, Washington. "Did she just...?"

"Hurry!" cried Singh. "Everyone off the back!"

The Captain saw that Mullins was not following and felt a deep sting of anger and grief. Dropping to the ground though, he swatted away some zoms who had gotten nosy.

As the tank's turret started moving, the rest of the team dropped next to him.

"This way," hissed Singh urgently and he led them around to the left side of the bus, away from the fight. He called over his earpieces. "We're clear!"

"Okay!" called out Bath. "Hold your ears sweeties!"

Singh put his hands over his ears.

Inside, Uncle Danny had regained himself. Tessy was buried somewhere in all the civilians. He arched his body protectively over the child while Frankline told everyone to duck down.

The tank fired.

"¡Ay, Por el amor de Dios!" hissed Danny and he fretted about his *amiga* above.

Liberty clamped her hands over her ears to stem the deafening noise, but she was still able to witness everything.

The world seemed to slow down for her.

Smoke from the cannon.

The Librarian saw something race past the pseudo-soldiers. The shell came at the metal wall at an angle, but it did not stop. It easily just punched through the scrap like it was paper. Past the wall, the shell must have connected with something more solid, like a brick.

The explosion turned the metal wall into a hailstorm of shrapnel and Liberty instinctively ducked her head, putting her arms over her beret. After a moment, a few bits of metal —*plink-plink*—fell from the sky.

Glancing up, Liberty saw with dread that the explosion had created a zone where nothing had survived. And a howling anger gripped her, the senseless stupidity of it all.

Someone was shouting, and she realized that it was Danny's voice.

"Medic! We need a medic!"

Even as fear gripped her, she scrambled across the left

side of the roof and peered over the other edge. Thankfully, Singh and his people there were still upright and alive.

"Medic! We need a medic in the bus!" cried Liberty.

Singh turned to Washington. "Go!"

Without a word, the medic dashed around the front of the bus to help.

"Liberty?" said Singh. "Can you keep an eye up top? Make sure that we don't have any more surprises."

The Librarian looked down through the roof of the bus, and the Captain seemed to read her concern.

"Lieutenant Washington was in his residency, already a doctor," said Singh softly. "They're in the best of hands." He suddenly looked over at the tank. Mullins was still laying on top. But he forced himself to look back at the Librarian. "Please keep an eye out. We don't know how many more are in that compound. Stragglers might come out, or even over the rooftops, looking for a fight."

Liberty stiffened. "True." And she nodded quickly. "Okay." Returning to her spot atop the bus, she watched.

While his steps were heavy, the Captain did not move slowly as he went back to the tank. Climbing up, he knelt beside Mullins' body. Her eyes were still open.

"Thank you," he said and suddenly he felt a searing emotion roaring up inside of him. Turning up towards the sky, Singh called out *"Akaal! Akaal! Akaal!"*, a Sikh prayer for the dying. As he stood, Ruiz and Bath both looked out of the tank, sadly. Singh cast his arms wide and called out *"Akaal"* once again for all those lost today.

"Dear Lord, please help those who have died today,"

added Ruiz.

"Amen," agreed Bath.

Straightening, the captain went over to the tank ladies and smiled.

"We will give her and Private Sondes a proper send off when we return, and Locke too, even though we had to leave him behind," said Singh with a heavy voice.

"Because he was so stupid," grumbled Ruiz, and the Captain could see that it was really the frustration talking.

Taking a deep cleansing breath, Singh looked at the tank ladies. "But first, good job."

Bath crawled halfway out of the Loader hatch to look forward. "Wow! I think some of that shrapnel almost reached here. Good thing we stopped when we did."

Singh looked around. "Okay! Everyone back on the tank! We roll in 90 seconds."

"We, Are GONE in 60 seconds," called out Bath with a bad Nicholas Cage impression.

The Captain gave a little smile and jumped off to check on the bus. Uncle Danny was standing just outside the door, hitting a zom with his cleaver.

"The locals are getting restless," said Uncle Danny.

"We'll be out in a minute," replied Singh. "What's it like in there?" The Captain saw Frankline in the driver's seat, alive. He had a cut on his face, but it didn't seem to be bothering him. And Collins was deeper in.

Liberty was suddenly looking over the edge of the roof. "Tessy? The kids?"

Uncle Danny nodded quickly.

"We got lucky," he replied to both of them. "Baby's okay..."

Singh chuckled. "Oh! I almost forgot about the baby in all this."

"All the kids are good," said Danny. "Mainly cuts from shattered glass but...Stephen got killed."

"Stephen?" asked Singh.

"He was the *hombre* singing when we had to go down that street," said Danny.

The Captain's face scrunched up. "The one with That Song."

"But it took everyone's mind off it. And it looks like he was putting himself between the shooting and everyone else, because he spread himself up and over, in front of everyone." The Big Mexican whacked another zom. "*¡Aquas!* I think it's time to go."

"Agreed," said Singh. "Okay, here's the plan."

As the Captain was returning to the tank, Uncle Danny looked up. "You okay *Mija?*"

Liberty nodded quickly. "I'm okay." But her face looked downcast.

"What's wrong?" asked Danny quickly.

Swiftly, Liberty told him about the guy who jumped out and tried to shoot her.

After she was done, Uncle Danny nodded slowly. "I know. I hate having to take a life too. But, he would have killed you."

"I know," sighed Liberty. "It's just...this whole thing. This whole fight."

"¡Orale! The whole thing was stupid," said Danny. "But we didn't pick it."

"True," nodded the Librarian. "Worse yet, he said I shot like a girl."

"Before or after you shot him?" asked Uncle Danny.

"Before," replied Liberty.

Danny gave a little bark of laughter, and she couldn't help but smile.

"Was pretty ironic," admitted Liberty.

"I'm just glad you're okay," said Danny.

"You too amiga," smiled Liberty.

Uncle Danny opened his mouth to correct her, but then he just smiled. "I better check on Tessy."

"Give her a hug for me," said Liberty urgently.

From the tank, Singh called out. "Okay! Head 'em up!"

Danny looked back up at her and grinned. "Break's over!"

"But I didn't get to finish my muffin yet, " grinned Liberty with a mock whine.

"Too bad!" said Uncle Danny. "Back to your place!"

Liberty returned to her spot feeling better.

The Big Mexican hopped up inside the bus as the tank started to move forward. Looking through the shattered front window, he saw Captain Singh pointing towards what was left of the scrap metal wall.

110

The main gun of the tank kept aim on the milia base, but Singh turned opposite, scanning a side street on the left.

"¡*Fíjate!* The Captain wants everyone to keep low, until we've passed this area," said Uncle Danny.

"Is there more trouble?" asked Giselle, and her voice rose in panic.

"Well, we're out in the middle of Zom Country," said Uncle Danny. "There's trouble all around us. ¡*Neta!* I'm trouble, and Liberty above, is *Gran Problema!* But the good news is…" And a slow grin spread across his face. "…we're on your side."

And the mood instantly whipped from rising panic to surprise.

Gisele squinted. "Kinda full of yourself, aren't you?"

"No," grinned Danny. "It's only bragging if you *can't* back it up! An' we can."

"Yeah!" cried out one of the kids, enamored with Tessy's stories.

"Whack! Whack!" cried another.

Gisele looked in horror at the kids.

"Now, I'm going to watch the door," said Uncle Danny, and he looked at Tessy. "I'm not going out, but just going to cover."

"Just in case?" asked Tessy with an uncertain voice.

The Big Mexican nodded. "*Si.*"

"Okay," nodded Tessy.

Uncle Danny saw that Simon, the tattoo artist, was holding the baby and making funny faces. Satisfied that they were as safe he could make them, he went to the door.

"We expecting trouble?" whispered Frankline.

"Captain's probably just being cautious," replied Danny in a low voice. He sat down on the top step of the bus and looked out. The glass in the door was gone—shattered— but there was still enough door there. And now it was like a slot to fire out of, like one of those old castles.

They reached the street where the metal wall had been. The pseudo-soldier's compound had occupied a long block, but no one came out. For a second, Uncle Danny saw movement halfway down, but then it was gone.

After the tank/bus moved past, the zoms started to saunter in, to re-occupy their land.

"*Hay días tontos y tontos todos los días,*" whispered Uncle Danny somberly.

## Chapter Twelve

As the tank-bus lumbered away, someone bent down to sniff what was left of Carl, the newly minted leader of the United States of America.

The alien-bird, Rakduson, straightened as several zoms lumbered towards her curiously. But she quickly side-stepped them and went into the compound. A mob of zoms was filtering through, like water filling a hole in the ground.

Further away, a big door opened in the far metal gate and a small group of people, including several children, ran out.

But she had no quarrel with them.

Taking to the air, Rak flew up to the rooftops and continued to follow the tank-bus.

## Chapter Thirteen

Once they were past the militia compound, Uncle Danny stood up to look out the front of the bus. The tank turned the main gun forward, which was fun to watch. But then, he suddenly leaned forward and was shocked to see a music store coming into view. He didn't even know that those still existed. Then, as the next store came into view, he immediately called up.

"*Mija!* Check right!"

Swiftly, Liberty aimed her rifle in that direction, but only saw store fronts. First, she saw the sign for the music store roll by. "Those still exist..." But then she saw it and shrieked with joy.

Below, Uncle Danny heard the noise and grinned because he knew he had done good.

Up above, Liberty cried. "A BOOK STORE! Oh my

God." However, then she spied something else too. "Hey! A sailing store!" She leaned over the front of the bus roof. "There's a sailing store nearby too. We totally have to come back here."

Inside, Giselle muttered. "Who would ever want to come back?" But she kept her counsel to herself

Unaware of Giselle, Uncle Danny continued happily. "*¡Hijole!* Next trip, we're going to make a point of coming this way." He called out the cross streets, and they repeated them out loud until they were cemented in their brains.

Uncle Danny glanced back. Tessy was sitting on the floor, looking really worried. He went over and knelt beside her.

"*¿Mande?*" asked the Big Mexican. "What's wrong?"

Tessy's little brow furrowed. "You're going to come back here? Even after we're safe?"

Danny knelt on the floor, a little slowly, because of his old knees. "We're pirates for the Fleet."

"What?" asked Tessy.

"Liberty and I do come back, but very, very carefully," he said.

"How is that even possible?" asked the little girl archly.

"So, last week, we moved fast, got some medical supplies that the doctors at the Fleet needed, and then ran for it," said Danny.

"You stole it?" asked Tessy.

"No, because no one owned it," said Uncle Danny. "Thieves steal from those who need it. We're pirates that take stuff that does not belong to anyone anymore."

115

"But...pirates?" said Giselle with distaste.

"*¡Neta!* If we found a hospital, still working on the coast, we would—And should!—do everything we can to help them. Food, water, ammunition," said Uncle Danny lifting his chin. "But we've only found empty buildings...except for the few poor souls that are zoms."

"So...you're the good guys?" asked Tessy.

"We work really hard to help everyone we can," said Danny earnestly.

With pernicious oiliness, Giselle asked. "And what about those soldiers back there?"

"I don't know what was up with them," shrugged Danny. "But they started that fight. And I wished they hadn't."

And the people around him saw the sadness in his lined face.

Tessy reached out to touch his hand. He looked up at her and smiled.

"Annnnnd....," she said at last. "Pirates are kinda cool."

"Right!" chuckled Uncle Danny. "That's what we thought. *Piratas son muy chidas.*" He leaned a little closer to the little girl. "*And!* We Don't want to get in trouble with *mi Abuela* for stealing like a thief."

Tessy's eyes widened and she nodded emphatically. "True!"

A shout came from the tank. "We're close!"

Uncle Danny started to get up, however he suddenly stopped to hug Tessy quickly. As he was disengaging, he stopped and gave her another hug. The little girl looked puzzled.

"That one was from *Tia* Liberty above," explained the Big Mexican.

Tessy grinned.

"Now, I need to go out, *but* I promise to be careful," he whispered.

The smile faded and the little girl nodded soberly. "Okay."

Standing, he turned and went to the front of the bus. Mostly, he saw tank in front of him, and the buildings beside them.

Once the bus stopped, Danny did have to boot a zom in the chest, to get it to back away from the door. Now that he had clearance, he jumped down as Frankline closed the door behind.

As Uncle Danny walked towards the tank, Liberty dropped down to walk beside him. However, neither was desperate to climb on it.

Contorting herself, Liberty stretched and felt a few vertebrae pop. "Ooooh, that felt good." She looked at Danny. "I really needed to stretch my legs."

"*Si*, me too," admitted Uncle Danny.

Liberty's nose wrinkled. "But we might not want to stand too close."

Uncle Danny followed her gaze to all the zom-bits, which were now embedded in and around the bottom of the tank. "*¡Orale!* I'm not going to argue."

A moment later, Captain Singh dropped down with Staff Sergeant Ruiz.

"I want to walk a little ahead to see what's around the Dyson building," explained Singh.

"*And* he's tired of being a passenger," said Ruiz in *sotto voce.*

"I am not," replied Singh archly.

"*Please!* You hate being a passenger," laughed Ruiz. "If you're not driving the boat, you get all squirrelly."

"You drive really fast," countered Singh.

"I do," agreed Ruiz. "But it doesn't really matter who's behind the wheel. Washington grandmothers putters over the waves, an' you still get all worked up."

"Speaking of which, can we get back to work?" asked Singh. He tried for an icy voice, but it just sounded like a complaint.

"Sure," replied Ruiz with a cute little chirp in her voice.

Singh gave her a scowl, but there was also the start of a smile. He turned to Liberty and Uncle Danny.

"You two know the area better," he said. "Can you get us to a good vantage point?"

Shortly, they were back on the roof of the pizza joint, near the Dyson Science building. Liberty looked at Uncle Danny.

"Feels like just yesterday," she said.

Danny smiled. "Funny that."

"This the way you got in?" asked Singh.

Liberty quickly explained how they went from the roof, onto the covered sidewalk and just walked over.

"I see a little problem with that," said Ruiz drily.

There was a gap where the alien ship had used its heat beam to melt a large section of covered sidewalk. And no one had bridged the gap in the meantime.

"Actually, we could drive the bus right into that gap," said Ruiz thoughtfully. "And then load everyone on."

"Yeah...," started Singh while he looked over the grounds around the building. "Good idea. But that's a lot of zoms."

Ruiz sighed. "Bath *is* going to freak if we ask her to run over that many zoms."

"She'll be more worried about the cable between the bus and the tank," said Singh.

"And she'd be right about that too," said Ruiz.

Singh turned to Liberty. "So, you said that you went over the bridge to the building to get in."

"Yeah," nodded Liberty. "Then they put us in a quarantine room on the first floor, for the people who have been bitten," suggested Liberty.

"It must be full of zoms by now," chuckled Singh, looking at the creatures crowded around the first floor.

"Oh! But it wasn't though," said Liberty thoughtfully. Her lower jaw jutted out, trying to remember. She looked at Uncle Danny. "How *did* they clear the quarantine area of zoms? It's like I can see it in my mind, and it was a pretty cool idea, but...." She bit her lower lip.

The Big Mexican snapped his fingers. "The fire alarm!"

"Oh! That's right," exclaimed Liberty.

Uncle Danny turned to the Captain and Staff Sergeant and explained. "Apparently, when they turn on the fire

119

alarm, the zoms inside head straight for the door."

"You're kidding!" said Singh.

"Makes sense," suggested Ruiz. "I mean, from elementary school on, it's ingrained in us to head for the exit when you hear that alarm."

"Like muscle memory? But that the zoms remember...that's really fascinating," mused Singh. "Well anyway, back to work. So, driving over zoms is not a good idea."

"How about putting a wooden or metal bridge over that covered walkway. Then we just bring everyone this way," suggested Ruiz.

"Take everyone down the fire escape and through the alleys?" said the Captain. "Let's check that route."

The path down and through the alleys was not that long.

"But I'm a bit worried about all the ways that zoms can wander onto our path," said Singh.

Ruiz scrunched up her face. "It would be better to plug those holes."

"If we had a bunch of cars," suggested Uncle Danny.

"But that's like seven or eight cars that we'd need," said Liberty.

"And just shooting anything that comes in is just a waste of ammo," mused Singh. "The cars might be the best, but then we have to fan out and get that many."

"With all those birds flying around," said Uncle Danny.

"And just the regular garden-variety zoms," said Liberty.

"There has to be a faster option," said Singh. "I don't

want to turn off the tank..." And his voice trailed off.

Ruiz looked at him. "You worried that it might not start back up again?"

Singh just shrugged.

Uncle Danny suddenly blinked and looked up at the sky.

Liberty lifted her rifle up. "Trouble?"

"*¿Mande?*" he asked in confusion. "Oh! No, no. I had...what if we use the fire alarm?"

"To scare off the zoms in front of the building?" asked Liberty.

"Then we could just drive up to the covered walkway and get everyone in," nodded Ruiz.

"But will the fire alarm move all those zoms?" asked Singh. He turned to his Staff Sergeant. "SAT phone?" Ruiz quickly took it out and handed it to the Captain. He dialed and someone came right on.

"Is everything alright?" asked Fred, the unofficial leader of Dyson.

"This is Captain Singh, and we're right down the block from you." He went on to explain how they were planning on moving everyone out of there, including using the fire alarm.

"Oh...," said Fred with a subdued voice. "Problem. The fire alarm *does* drive any zoms out of the quarantine, and they will back away, *but* they don't leave. We think the sound has to be more immediate."

"Immediate?" asked Singh.

"Right on top of them," said Fred pensively. "If it's right

there, then they go, but as soon as they are a little away, they just mill about."

Singh relayed this to everyone else there, and Fred took a moment to ask Liberty about Dr. Tagg, who had come from Dyson. But the Captain quickly got them back on track.

Liberty asked. "Do they come back to the door?"

There was a short pause, and then Fred said. "Only after the sound has gone away. But if the creatures don't go that far..."

"Is it enough to open up a path all the way to the door?" asked Singh.

"Sorry, no," said Fred.

"Have you ever tried amplifying the sound?" asked Singh.

"To see if we could clear a larger area?" asked Fred. "No, but it's worth checking out."

"If we can open a path to the covered walkway, we can drive our bus right up," said Singh.

"Are there any external speakers on the building?" asked Uncle Danny.

"No," replied Fred. "But maybe we can see if there is something we can use here. I don't know if we have anything bigger than a boom box here. And even that might not work anymore."

"Okay," said Singh. "If you can dig at your end, then we'll work on the problem at our end as well."

After they had signed off, the four moved back towards the tank.

"I saw a music store back a little ways," said Uncle Danny. "I want to check it out."

"I could send a couple of people with you," said Singh.

"Um, I was just going to ask Liberty if she's up for it," said Danny. "It's just a quick trip anyway."

"And you can always come back for extra arms if you need it," nodded Singh. "Meanwhile, we'll keep noodling over the problem here."

"Sounds good," said Uncle Danny. He started off with Liberty at his side, but then he said. "I just need to do one thing."

Reaching the edge of the bus, he asked if Liberty could hold his shotgun. The moment his hands were free, Uncle Danny leapt up to one of the windows that no longer had any glass and did a chin up.

"Hey Tessy!" he called out.

"*Tio* Danny?" she laughed. "What're you doing?"

"Me and *Tia* Liberty are just going down the street a little ways," said Danny. "We need some kind of sound system to scare off the zoms."

"Are you going far?" asked Tessy with great concern.

"Okay, my arms are getting tired," said Danny. And he dropped to the ground.

Tessy came to the window though.

"We're just going a little ways," said Uncle Danny. "And I promise to be careful."

"You go off on a lot of missions, don't you?" asked Tessy.

"I need to help people," said the Big Mexican. "*Tu*

123

*bisabuela,* up in Heaven...she is watching, and..."

"She's got a shoe in her hand, right?" chuckled Tessy. "That's what Papa always used to say."

"Right, and she expects me to help as many people as possible," said Danny. "Or Else!"

"Do you think Papa and Mama are with her?" asked Tessy softly.

"Of Course!" smiled Uncle Danny with authority. "Absolutely."

Tessy nodded. "And you're going to be real careful."

"I'll keep an eye on him," said Liberty. "I promise."

"And I on her," said Uncle Danny. "That's how a team works."

Liberty called out a warning. "Zoms closing."

"See! She is doing it already," grinned the Big Mexican.

Satisfied that Tessy was good, they moved away from the bus, and the encroaching zoms, who were looking for a light snack. Tessy did move to the back of the school bus to watch them. Liberty caught the movement and tapped Danny's arm.

"Wha...," started Uncle Danny, but then he looked back and saw his niece. He gave a big, slow wave, and she waved back tentatively.

"She'll be alright," said Liberty and she grinned. "As long as I keep you in one piece."

"¡*No manches!* Good luck with that," chuckled Danny as they weaved in amongst the zoms.

"*Actually,* for that matter, what are we doing out here?"

asked Liberty.

With a mischievous smirk, the Big Mexican looked sideways at her. "You don't feel guilty for going off on our own, do you?"

Liberty looked down and away. "Um, kinda."

"We don't work for them," said Uncle Danny. "We work with them, but...we're like private contractors."

The Librarian looked up at him with a grin. "Hey, that's right." She looked down. "I was starting to feel like we were out of place with my red beret and your tan coat, like we should be wearing some sort of uniform."

"Do you want to wear a uniform?" asked Uncle Danny with genuine curiosity.

Liberty opened her mouth and then closed it, deep in thought. "Not really. Do you?"

"No," said Danny flatly. "I like what we do." He gestured at the street ahead. *"Dos amigos,* back on the road again."

"Filled with zoms?" chuckled Liberty.

Uncle Danny sniffed. "It's not perfect. *But*...helping like this secures our place in the Fleet. If we're on the Rear Admiral's good side, that makes it easier for Colin, Tagg and Smalls. And soon Tessy too."

"That's true. I never thought of it like that," nodded the Librarian earnestly.

"Which is one reason I keep coming back to this lovely place," smirked Uncle Danny, waving a hand at the zoms nearby. Then he added with mock gruffness. "Annnnnd, We Do Good Work Out Here. And don't you forget it!"

"Yes sir," laughed Liberty.

"But...if we become part of their army," he continued slowly. "We can only do what they want. Like policing."

Liberty wrinkled her nose. "I don't think I'd like that." She pointed with her rifle. "Oh! There's the sailing shop."

They reached the open door for the 'High Seas' shop. Uncle Danny went in with Liberty following close behind. She fanned out, checking the aisles. Narrowing his eyes, he squinted at her.

"What're you doing?" he asked with a trace of annoyance.

"What?" she replied innocently.

"Aren't you going to the bookshop?" asked Danny.

"In a moment," said Liberty. Slinging her rifle behind her back, she drew her handgun for close quarters.

"You don't have to do this," rumbled Uncle Danny icily.

"Yes," she said airily. "I believe I do." Then she disappeared down an aisle.

Uncle Danny's face twisted in annoyance. But she was soon back.

"Stockroom is clear, and the back door is locked. I'm heading over to the bookshop," she said casually.

"What was that?" asked Uncle Danny, annoyed.

Liberty stopped, but she did not look up at him. However, she did have a small smile on her face.

"I made a promise," she said.

For a moment, the Big Mexican was going to snap at her, but then he stopped himself.

126

"Tessy?"

"I'm going to close the front door behind," said Liberty. "We better go quick. We don't want the tank/bus to worry."

After she left, Uncle Danny gave a small smile and looked up. "Well, *Abuela,* I got good friends. That's a blessing. Or...did you arrange that?"

## Chapter Fourteen

Less than ten minutes later, the two met back out in front. Her Dora the Explorer and his Avengers backpack were both stuffed to the gills.

"Arrr, did yah find some good loot?" asked Liberty.

"I found many a Spanish Doubloon," replied Uncle Danny. "Or whatever it is."

Liberty grinned and the two moved down to the music store.

"What are we looking for again?" she asked.

"Anything that can be mounted to the front of the tank," said Danny.

"Like a pair of steer's horns," said Liberty."

Uncle Danny looked at her questioningly.

"Oh, out in Texas, some men would put a pair of horns on the front of their car," explained Liberty.

"That'd be cool on the front of the tank," nodded Uncle Danny as they slid into the music store.

"Pimp my tank," giggled Liberty.

There was one zom in the music store, who was easily dealt with. They stopped in front of what could have been a section for musical equipment, but it was utterly barren.

"*¡Hijole!*" said Danny as they were heading towards the front. "Well, we tried."

"Wait!" cried out Liberty.

Uncle Danny swung around; shotgun ready.

"Harmonicas!!!" hissed Liberty breathlessly.

"Wait, what?" asked Danny, and he added with a growl. "I thought we were in *danger.*"

"Nope," chirped Liberty. "Just harmonicas."

Finding a chintzy string bag, she dumped a box of metal harmonicas into it and then tied it to her Dora backpack.

"Come on," she said. "Hurry! Tessy's going to get worried."

Liberty zipped out of the store and Uncle Danny followed.

"Can you...," started the Big Mexican.

"Wait!" she said urgently.

Danny was about to ignore it, believing that she was crying wolf again. But then she raised her rifle, back towards the militia compound. He immediately raised his weapon.

"What?" he asked softly.

"Let's head back slowly," said Liberty. "Can you lead me, while I walk backwards? I want to keep an eye on our tail-feathers."

As she watched the street behind them, Uncle Danny took ahold of her backpack.

"Clear in front," he reported with a soft voice, ignoring the zoms shambling towards them. "I'm leading you."

Slowly, they moved back towards the bus.

For almost 20 feet, Uncle Danny led her. Eventually though, she lowered her rifle.

"Come on," she said. "Let's get outta here."

Silently, they walked for a while on high alert. Soon, the bus was in sight and Liberty relaxed a little more.

"I thought I saw something moving back there," explained Liberty. "Maybe a bird."

Uncle Danny looked at her in surprise.

"I don't know if it's one of the ones you met," said Liberty.

"That's okay," said the Big Mexican. "Better to be safe than sorry."

Uncle Danny suddenly saw Tessy in the back of the bus, waving furiously. He waved back happily.

"Oh!" he said. "Why harmonicas?"

"Huh?" started Liberty, but then she remembered. "Oh, I'm going to give them out. For kids to play with. And for musical adults. But, mainly for kids. I think learning music is an important part of a child's education, even if you suck at it, like me."

Uncle Danny grinned. "That makes sense." Then he frowned. "They're collecting quite a crowd of zoms."

Once close, Singh, almost upset, called out. "What took you so long?"

Uncle Danny raised an eyebrow at that. *"¿Neta?"*

Singh saw the look and remembered their lack of uniforms. He tried again. "We were just starting to get worried about you."

"Got to go carefully," replied Uncle Danny.

"We don't want to blunder into trouble," added Liberty.

The Captain noticed that their backpacks were full, but he wisely decided not to comment on it.

"Any luck?" called out Singh.

*"Nada,"* replied Uncle Danny. "Someone has a sweet stereo set-up somewhere, but not here."

"We appreciate your help," said Singh.

"You guys might want to move soon," suggested Uncle Danny. "Looks like you're getting quite a crowd."

"We were waiting on you," said Singh without heat.

"We're jumping aboard," said Uncle Danny as they got onto the bus.

The moment that they were on, Tessy appeared and hugged him.

"You took too long," she chastised.

"Sorry," he said gracefully as he hugged her back and whispered. *"Por favor, no te enojes conmigo."*

131

The tank-bus started moving and Liberty and Uncle Danny put their backpacks under the front seat.

"Looting?" asked Giselle with scorn.

Tessy turned with fire in her eyes and said, icily. "They're pirates. Get it right!"

The older woman was so surprised that she couldn't find the words.

"Now, now," said Uncle Danny softly to the girl. "Be nice."

"But…," started Tessy.

However, Uncle Danny just gave her a hard look and made a little nod towards Gisele. The little girl's shoulders slumped.

Tessy turned to the older woman and mumbled. "Sorry."

For a moment, it looked like Gisele was going to say something snotty, but she caught Uncle Danny's eyes.

Over his Niece's head, The Big Mexican mouthed. 'Be nice.'

Blanching, Gisele said to the little girl. "It's all good sweetie."

Not wanting to push his luck, Uncle Danny turned with Tessy toward Liberty.

"I should probably go back up," said the Librarian, but she didn't want to, and it showed in her voice.

"We're not travelling far *Mija*," suggested Danny. "Might as well stay for now."

Liberty leaned heavily against the metal pole by the

door. "Okay. If you insist."

Letting go of her Danny, Tessy stepped over a little tentatively to Liberty, who gave her a weary smile. Then the little girl went in for a hug. It was a great, big, solid hug.

"Thank you," murmured Liberty as she hugged Tessy back.

Uncle Danny saw Singh answer the SAT phone on the tank. Soon, they were stopping, and Tessy stepped back with a beaming smile, which the Librarian returned in full.

"Now that I got a Tessy-Hug-Full-Of-Power," said Liberty as she looked up at the Big Mexican. "Let's go and see what's going on."

"What about my hug?" asked Uncle Danny with a big whine.

After Danny had gotten Tessy-Hug-Full-Of-Power, they left the bus. This time they got onto the tank.

"So, what's the story?" asked Uncle Danny.

"We got a hit," said Singh. "Kind of."

"Kinda?" chuckled Liberty. "That sounds like a normal day for us."

"Probably a Tuesday," smirked Uncle Danny with mock seriousness.

Ignoring them, Singh continued. "One of the grad students at Dyson said that he knows where the ...," But he stopped, and his eyebrows collided together in disbelief. "...'the sickest sound system ever' is."

From inside the tank, Ruiz called out. "You're just old!"

"Hey," replied Singh swiftly with a mock growl. "Remember who's in charge."

"SIR! You're just too old. SIR," came the immediate reply.

Singh sniffed. "That's better! Anyhow, this grad built it to be completely portable, so that he could take it home on the weekends. So, one person should be able to easily carry it."

"Where is it?" asked Liberty.

"It's in his dorm room nearby." Singh pointed towards a nearby building sticking up. "That's the one. Room 312. I was originally thinking of driving over."

"That'll cost fuel," wondered Liberty carefully.

"Exactly. Which is why I'm planning on sending a team over right now," said Singh.

"Do we need that many," suggested Liberty thoughtfully.

Singh looked at her curiously. However, Liberty looked over at the Big Mexican., and he shrugged.

Danny grinned. "Why are we still here *Mija?*"

"Don't you want any help?" asked Singh with concern, and then he added. "I wasn't trying to get you to volunteer."

"You didn't call us over!" smiled Uncle Danny reassuringly.

"We're used to moving about," added Liberty.

"And above all, we need to protect the bus," said Uncle Danny. "An' the more soldiers, the better."

"That's true," nodded Liberty.

Liberty and Danny climbed off the tank, basically ending the discussion. The Big Mexican power-walked back to the bus to tell Tessy where they were going.

To Singh on the tank, Liberty said. "We'll be back 'A-Sap', isn't that what they say in military movies."

"It works," smiled the Captain. However, he warned. "We're going to have to move periodically."

"Hopefully we won't be that long," said Liberty. "And it was Room 312, right?"

They were soon out of earshot, moving as quickly as they dared.

"We better take the main streets getting there," suggested Liberty.

"At least that way we can see what's coming," agreed Danny.

Moving around the corner, Uncle Danny gave a low whistle.

"Good thing we left the tank at home," he muttered.

There was a maze of cars. Two people could slide through, but the tank would have had to try and shove them all aside.

Reaching the grad dorm, they had to bypass a zom or two. The glass doors in front had been shattered, so they just walked in. Liberty covered left with her handgun.

"Got a few," she said as zoms started shambling towards them.

"Stairs!" called out Uncle Danny.

135

Reaching those, he stepped to one side and whipped the door open.

A zom lunged out, but only found empty air. Uncle Danny slammed into the zom from the side and knocked it over. In no time, they were inside the stairwell and heading up.

As the stairway door closed with a boom, the zom, that had been knocked over, managed to stand back up. But it found itself face to face with an alien-bird, topped with a red tuft.

"Urrrr?" muttered the zom.

On the stairs heading up, Liberty and Danny moved as fast as they dared. Turning a corner, they saw a zom halfway down the stairs. It saw them and started to move carefully.

"I wouldn't think they'd be able to do stairs," muttered Danny.

"Well, I could…," started Liberty, and she started to raise her handgun.

"Actually, if you move to one side," suggested Uncle Danny. He gestured to the other side of the landing, so she stepped aside.

Going in, Uncle Danny shot up the stairs. The zom started to reach out. Keeping low, the Big Mexican grabbed the zom's ankles and yanked them. He dove aside as the zom fell backwards onto the hard stairs and skidded down.

As soon as it reached the bottom, Liberty jumped past it and ran up to him.

"Ow," she said without heat.

"Yeah," nodded Uncle Danny unhappily as they kept moving. "I didn't want to just kill'em, but...I hope they didn't feel that...you know, like 'feel' feel." He turned to the zom that was struggling to get up and said, embarrassed. "*Me disculpo de verdad.*"

Liberty just patted his arm. "I don't think it felt a thing, and really you were trying Not to kill it."

On the third floor, they opened the fire door, but there were two zoms close by.

"Probably best not to get cute with these guys," said the Big Mexican. Uncle Danny just raised his shotgun and put them down quick.

They stepped over the bodies and quickly found room 312. A deer slug from the shotgun opened it right up. Turning from the window, a zom wearing only a t-shirt swiveled to face them.

"Got it," said Liberty and she fired once.

Swiftly, they checked the rest of the small dorm, but it was clear.

Liberty made an unhappy noise. "Um, could you...,".

Puzzled, Uncle Danny looked at her, and then saw that she was pointing at the extremely-dead zom. It had dropped on its back, naked from the waist down.

"*¡Orale!*" nodded her friend. He grabbed an old blanket and threw it over the zom.

"Thanks, that was...," began Liberty, but her voice trailed off.

"It's okay *Mija*," said Danny, and it was. He stepped towards the desks.

There was a noise from out in the hall, and they looked at one another.

"Was that the fire door?" asked Liberty soundlessly.

Uncle Danny started towards the door, but then he stopped. Whoever it was, they were close.

Liberty nodded towards the bathroom. There was barely enough room for one person as she went in first, edging around the crusty toilet.

"That's scary," she hissed softly in true horror, nodding at the toilet.

"You get in the shower," whispered Uncle Danny.

"No! You get in the shower. I'm supposed to be keeping you safe," replied Liberty at the same volume.

Uncle Danny turned his broad back towards her and started backing up. She had no choice but to step into the mildewy shower, or else get knocked over.

As the Big Mexican crouched down, shotgun towards the bathroom door, her nose wrinkled in annoyance. She glared down at him.

"I think you're getting a bald spot back here," she murmured testily.

"Ow," he replied softly, sadly. "That one really hurt."

Out in the hallway, came footfalls. Both could tell that it was too fast to be a zom. However, it stopped.

More noises were coming from the hallway. More alien-birds.

Uncle Danny made sure that his shotgun was ready to fire. Liberty aimed her Glock over the crouched man.

Something started into the main room.

"TASS!" cried out a desperate voice from in front of the building. "TASS! TASS!"

Suddenly, loud sounds erupted from the hallway. The noises headed away, and then there was the sound of a fire door being thrown open, which banged against the wall.

"Is that...?" asked Uncle Danny.

"Go!" hissed

Liberty urgently. "Whatever it is, this might be our best chance."

Moving out, Liberty went first to the door to check the corridor. There was another fire door opposite the one they had come through. She ducked back in and saw a sleek sound system on a shelf. It looked like something out of Star Trek.

"Must be it," she muttered. Quickly taking it and wrapping the power cord around it, she noticed that Uncle Danny was still standing at the window. He had a stunned expression.

"We gotta go," she said.

But he did not reply at first.

"Daniel DeSantos Rameriez!" she hissed in her You-Cheesed-Off-The-Librarian voice.

Jerking awake, he blinked at her.

"Come on!" she continued, more gently.

Nodding, Uncle Danny moved to follow. He did not even question why they were going in a new direction.

Through the little window in the fire door, she saw a

zom looking at her. Giving the door a big kick with a 'hi-yah', she knocked it open. The door unbalanced the zom who fell back onto the landing.

Sweeping with her handgun, she found it clear of anything else. The zom on the landing was flailing a bit to get up. She stomped down with her clodhopper boot, which rapped its head against the Formica. Dazed, it lay still, but it would survive. Nonetheless, Liberty still felt sickened by the violence of it.

Pushing herself to keep going, Liberty led Uncle Danny down. She was grateful that she now had the silencer, however she still did not want to push her luck.

"Why are we on the stairs?" blinked Uncle Danny behind her.

"Leaving," she replied, concentrating on the environment.

Liberty led him out the back to a small parking lot.

Uncle Danny suddenly started with sudden concern. "Wait, do you have the…?"

Turning around just enough, the Librarian showed that she carried the 'sickest sound system ever'. Then she led him carefully across the parking lot.

"Oh shit, I got lost in my head," said Uncle Danny. "I'm sorry."

"It's okay," said Liberty and it was. "Let's just get out of here. There's an alley up ahead going in the right direction."

"Worth a shot," said Uncle Danny. His voice now back to business. He tapped his earpiece. "Captain Singh, this is

Danny. Liberty and I are heading towards you with the sound system, but our friendly little neighborhood birds are around, so be careful."

"Copy that," said Singh. "We're not far from where you left us. Singh out."

"I didn't even think to warn the tank," said Liberty with embarrassment.

"But you got me out," said Danny. "Teamwork!"

And Liberty gave him a grin.

They reached the alley, and the Big Mexican took the lead. He moved close to a big green commercial garbage bin when a shadow shot over the alley from rooftop to rooftop. Using hand gestures, Uncle Danny suggested that they go next to the bin and Liberty nodded.

They both hunkered down close to the side. Since it had been a long while since anyone put any garbage inside, the bin actually didn't smell bad, for which Liberty was grateful.

Another shadow whipped by overhead.

Soon though, they heard sounds above, just out of sight. It sounded like claws on the edge of the roof. Uncle Danny pointed himself up and then Liberty out. She nodded and he raised his shotgun to the noise, which was coming closer. Setting down the sound system, she covered the alley with her rifle, just in case.

"Hey!!! This is Colonel Sanders," cried the distant voice of Sergeant Bloodbath. Danny and Liberty looked at each other in surprise as the voice continued. "The Lord has Risen me from the dead, with eleven herbs and spices, to stomp your sorry asses! Praise the Lord and pass the honey mustard!!!"

Gunshots rang out.

Suddenly, they heard the birds around them taking flight.

"I was worried...," began Uncle Danny.

Liberty started to turn back to him.

An alien-bird leapt down from the roof, slamming into the top of the metal dumpster. Her razor beak whipped over the edge, and the bird snapped at him.

As Uncle Danny tumbled back, he felt the beak get his shoulder, which exploded in pain. He accidently dropped on top of Liberty pressing her face-first into the alley. Quickly, he rolled off Liberty's back just as the alien-bird dropped next to them.

The creature lifted one leg to smash down on her. Liberty's rifle was trapped underneath her, but the barrel was pointed in the direction of the alien-bird. Quickly shifting it, the rifle went off.

The bullet hit the leg, which was still on the ground, and shattered the tarsometatarsus bone.

"Ratt-Tuh!" screeched the alien-bird as she tipped to the side. Despite slamming down hard, the bird was still too freaking close to Liberty.

With no other choice, Liberty let go of her rifle and scrambled backwards as the bird pecked at her. She tried vainly to grab her rifle but had to abort at the last second. The bird's razor beak scored a hole in the concrete where her hand would have been.

Uncle Danny's shotgun went off.

The alien-bird tried to peck more, but her movements grew sluggish. Then the bird slumped down and did not move any more.

Snatching her rifle, Liberty was relieved to see that it was not damaged. "Thank God. I don't know what I'd…" But she could not find the words.

"It's okay *Mija*," said Uncle Danny with heavy words.

Liberty turned to glance at him, and then she did a double-take. "Your shoulder!"

"Ow," he muttered with a smile.

The Librarian leapt up. There was a gash going upwards from his chest to his left shoulder. Blood stained his tan coat.

Slinging her rifle behind her back, Liberty reached for his coat. He backed off, a little reflexively. The Librarian snatched the unbloody side of the coat to hold him still.

"Quite fussing," she ordered.

Opening up the coat she saw the torn shirt and some of the cut.

"It's not bleeding very heavily, and you're upright. Thank God!" she assessed. She let go of his coat. "Let's get you to that nice Medic…damn it, I can't remember his name."

"Probably a good idea," admitted Uncle Danny reluctantly. "And it's Washington."

"That's right! Thank you!" She immediately moved opposite his wound and pulled his arm over her shoulders.

"I'm not an invalid," grumbled Danny.

"No, you're THE Uncle Danny. A Force of Nature. And don't you fucking forget it!" replied Liberty fiercely. He looked down at her in bemused astonishment as they moved towards the far street. However, Liberty suddenly smacked her hand against her head.

"I'm a dummy," she declared.

Confused, Uncle Danny watched while she set him to lean against a wall. Then she power-walked back down the alley. Immediately, she returned with the "sickest sound system ever", and he chuckled.

Liberty was grumbling hard, but really only at herself. "I can't believe I almost forgot it."

"It's okay *Mija*," said Uncle Danny kindly. "What can we say, it's been a long day."

"A ten hour nap sounds good about now," chuckled Liberty wearily.

"At least 10 hour," agreed Danny fervently.

They reached the end of the alley, and the street beyond. The sound of gunfire was getting sharper, so she put him against a wall again.

"Let me look first," she said.

"'Kay," he replied.

The easy acceptance worried her. She moved to the edge and drew her Glock since her other arm was full of stereo. Glancing out, she saw a bird hightailing it down a side street while Singh shot at the alien.

Then it was all clear, except for some garden-variety zoms.

Turning, Liberty saw that Uncle Danny was still leaning

against a wall. But he was eyeing the zoms as they shuffled closer, ready to fight.

"Come on," she said to him. "No lollygagging."

Shifting him from the wall hurt, but the Big Mexican stood upright. Soon, Liberty had him out of the alley and dodging the zoms, who had been getting a little too close.

Liberty called out to the tank. "Hey!"

They were moving a little quicker than Danny'd like. But he could tell from her pinched mouth that she was worried. To be fair, he was a little worried about him too.

Suddenly, Uncle Danny stopped, and she nearly dragged him off his feet.

"What...?" muttered Liberty, and she followed his gaze down. He was looking at a dead bird. Danny was trying hard to focus on the tuft on top of the alien's head. Finally, she understood.

"It's more orange than red," she said urgently. "Like burnt umber."

Blinking, Uncle Danny nodded. She was right. It wasn't Rakduson. It wasn't the one that he had crippled; left screaming in pain. But then, the Big Mexican wondered, when he shot the device in the back of her head, *had* he crippled the alien-bird?

"Come on," urged Liberty, and they kept going.

Haltingly, Danny said. "We heard—back in the dorm— one of the birds calling from outside." Man, he felt bone-tired.

"Yeah, I wondered what that was all about?" grunted Liberty, weary from her effort.

145

"When I looked out the window, I saw Rakduson walking around in a circle, hobbling...calling out," said Uncle Danny, and she almost stopped walking.

"Rak? As in Red Tuft?" asked Liberty with surprise.

"¡Orale! But she was only playing," said the Big Mexican. "Pretending. I don't know how I knew, but..."

Now that they were close enough, Liberty called out to the soldiers on the tank. "Paging Dr. Washington, paging Dr. Washington!"

Uncle Danny chuckled at that. "Dr. Washington to the Geriatric department."

"Stop that," chastised Liberty, but with a hint of a smile.

The two had to go around a knot of zoms, who looked befuddled by all the humans around. A giant buffet that they could never catch.

Singh came over the edge of the tank as they passed, and Liberty handed him the stereo system.

"Thank you," said the Captain sincerely, and he turned. "Sergeant BloodBath. Front and Center!"

By the time the two reached the bus, the medic was there, and Frankline had the bus door open.

"This way sir," said Washington. He worked to get the Big Mexican up and onto the bus.

"Here, I'll keep that safe," said Frankline as he took Uncle Danny's shotgun without a protest from the wounded man. Carefully, the private laid it across his lap.

Washington settled the Big Mexican into the first seat.

"Wait!" cried out Danny, and he held out his right hand

146

to keep the medic away. "You need to double glove."

"Okay," replied Washington calmly.

"Shit!" cried Liberty from outside the bus.

"Language," hissed Gisele from behind Danny.

The Big Mexican was about to get up to check on Liberty when she stuck her head in the door.

"That's right," she moaned. "He's got the zombie virus. Sorry! You need to be careful."

"It's okay," said Washington confidently. "I volunteered at an HIV clinic in high school. So, no problem. But thank you both for the heads up." And he did double-glove.

Suddenly, Tessy was standing beside Uncle Danny, though she was too short to loom over him.

"What happened?" she demanded.

"He's okay," said Liberty as she stuck her head in the door again.

Slowly, Tessy turned to glare at Liberty with a cold fury in her eyes.

"He just got scratched up," replied the Librarian immediately, defensively.

"You promised!" growled Tessy.

"Be gentle," said Uncle Danny to his niece. "She saved me—twice!—out there."

Tessy turned on him. "You shouldn't have gone!" There was still fire in her eyes, but now it was tinged with fear.

"It's going to be...," started the Big Mexican. But he gave a hiss when the medic pulled his coat away from his wound with a sticky noise.

147

"I'm afraid I'm going to have to ruin this shirt," said Washington.

"*¡Sale!* It's pretty ruined already," chuckled Danny, however he winced because it hurt to move.

"Why are you laughing?" demanded Tessy, stamping her foot.

"It only hurts when I laugh," replied her uncle merrily, which made him chuckle and so he winced some more.

"Stop it," insisted Tessy and she stamped her foot.

Uncle Danny looked at her more seriously. "*Mi Mariposa Unicornio*, this is okay. I'm going to be okay."

"But you don't know that!" said Tessy, almost pained. "Not for sure!"

Reaching out a hand as Washington cut his shirt open, Uncle Danny said. "I could use someone to hold my hand right now."

Tessy grabbed it, quickly and fiercely.

Smiling, Uncle Danny looked at her and tried to ignore the pain as the medic worked.

"There, that makes me feel better," he smiled wanly. "To have you holding my hand."

Washington caught a tender spot and Uncle Danny's face twisted for a second.

"Does it hurt?" asked Tessy with great concern.

"I told you, 'only when I laugh'," said Uncle Danny with mock seriousness.

"Stop that," grunted Tessy and she used her other hand to whap his arm lightly.

Liberty took two steps into the bus. She vacillated on whether or not to go to the little girl. She didn't like to see Tessy so unhappy, but at the same time, the Librarian did not want to make the situation worse.

Uncle Danny glanced up and caught her eye. He smiled gently and mouthed. 'She'll be okay *Mija*.' Liberty gave a wan smile and nodded. She suddenly needed to get her frustration out, and there was a skanky zom in a wifebeater closing on the door. Her eyes narrowed.

As Liberty disappeared out the door, Giselle, seated behind, leaned forward to look over the Big Mexican's left shoulder.

"Oh, I was worried there for a moment," she said blithely.

Tessy blinked at her. "What?"

"It looks like a minor laceration, but it shouldn't even need stitches," explained Giselle to the little girl with a gentle tone. The older woman moved to the edge of her seat to be closer to the girl. "It's an annoying wound, but he should be fine as long as we keep the wound clean and give it time to heal."

"Really?" asked Giselle and Uncle Danny, almost together.

"She's right," agreed Washington. "Sorry, I should have said, but I just wanted to get you fixed as fast as possible, in case we have to move."

"Nothing to apologize for," said Giselle to the Medic. "You're working, I'm just an old busybody who was pre-Med." She looked at Tessy. "But, you want to know what the worst part is?"

149

"What?" asked Tessy. Her eyes grew wide with muted horror.

Giselle said, in almost a whisper. "The Itchies."

Tessy blinked in confusion. "The what?"

With a gentle smile, Giselle went on. "There's an Old Wives Tale that..."

"An Old Wives Tale...?" asked Tessy quickly.

"It's a story from a long, long time ago, that people usually think is not real," explained Giselle smoothly. "And this one said that when a wound begins to itch, that that means that it's beginning to heal."

"So...it's not real?" asked Tessy.

"That's what's so funny," chuckled Giselle. "It *IS* true."

"Really?" asked the little girl. She was still holding on to her uncle, but her death grip had loosened.

"Even now, his body is trying to repair the damage," said Giselle. "It's sending inflammatory cytokines, like fire engines, to the cut. But these are going to cause it to itch, or at least, feel like he needs to itch."

"*But* he is so not allowed to scratch this itch," added Washington. "Even if he really wants to."

Giselle looked at the little girl. "Someone has to make sure that he doesn't itch himself. Do you think you can do that?"

Tessy nodded emphatically. "I can."

Giselle gave a warm smile. "I thought you'd be up to the task. "Now, as soon as..."

There was a sudden and blaring cacophony of noise

from the tank, and everyone jumped, except Danny and Washington, who weren't that easily startled.

"What in God's name?" bellowed Giselle and the sound disappeared.

Satisfied that Danny would be okay, Liberty moved away from the bus.

From the tank, Bath called out. "Sorry! Someone had the stereo cranked way up!"

The mechanic, with an embarrassed look on her face, turned back to the sound system. It was now set on the front of the tank with wires leading inside.

"This is actually beautifully designed," she murmured. "Simple and elegant. If this is made by a guy, I want to date him." And she licked her lips a little. "Heck, even if it's a chick."

"Only a guy would make something like that," said Ruiz dismissively.

"Hey!" scolded Bath. "Don't be sexist. Girls can build kickass sound systems too if they want."

"I'm not saying that they couldn't," started Ruiz defensively. "I'm just saying…"

Singh cleared his throat and said with a warning tone. "Sergeants. Staff and non-Staff."

"Oh-oh," smirked Ruiz playfully. "We're in trouble with Dad." She gave Bath a mock glare. "It's all your fault."

"My fault?" retorted Bath with mock outrage. "You…"

The Captain cleared his throat noisily, and the ladies held their tongue. But they smirked at each other with great amusement. Singh wisely let that go and said. "Okay, so we have a sound system."

"Which is pretty 'sick'," added Bath quietly.

Singh gave a quelling glance and then kept going. "But do we have a recording of a fire alarm?"

Bath opened her mouth, but then closed it. "Oh."

"If I had my iPhone, I'd just download an app that plays one," said Ruiz sadly.

Because a zom-stalker was trying to get a little handsy with Liberty, she climbed up onto the tank. Carefully though, she avoided the plastic wrapped body of Mullins.

Reaching Bath, she said. "Excuse me, but what kind of media does the stereo take? I didn't get a chance to really look at it before. Just grabbed and ran."

"Oh! It'd take an iPhone, but who has one of those anymore," said Bath and she examined it closer. "Oh wow! It takes CD's. Who had CD's before everything fell?"

Liberty looked at the Captain. "Can we call Dyson?"

Less than two minutes later, the de facto leader of the science building, Fred, had to put them on hold while he asked around for a fire alarm sound. In the meantime, they had to move the tank/bus a few more times.

Finally, Fred came back. "Carson, who's sound system that you're using, just burned the sound to a CD. I guess he likes to put his DJ-ing sessions on CD to review them." They could almost hear his eyes rolling. "Everyone's a DJ these days."

"That's true," said Bath sympathetically.

"Anyway," said Fred. "We're going to get it to you. I'm not sure how…" And his voice trailed off.

"Our drone finally died. You wouldn't happen to have one, would you?" asked Singh.

"I wish!" called out a voice from the background. "Our drone died a year ago."

"Carson," said Fred repressively.

"Sorry dude," came the reply from Carson in the background.

To Singh, Fred said thoughtfully. "No, we have another plan, one we've kept in case of emergency, but we never tried it."

# Chapter Fifteen

Private Frankline grinned. "I can't believe that I won. I never win anything."

"Have to admit," said Staff Sergeant Ruiz softly. "When the captain said we could draw straws for this duty, I figured I'd be sitting in the tank."

"At least you're sitting inside a tank instead of a school bus," replied Frankline kindly.

Ruiz was tempted to comment on why Frankline got bus duty-- after losing his M4 Carbine-- but she went on. "This should be interesting."

"Interesting? Oh man! I've *always* wanted to try this!" grinned Frankline.

Ruiz tried not to smile, but one escaped, nonetheless. "I've always wondered if this would work too. Especially since I've got a good throwing arm."

"Did you play ball?" asked Frankline with genuine curiosity.

"For a little while," admitted Ruiz.

"What position?" asked Frankline

"Pitcher, most of the time," said Ruiz.

"No shit!" said Frankline. "That's cool. I did some catcher, but really, I was a benchwarmer. But I was Benchwarmer Number 1, so there's that."

Ruiz just managed not to laugh out loud at that. "Did you play high school?"

"Yep," said Frankline. "We were decent. How long did you play?"

"I played a little college," said Ruiz. "But...long story, I ended up here." And she gave a little, sad sigh.

Frankline shrugged. "Maybe saved your life."

Ruiz blinked, and then looked at him in surprise. "I...I never thought of it that way."

Rising up before them was the Dyson Science Building. However, the front door was obscured by all the zoms in front.

Ruiz sized up the mob. "The distance to the front door has to be at least 50 feet, and all full of zom." She pointed to a car, closer to the mob of zombies. "At some point, we may want a higher vantage point."

"Yes Staff Sergeant," replied Frankline automatically. She glanced at his quickly, but he seemed really sincere.

They sidestepped a zom and moved a little closer. Here,

there were just small knots of zoms, but it was still somewhat dangerous.

Excitedly, Frankline jumped in place. "Oh! Come on! When's the signal?" It came out like a whine, and he heard it too. Embarrassed, he deepened his voice and stopped fidgeting. "I'm just ready to go."

"I understand," said Ruiz patiently.

Frankline glanced at her with a happy, little smirk. "I see, playing it cool over there."

Ruiz chuckled. "Just saving my energy, just in case."

"I'm happy they decided not to use the cannon," said Frankline after a brief pause.

"Me too," said Ruiz. "For many reasons. Though, mostly because shooting an explosive that close to the people who we're trying to rescue...could go very badly."

Frankline blinked. "How?"

"I'm not so worried about Sergeant Bath...," began Ruiz.

"You mean Sergeant Bloodbath?" asked Frankline, straight-faced.

Ruiz suppressed a smile. "Of course. No, I'm worried about one of those rounds hitting the ground at a shallow angle and ricocheting. Skipping like a rock and going right into the building."

"Ooooh, that would be bad," agreed Frankline. He glanced at her, looked back at the zoms, and then returned to her, before looking away again.

Without looking at him, Ruiz ordered. "Out with it, Private."

156

"What?" asked Frankline. "Out with what?"

"You got a question," said Ruiz, and her voice was guarded. "Usually it's, 'are you a lezzie', since I'm in the army, *and* now you know that I played softball....."

Frankline started in surprise. "Wha..." But then he paused. The Private took out his earpiece, taking him off the grid.

"What're you doing?" asked Ruiz with concern.

"I actually didn't think you were..." He cleared his throat. "Well ma'am, since you ordered me...actually I was wondering what you would say if I asked you out."

Now it was Ruiz's turn to look surprised. "Seriously Private? While we're out in the field?"

"I think you're cool," said Frankline. "And why not?"

Ruiz looked at him quixotically. "You're serious?"

Frankline rolled his eyes. "Not asking to get married. Just coffee on the deck at sunset."

"Is that where you take all your dates?" asked Ruiz with a little smile.

A little laugh burst out of Frankline. "Usually I'm just up there myself, unless you count the seagulls."

A flash of delight shot through Ruiz's eyes, but then her face fell. She chewed her lower lip for a moment in thought. "You're under my command. It's frowned upon."

"Maybe that's the old rules," suggested Frankline.

Ruiz thought for a second, but then shook her head. "Unfortunately...and I'm not just saying this, because really unfortunately, I still think it's a good rule." And she took that moment to move them away from a knot of zoms that was getting a little too interested.

A distant fire alarm went off.

"That's it," said Ruiz. "Get ready."

All business once again, Frankline put back in his earpiece. "Yes Staff Sergeant."

Ruiz moved a little closer to the science building and Frankline followed. She checked again, but he seemed sincere and professional, and not pissy that she had rebuffed him. Then she pulled her attention back to the job. If he wasn't so damn cute, she lamented and added. In a naughty puppy sort of way.

In the distance, they heard doors opening and the sound of the fire alarm grew louder.

"You remember the drill Private?" asked Ruiz, all business.

"Yes Staff Sergeant," replied Frankline, and he looked like a greyhound ready to sprint.

"Throw at will!" ordered Ruiz.

The Staff Sergeant pulled the pin on a grenade and threw it. It arced towards the door, but it was meant to fall short, and it disappeared amongst some of zoms. The explosion tore open a ghastly hole in the mob of zoms.

Frankline threw the next one into a closer group and tore open another hole.

"Up here," ordered Ruiz. She power-walked down the street, a little closer to the mob and jumped up on an abandoned car. Frankline came up behind her. She pointed to a spot that was crowded with zoms. "Can you nail that spot?"

Hastily, Frankline threw a grenade. But it went too far and exploded a little outside the path that they were trying to create.

"Dammit!" growled Frankline. "Sorry."

"It's okay," said Ruiz, with a measured voice that she used for training. "Take a second to aim."

Frankline took a deep breath and threw the next grenade more carefully. It appeared to land a little short, and he held his breath. But it bounced smack-dab into the zoms and knocked them back.

"Yes!" he howled.

"Nice work," smiled Ruiz and for a moment, they both looked at each other. And the moment lasted longer than was strictly normal. She quickly cleared her throat. "Okay, we gotta keep going."

Soon, they had cut a rugged path to the door.

"Huh! That worked," she uttered with surprise. Then she blinked and called through her earpiece. "Okay Captain, we're good."

"Good job Staff Sergeant," replied the Captain. "I'll tell Dyson."

Ruiz looked at the Private. "How many grenades do you have left?"

"I'm out," said Frankline as he held his empty hands up.

"Shit, if only we had one more," said Ruiz.

A few zoms were trying to move into the path.

Ruiz spoke up, as if the people in the building could

hear her. "Come on! That path isn't going to stay open for long."

"I got a question," said Frankline as he took out his earpiece again.

"Shoot," replied Ruiz, watching the path.

"If I wasn't under your command," said Frankline. "Or, if I was in a parallel command next to you, I could take you out, right?"

Ruiz blinked. "Wait? What?"

"If I didn't work for you, basically," said Frankline.

"Now?" asked Ruiz, exasperated.

Frankline waved his hand at Dyson. "They're going as slow as molasses."

Ruiz was ready to snap, but then she stopped herself and thought about the question. She shook her head quickly.

"You're not talking about quitting, are you?" she asked.

Frankline chuckled. "And leave in the middle of a fight? Hell no, Staff Sergeant!" He started to speak, stopped, but then started again. "I don't know how. But I need to know that if... I mean, as long as I'm not under your direct command, that I can ask you out for coffee, or whatever I can find."

Ruiz looked up thoughtfully, but then she spied something. "What the heck?"

Frank did a double-take and grinned.

"Okay, that's awesome sauce," he said as he put back in his earpiece.

The Staff Sergeant called out over hers. "Captain, I got movement from Dyson. At least, I think that's what I'm seeing. Or maybe I've gone crazy."

"She's probably gone crazy," chimed in Bath. "It's the stress."

"Shush Bath," said Singh, without heat. "Ruiz, what're you seeing?"

"It's...it's...," started Ruiz, who didn't want to finish.

"It looks like someone in a suit of armor, Sir," said Frankline, giving the assist. "Like, an old medieval knight."

"You're kidding," replied Singh, shocked.

"Oh-oh!" cried Liberty over the earpieces. "I thought we mentioned that Dyson has a suit of armor. Maybe."

"Someone probably left it out of the official report," interjected Uncle Danny with humor. "Thinking we'd gone *muy loco*."

"Regardless!" called out Singh. "Ruiz, Frankline. Get down there and help them."

"Yes Captain!" called out Frankline and he scrambled to the ground. He was so eager and keen that Ruiz was shocked for a moment. The Private turned and grinned. "Come on Staff Sergeant!"

Shaking away her surprise, Ruiz jumped down after him. She had a second to wonder if the 'Staff Sergeant' was a passive-aggressive bite for rejecting him. But then, as she caught up, he looked over at her and smiled warmly. He was enjoying himself.

Before she could think anything more on it, they were at the end of their ragged little grenade-path.

161

"Coming!" called out a terrified voice.

The suit of armor stepped through the fallen zoms, some of which still pawed at him. A zom had moved from the side and onto the path. It headed straight for the knight.

Ruiz and Frankline raised their handguns.

"I got it!" called the suit of armor. "I think!"

As the zom closed on them, the suit of armor swung a big cast-iron skillet. The soldier could hear the clang from where they were.

"Oooh. That's gotta hurt," chuckled Frankline. "Reminds me of my Memaw."

More zoms were filtering in. Too many for one knight.

Frankline took a shooting stance. "At your command, Staff Sergeant."

Ruiz glanced and then realized that he was talking to her. "Head shots only."

"Yes ma'am," said Frankline. "Tell me when."

Ruiz was still puzzled by his new attitude, but she pushed it aside. Work first, she thought.

"Fire at will," she ordered.

Frankline immediately took a shot dropping a zom. The knight stopped for a moment in surprise.

Ruiz called out to them. "Hey! Hurry! Move your butt!"

The knight jerked forward, swinging his skillet.

Frankline grumbled. "Damn, missed." He fired again. "Got 'em."

Ruiz said. "Let's move a little forward. Open up the path."

"Yes Staff Sergeant!" said Frankline. He moved forward so that they were almost back to back.

The knight stumbled for a moment and Ruiz's heart clenched. We don't have that many bullets, she thought. But the knight got his footing again.

"Man, I thought we were toast for a second there," grinned Frankline. He glanced around. "Um, the zoms *are* getting really close."

"We can do this," insisted Ruiz bravely.

Frankline was eyeing the knight. "Come on, you brilliant, tin-plated bastard."

Ruiz tried not to laugh.

"Next Last Stand, I'm bringing two guns!" said Frankline.

"You do that!" said Ruiz.

It was now getting too easy to shoot, because the zoms were too close.

The knight was still trucking along. But it looked like they were slowing a little, tiring out.

Frankline shot two, but there was a third, almost on top of him and he was out.

"Reloading," called out Frankline. He popped the magazine and put in a fresh one.

The zom was too fast.

Frankline wanted to call for help, but Ruiz looked like she was just barely holding them back. He kicked the zom in the stomach and knocked it back a few steps. But it quickly straightened up.

"They're getting tight over here," he warned.

"We need to hold," said Ruiz. "We're outta grenades. This is our best chance."

"Then we hold," growled Frankline with determination. And as the zoms closed, he fired as fast as he could. The zoms were so close, he could see the clear braces on one. But he would not run. Even if...

A sniper's bullet went through the head of one zom, and then hit another.

"What the...," cried Frankline.

"Reloading," called out Ruiz behind him.

Sniper bullets hit more on his side, so Frankline twisted and fired at the zoms coming towards Ruiz.

"Ready!" said the Staff Sergeant. She lifted her gun and kept firing. Frankline turned back to his zoms as the sniper culled the mob on either side of them. But then the cover fire stopped. Even as the knight got closer, the zoms were even closer.

"Maybe a rifle jam...," started Frankline.

More gunfire came. The full throated roar of M4 Carbines. As zoms fell down on either side of them, the knight reached them.

"Sorry, sorry," sputtered the knight. And he handed out a CD-R.

The Private glanced at Ruiz.

"If you want to take the disc, I can get King Arthur back

to the bus," suggested Frankline.

The Staff Sergeant looked torn, but then she took the CD.

"Be careful," she said, a little more earnestly than she originally planned.

Turning, Ruiz power-walked back towards the tank. She ducked between Singh and Washington, who had been giving her and the Private an assist.

Not dawdling, she was soon back on top of the tank.

"There you are!" cried Bath, relieved. "I was just starting to get a *little* worried." Unable to help herself, she gave Ruiz a swift hug. "Don't do that to me again!"

"Yes Sergeant," said the Staff Sergeant with mock contrition, and she handed over the CD-R. "Sorry Sergeant."

Someone murmured with a long drawl. "I do not know if I believe her."

Ruiz looked over and saw Liberty atop the tank, covering the guys.

"Guardian angel, I presume?" asked Ruiz.

"Trying to be," said Liberty, but then her face grew contrite. "Sorry I didn't notice sooner. I didn't think the suit would take as long as it did."

"They *were* wearing full armor," suggested Bath kindly, without looking up from the stereo.

"Yeah. I know, but...I kinda figured that they would've been more used to wearing it," said Liberty. "Maybe— whoever it is—doesn't wear it that often."

"Would you?" asked Ruiz curiously.

"If lives depended on it," nodded Liberty seriously. "I'd wear it as often as I could. So, I could move as quick as I could. I mean, I'd have too."

A fire alarm went off—Like really, really loudly!—and Liberty nearly jumped out of her skin.

Bath turned it down quickly. "Ummm, it works."

"I couldn't tell," said Ruiz with mock iciness.

"Hey!! Check out the zoms near us," said Liberty.

As Ruiz looked around, she saw that the zoms closest to them were backing away, in a haze of confusion and mindless concern. Then the Staff Sergeant saw that Frankline getting close.

"What was that for?" asked Bath with a mildly accusatory tone.

Ruiz blinked and looked down with cautious confusion. "What?"

"You smiled," said Bath. "That's something you don't normally do."

"You and I have only known each other for a day," replied Ruiz with affront.

"I'm just sayin'," grinned Bath with mischief.

Liberty piped up with mock seriousness. "She does seem rather defensive now."

"Totally," agreed Bath. "And for a while there, it sounded like you and the Private were talking, but we couldn't quite hear you."

"And we couldn't hear him at all," purred Liberty, lounging like a panther.

Focusing on Ruiz, Bath asked, like an accusatory mother. "What were you talking about, young lady?" And she arched an eyebrow perfectly.

Keeping quiet, Ruiz put on a neutral face as Frankline arrived with the knight. The two were flanked by Singh and Washington.

The knight was talking really fast, out of breath. "We thought about making an improvised explosive, but then we thought...we might end up blowing ourselves up, so we better not. Unless things got really, really bad."

"I'm glad that you didn't," said Singh sincerely. Then he turned to call out. "Sergeants, Staff and otherwise. I want to move out as soon as everyone is on board."

"Yes sir!" replied Ruiz.

"Sure," said Bath, but then she hastily added. "I mean, Yes Sir. Wow! I didn't think that I was out that long that I forgot that."

"Real smooth," smirked Ruiz to the mechanic.

Bath turned and stuck out her tongue at the Staff Sergeant.

"It's all good," smiled Singh. "Just be ready to go."

While Liberty scrambled off the turret and headed towards the bus, Bath jumped down the loader's hatch to get into the driver's seat .

Frankline was aiding the knight into the bus, but Ruiz saw him glance at her quickly. Then he was inside.

With his soldiers on the tank in their Now Usual places, Singh saw that Liberty was already on the hood of the bus. She was crouched down to look in the front window.

Liberty's eyes bore swiftly into Uncle Danny.

"What're you doing up?" she asked accusingly, and there was no 'mock' in it.

The Big Mexican turned carefully. He was leaning on a seat, having recovered his shotgun. He motioned to the knight, who had collapsed into his old seat and was trying to get off his helmet.

"I tried to come and help you, but they wouldn't let me," said Uncle Danny, a little defensively.

"We practically had to hold him down," sniffed Giselle.

Uncle Danny shrugged and admitted. "They were worried that I'd undo all of Dr. Washington's good work." But then he waved at the knight. "And right now, he needed that seat more than me."

Tessy, who was holding her uncle's free hand, turned to Liberty.

"And he won't take any of the other empty seats," grumbled the little girl.

"Ah! But *Mi Unicornio Mariposa*, these seats are going to fill up fast. Besides, I can rest once we get back onto our little unnamed boat," said Uncle Danny, unconcerned.

"Liberty?" called out Singh from the tank.

"Oops. There're playing my song," grinned the Librarian. She climbed up onto the roof again.

Once she had settled on top, the captain called out. "Okay, head 'em up, an' move 'em out."

The tank towed the bus once again towards Dyson. The M1A2 Abrams was taking a wide turn when there was a crash. The tank immediately stopped, and the bus slowed to a halt, almost rear-ending it.

The tank's turret had pierced the side of a semi-truck, right by the hood windshield.

Atop the tank, Singh winced, but didn't say anything.

Bath's voice called out from inside the tank. "Sorry! Still get used to cornering with a big gun in front. My Chevy wasn't that extra."

Since the bus was resting close to the tank, the mechanic had to be careful. Backing a smidgen and then turning, the tank tore open the side of the truck taking the door with it.

Crawling across the cab, a male zombie in a "My Little Pony" t-shirt peered out. "Errrn." It began to climb out the hole in the truck.

The tank stopped momentarily, and Bath stuck her head out of the loader's hatch to call out to the zom as they were getting up. "Sorry!"

"Sergeant," said Singh with a gentle voice.

"Oh, yeah!" said Bath to him. "Sorry sir."

The mechanic dropped back in and started to drive again. But she called out over the earpieces. "And no one shoot that zom. He's probably been stuck in there awhile and needs walkies."

"Are you adopting him?" asked Ruiz with a chuckle.

"Yes," replied Bath quickly, and then she repeated it with more authority. "Yes! He's mine. His name is Bob. Don't shoot him."

"Bob?" asked Ruiz.

Bath sniffed. "I always liked the name. Don't judge

me."

Back in the bus, as they passed Bob and his Semi, Uncle Danny called out over the earpieces. "Hey Liberty! At least that zom hadn't been stuck in a KIA. I still argue that it would be terrible to be locked in one of those for all eternity."

It took Liberty a moment to remember that conversation from a lifetime ago. But she soon replied excitedly. "Oh yeah, if you got too sick, I was to lock you in a nice car, but no KIA."

"Not just a nice car!" huffed Uncle Danny, insistently. "A really, really fancy car."

"Oh, that's right," said Liberty.

"This is important!" said Danny with mock sternness.

"Yes Uncle Danny," replied Liberty, feigning meekness.

Atop the tank, Singh almost asked them to cut the chatter, but he immediately stopped himself. They were helping and being a big help too. So, he let them go and crouched by the loader's hatch. The fire alarm noise was loud, even with the speaker pointed away.

"I want to see if the crowd disperses with this noise too," said the Captain loudly.

"Inching forward, sir," replied Bath. She was getting back in the armed forces mode. Like driving a car for the first time in months, she thought. Just needed to get back into the swing of things.

As the tank stalked towards Dyson like a chonk cat, the zoms turned away from them and began to shuffle away.

"That's amazing," said Liberty over the mike. "Danny?

Are you seeing this?"

"I had to take a chair," said Uncle Danny with a small sigh. "Dr. Tessy insisted."

"Tell Dr. Tessy that she's my new favorite person," said Liberty.

"What about me?" asked Uncle Danny with mock hurt.

Liberty gave a big sniff. "My statement stands." But, then her voice changed to a work tone. "We're going to need some kind of sound system when we come back to the coast."

"We could get one of those big boom boxes," said Uncle Danny, and she could hear his grin. "I could walk down the street like that guy in 'Do The Right Thing'."

"Um, didn't something bad happen to him?" asked Liberty.

"No *policias* out here are going to harass me," shrugged Uncle Danny.

"Was that a prob...," started Liberty, but then she made a little noise. "Oh, that's right. You were...kinda over your Visa thing."

Uncle Danny sighed. "If I had left...my brother's garage would have gone belly-up. Everything he worked for."

"He was so proud of it," came Tessy's voice.

"True," agreed Danny. "Still, I hated doing it. *Mi Abuela* will certainly have words for me when I get up there." However, he paused. "Not that my brother's garage hasn't crashed anyway." He looked down at his niece. "But, if I had been in Guadalajara..." With a smile, he hugged Tessy to his side.

171

"Looks pretty clear," Bath over the earpieces. "Should I just go to the front door? I mean, I'd have to turn the tank and bus around, but I could do it."

"Let's stick with the original plan and use the hole in the covered sidewalk," said Singh. "There are still more zoms than I'd like."

Liberty watched as Bath maneuvered the tank/bus. The lawn in front was a lot less populated, but then she noticed something odd.

"I would've thought that there'd be less zoms," said Liberty over the earpieces. "I wonder why they don't all go."

"Hearing troubles could be part of it," mused Washington.

"Or some could have a kind of immunity to it?" wondered Liberty out loud.

"OR" said Uncle Danny, and she could hear his smile. "Some people in life might've been too stupid to recognize danger. At least, until it bit 'em."

"Literally, in this case," said Washington.

Singh continued thoughtfully. "Regardless Liberty, can you go to that upper door and get them moving." He saw that the tank was still lining up to get the bus in the right spot. "When we get to the walkway."

"Sorry sir," said Bath. "I just want to get it kind of right."

"You're fine," said Singh instantly. "I don't want to swing around. So, in your time."

"Thank you," said Bath gratefully.

172

"Why is there a door on the second floor again, with a covered walkway?" asked Washington.

"Apparently the architect planned for not only earthquakes, but zombies and alien invasion," supplied Liberty. "The covered walkway provides a bridge from a nearby building to the second floor door."

"How'd it get that big hole?" asked Washington as the tank started to thread between the hole in the covered walkway.

"Pissed off alien," supplied Uncle Danny over the earpieces. "Their ship melted this spot."

"And yet, it's perfect for our purposes," chuckled Singh. "Thank you evil aliens."

Washington asked. "Hey Liberty? Is the architect in the building right now? Did he get here safely?"

"I don't think so," said Liberty.

"Tsk. Poor guy," said Washington. "That's not fair."

"Liberty?" called out Bath. "Can you help? How's the bus in relation to the walkway?"

Between the two, they found a sweet spot, so people could step right off the walkway and onto the roof of the bus.

Hopping over the gap, Liberty slowed to a halt. Looking around, she smiled and called over her earpiece.

"Hey Uncle Danny."

"You okay up there *Mija*?" asked Uncle Danny over the earpieces.

"Don't get up," insisted Tessy's voice in the background.

Liberty saw Singh looking at her in concern and she instantly became embarrassed.

"Oh no! Everything's okay! Nothing bad!" she said quickly.

"*¿Mande?*" asked Uncle Danny simply.

"I was just going to say how weird it is to be back here," said the Librarian quickly. "It feels like a lifetime ago that we appeared with Colin and left with Tagg as well. Anyways! Sorry. I'll just go now Sorry!"

Uncle Danny chuckled. "*¡Hijole!* I guess it wasn't that long ago." he agreed.

Self-consciously, Liberty walked swiftly across the covered walkway and through the second floor door.

Once inside, she stopped on the stairs. The doors above and below were closed and before her, a glass wall. In the distance, she could hear the heavy breathing of someone running.

Suddenly, Renoir burst into view.

"IT IS YOU!" he cried joyfully. "The *Liberté* has come. It is like Bastille Day all over. I cannot tell you how thrilled I am to see you."

"I said I was coming," said Liberty, with a bemused, though gentle, rebuke.

"Yes, but...," started Renoir, in his French accent. "To come and save a boy who may hold the key to the zombie infection, or our Dr. Tagg, who is handsome and might find a vaccine. That...that is one thing. But for me...I wasn't sure I was important enough."

"HEY!" said the Librarian, unconsciously slipping into

174

her You-Cheesed-Off-The-Librarian voice. "Everyone is important. Everyone! In these times, we *must* stick together. So, I do not want to hear any more of that. 'I'm not important' shit..." Suddenly, she stopped. "Oh, I'm sorry for swearing. But I..."

Renoir smiled with a moist eye. "You are right, of course. We must stick together." He motioned for her to go up the stairs. "Please! Come in."

The door at the top of the stairs opened remotely. Liberty had never gone up, so she was kind of thrilled. Stepping through the door, there was cheer from the small group of people gathered there, which startled Liberty for a moment. She didn't normally like to be the center of attention.

"Um...," she began.

"There she is!" called out a voice to the left.

Pelting around a corner came Renoir in the flesh. He leapt up to her and grabbed her upper arms. She was about to get defensive when he placed two air-kisses, one on either side of her cheek.

"We are saved!" cried Renoir, and he hopped back quickly. He went over to a lady with a sweet face and tugged her by the hand. The lady, for her part, looked bemused. But Renoir gestured to her like a presenter. "Please *Mademoiselle* Liberty. Allow me to present the great Dr. Milton." And then, Renoir touched her tummy. "And there is *le petit haricot.*"

"The Little Bean," supplied Dr. Milton to Liberty. "Hi, I'm Emmy, and you must be the great Liberty."

Liberty blushed. "Well, I don't know..."

175

"How's it going in there?" asked Singh over the earpiece, and Liberty straightened, almost guiltily.

To everyone, she held up a finger and said. "One moment please." And then to her earpiece she replied. "Getting them moving. Already have some here. I'm going to start sending them out."

"Roger," replied the Captain.

Liberty was pretty sure that 'Roger' meant, 'okay' or something like that. She never watched movies with lots of military in it. Regardless, she pushed ahead.

"I'm sorry," she said. "We need to get everyone onboard as soon as possible. We don't want to run out of gas."

"Is that a danger?" asked Dr. Milton, concerned.

"Not if we move," said Liberty swiftly.

"Then let's start," said Dr. Milton instantly. She reached down to grab a suitcase, but Renoir was there.

"No, no," he declared with a fussy voice. "I got it."

"I can carry a suitcase," said Dr. Milton frostily.

"Come on guys!" said Liberty before the two could get into it. She jumped forward and grabbed the suitcase. "Follow me."

Soon, Liberty went back across the walkway, not knowing if people were following. But she figured this way, she could figure out how to get people in. Just as she stepped onto the bus roof, a voice called out.

"¡Oye!" came Uncle Danny's voice. "Over here *Mija*."

Liberty walked to the front of the roof and looked down. Uncle Danny leaned out the broken front window, which no longer had a window.

"Yes!" cried Liberty happily. "Good idea!" She started to hand down the suitcase but froze. "Wait! You need to get back."

"¡Neta! Come on," said Danny. "I can handle a little suitcase."

"Private Frankline?" called out Liberty.

Frankline immediately clamored to the window and stuck his head out, radiating keenness. "Yes Ma'am?"

While Liberty was thrown for a second, mostly about being called 'Ma'am', Frankline glanced towards the tank to see if Ruiz or Singh were there. The Captain was watching.

Frankline could tell he was overdoing it, so he dialed it down. "I mean, how can I help Ms. Liberty?"

"Oh! Can you get this suitcase?" asked Liberty.

"Absolutely," said Frankline and took it.

"I'm going to be sending more people down and through the front window," said Liberty. "Could you come out on the hood to make sure they get into the bus okay?"

"Can do," said Frankline. "Just let me just drop this off."

As Frankline disappeared, Uncle Danny grumbled. "I could've helped."

Liberty got down on one knee and bent over the front of the roof. "You're tough as nails, but I need you to *not* get hurt—more hurt!—right now."

"Because of the little one?" asked Uncle Danny, eyes narrowing.

"I already got in trouble once today," said Liberty. "And

more importantly, I can't have my best-friend-in-the-whole-world getting hurt again this quick."

Uncle Danny gave a little chuckle. "You smooth-talker you. *¡Orale!* How about if I help coordinate inside?"

"Thank you," said Liberty sincerely.

Uncle Danny disappeared and Frankline threw something partly onto the hood. Then he climbed out. Liberty leaned down.

"I borrowed Mr. Danny's coat," explained Frankline. "There are still a few small shards in that window, and I didn't want to see anyone else getting hurt."

"Good idea," nodded Liberty, and she turned to see the eager, nervous people from the Dyson Science Building. She gestured with a flourish. "Your chariot awaits."

Between Liberty, Frankline, and Uncle Danny, they got everyone on board. Danny was further assisted by Tessy who kept an eagle-eye on her uncle, lest he pick a fight with a zom or fowl.

Pretty soon, the bus was well packed.

Uncle Danny leaned his head out. "Anyone else?"

Liberty turned to see the de facto leader, Fred, heading over with a backpack.

"Anyone else?" she asked.

"That's it," said Fred. "Thank you!"

"Good. Now, let's get you off the coast," said Liberty. "Then, you can thank me."

However, Fred abruptly stopped and cried out. "Oh! I almost forgot to lock up."

"Is that really necessary?" grumbled Liberty.

But Fred was already gone. He trotted back to the door and made sure that it was locked.

With the building secure, they got him into the bus. It was so packed, Uncle Danny and Tessy had to sit on the top step of the bus stairs. People even had to sit in the very back row, right before the bodies of Private Sondes and Stephen the entertainer, who were stacked against the back door.

Satisfied that Uncle Danny was all settled, Liberty waved to the Captain.

"We're good!" she called out.

Singh waved back as Liberty lay, once more, back down on the roof with her rifle. Turning, the Captain went over to the loader's hatch.

"We can kill the fire alarm," he said.

"Thank God," exclaimed Bath. She went to the sound system, on the front of the tank. After she had turned it off, she moaned. "I'm bringing ear plugs next time."

"Good idea. Now, how're we doing on gas?" he asked as she settled back into the driver's seat.

"Okay," replied Bath wearily. "But we better get there soon."

"Everyone's on board," said Singh.

The tank mechanic looked up with a smile. "The marina?"

"Take us back to where we started. Nothing fancy."

"Sir! No donuts in the parking lot, Sir?" asked Bath with

179

mock disappointment.

"Just a straight shot, or as straight as possible," said Singh with a little smile. But then his face darkened with a mock fierceness. "That's an order Sergeant."

"Yes Sir!!" grinned Bath.

The tank/bus got going and maneuvered back onto the main streets. They had to skip a couple of streets because they were so clogged with cars. Nonetheless, they were getting closer.

Again, Singh crouched next to the loader's hatch and asked softly. "Gas?"

"We're running on fumes," replied Bath.

"Just do the best you can," said Singh. "Next time, we'll have to bring more gas."

"To be fair, we weren't even sure we'd get this far," said Bath. "Or that the tank would even start."

"True," smiled Singh. "Well, if all else fails, I'll get out and push."

Bath laughed and it helped take her mind off the gas, at least for a second.

As Singh moved back down the tank, she gently petted the tank. "Come on baby, just a little bit further. You can do it."

Suddenly, Bath sat up straighter and blinked. She called out over the earpieces.

"I see it. I see it. I see it!"

"Slow down," said Singh gently. "What do you see, Sergeant?"

180

Liberty cried joyously from atop the bus. "It's the marina! Sorry, I was looking for trouble an' I didn't notice right away."

Singh stood and looked towards the marina. They were still at least three blocks away with zoms and who knows what else. He said a quick prayer and then turned back to Liberty above.

"Are all the boats still out there?" asked Singh over the earpieces. She used her scope to look for their little home that floats and the other boats.

"Yes! Thank God!" replied Liberty.

The Librarian did not know why she glanced back behind her.

Heart skipping a beat, she tried to dig in her toes, but she could not immediately get purchase. Liberty dug harder and suddenly she sprang forward, rifle in hand. Diving off the roof, the Librarian dropped hard down onto the hood.

"What...?" began Frankline from the driver seat.

Up above, right where she had been a second ago, an alien-bird hit the roof. Talons scored furrows across the metal. The alien with a rust colored tuft stopped at the edge and bent forward, over the edge of the roof.

Without thinking, Liberty dove through the open window of the bus, just as the Rust Tufted alien snapped at the empty air, left in her wake.

The Librarian was about to drop on top of Uncle Danny's bad shoulder. Without thinking, she twisted out of the way, but that meant bouncing across the floor pretty hard.

Private Frankline cried out in surprise.

Not bothering to check for damage, Liberty scrambled back up.

The alien's head snaked inside, and the angry buzzing from the device in the back of Rust Tuft's head squalled. He snapped his beak at her, but the bird was not close enough yet. The alien began to lean further inside when Frankline shot the bird in the neck. The alien jolted to the side, but he wasn't dead.

Rust Tuft opened his razor sharp beak and lunged at the nearest person, Uncle Danny.

However, the alien found himself staring into the barrel of a shotgun.

Uncle Danny hesitated for a second.

Behind there was a high-pitched screech, which turned out to be Private Collins. "Shoot It! Shoot It!"

But Danny was looking up at the alien-bird's tuft, and dreaded that it might be red.

The alien snapped down on the end of the barrel, but only managed to scrape it.

That spurred Uncle Danny to action.

Tessy cried out as the weapon went off. Partly because of the noise, which was thunderous in such tight, confined space, but also because of the blue bird-blood that splattered about.

The little girl suddenly jolted as an arm wrapped around her middle. She cried out. "What!?!"

Liberty pulled the squirming Tessy deeper into the bus.

"It's me! It's me, sweetie. I got you!" whispered the Librarian to the little girl. "You're safe."

Tessy, for her part, grabbed the arm around her and held on tight.

Uncle Danny backed up too, until they were all well away from the bird.

Private Collins, guarding his open window, was now looking at the dead bird, white as a sheet. But the soldier wasn't hurt.

The Big Mexican turned too quickly, and his shoulder flared in pain, but he brushed it away to check on Tessy and Liberty.

Finding that the little girl was unharmed, he pulled Tessy into a hug, who was between furious and scared out of her wits. He spoke to her softly, soothingly, in Spanish. But his eyes kept going back to the alien-bird to reassure himself that the tuft was rust, and not Rakduson. He wondered why it worried him so. Suddenly he remembered, like a lightning flash.

"*Mi Abuela*," hissed the Big Mexican in surprise.

Tessy and Liberty blinked in confusion.

"I've been trying to figure out why it's been bothering me," said Uncle Danny, but then he saw their questioning gazes and swiftly added. "About helping that bird..."

"Helping the horror birds?" whispered Private Collins in shock.

"...Rakduson?" continued Liberty.

"*Si*. And it's because of what *Mi Abuela* said," explained Danny quickly. "She said 'Help those who need it, *not*

183

because the Lord is watching, but because you can'."

"Was she holding a shoe?" asked Tessy. She still looked frazzled, but this was helping her focus on something else.

"Nope," said Uncle Danny. "That's how your Papa and I knew how much this meant to her." He leaned forward and stressed his words. "How important it was!"

"So, with these aliens...," started Liberty.

But they heard Singh calling from the tank.

"Hey! Is everyone okay back there?" asked the Captain.

"We're fine!" replied Frankline over the earpieces, though he did not sound like he believed it. "No one's hurt." He was staring at the dead bird, half in the window. Blue blood dripped onto the bus stairs. "Well, the bird's having a bad day."

"Liberty?" asked Singh. His voice was tight with concern.

"I was tired of being outdoors," replied the Librarian, trying to sound nonchalant, but not succeeding. "So, I decided to come in for a while." Her words sped up. "Outdoors is dangerous. There're bears out there. And sharks. One time I'm sure I saw a bear shark..."

The Big Mexican reached out and touched her shoulder. Liberty jumped for a second, but then she focused on his rough, lined face.

"Everyone's okay," said Uncle Danny softly.

Letting out a long, cleansing breath, Liberty gave a little chuckle. "Sorry. That spooked me a bit."

"Understandable," nodded Danny.

"What happened?" asked the Captain.

"Um, it just glided in behind me," started Liberty, returning to herself. "Perfectly quiet. Not even sure why I looked behind me."

Over the earpieces, Singh said. "Best not to question it too far. Glad you're all..." The Captain felt something through his boots. He paused before saying. "One moment."

Singh turned from the bus to the front of the tank as Washington's rifle watched the sky. The captain crouched by the loader's hatch.

"Sorry! Sorry! Sorry! Sorry! Sorry," came Bath's voice.

"Not your fault Sergeant," said Singh quickly. "You did good! Really." He looked forward to the sound system. "Can we take our fire alarm with us?"

"Um," said Bath. "It's hooked up to the tank by spit and baling wire as is. And without the tank going..."

"Okay," said Singh. I don't think we have to worry about carjackers..."

"Tankjackers," suggested Bath, and then looked down. "Sorry.

"It's okay," said Singh. "Can you stow it in the tank, and then get ready to move."

As the tank had slowed to a stop, so did the bus behind.

Ruiz looked at the Captain. "Abandon ship?"

"Get ready to move quickly, Staff Sergeant!" ordered Singh.

Ruiz nodded towards Mullins' body and asked. "Sir?"

Singh's eyes went first to their lost soldier. "We need to get the living to safety." But then he looked towards the bus.

The Captain moved over to his dead Marine and took her weapons. Somberly, he scooted her to the edge of the tank  Trusting his Staff Sergeant to get everyone there moving, Singh knocked back a curious zom and then slid off the back. He. He was tempted to shoot it, but that was just the anger and frustration talking.

Inside the bus though, he heard the man named Ted talking loudly.

"Wait! What're we doing?" cried Ted.

Before Uncle Danny or Liberty even said anything, Private Frankline stood up. "The tank has run out of gas." Voices started to swell with panic. "BUT! The marina is not far away."

"Don't you have any more gas?" asked Ted in exasperation.

"Right now! We're going to leave the bus," continued Frankline, authoritatively. "And just walk to the marina. It's right over there. If we move slow, we're going to be just fine!"

"But...," started Ted.

"NOW! Here's the plan...!" began Frankline.

Captain Singh went back to what he was doing. Braving the tank, which was really starting to reek, he brought Mullins' body down, though he almost dropped her once.

Singh got her into a fireman's carry.

"Sorry, this is not dignified," he whispered to her just as

186

the bus door opened.

Frankline jumped down first and began to fire, but not wildly. Taking careful headshots, he cleared a space around the bus. Finally, he turned to cover the rear of the bus and called out. "Clear!"

Backpack on, Liberty hit the ground next with her rifle ready.

The Captain moved past her and, without a word, handed the Private a rifle, Mullin's M4 Carbine.

Taking it cautiously, Frankline started. "Sir, I'll...."

"It's okay, " said Singh, and it was okay for now about the lost rifle. They would probably talk later, but it would probably be a short one, if Frankline kept stepping up to help like he was. The Captain turned to Liberty at the bus door. "What's going on?"

But in the bus, Uncle Danny called out. "Keep moving *Mija*."

Liberty moved out of the way.

With his backpack too, Uncle Danny came down with his niece and more people.

Liberty turned to the Captain and asked. "Can you start the people there? Frankline figured you'd like to be in front, so he asked if I would help him cover the rear."

"Really?" asked Singh with pleasant surprise.

The Private instantly looked nervous, remembering who he worked for. "Um...Sir? If that's all right." And then he added. "sir."

Singh nodded. "Good initiative. Carry on!"

Relieved, Frankline could not help looking past everyone to Ruiz. He almost waved, but then he remembered himself. Hefting his newly acquired rifle, he turned to watch the back of the bus.

As people exited the bus, they tried not to look at the body Singh was carrying.

"You need a hand?" asked Uncle Danny softly.

Mullins was getting heavier by the moment, but Singh shook his head. "I got her."

When it seemed everyone was off, Singh climbed onboard the bus. He used the tops of seats to keep both he and Mullins upright. Distantly, he noticed that there was one passenger left, but right now it was a slog to get to the back of the bus.

A memory of Mullins excitement came back to him. She had loved singing competitions on TV, and she was so geeked when they one aboard the carrier. Not that she could really sing, she just liked to watch.

Finally, he reached the back and, cradling her head, set her down carefully.

After taking a few deep breaths, the Captain looked at her and then at Sondes' body, partially obstructed by another corpse. Tiredly, he couldn't remember that it was Stephen the entertainer, which bugged him.

"I'm sorry," he said simply to his people. "We're coming back for you though."

Turning, Singh walked back to the front carefully to make sure everyone else was gone. When he reached the front, he turned to Collins, who saw him look.

188

The soldier jumped up and said as he went to the bus door. "Coming sir!"

However, Collins hesitated at the door, but went. The moment the soldier reached asphalt, he appeared to try and look in every direction at once.

"Collins," said the Captain as he descended behind him.

But the private did not appear to hear him as Collins started to watch the sky.

"Collins!" said Singh more loudly.

The Soldier jumped and turned to the Captain.

"I want you in the middle of the group," said Singh.

"Yes Sir," replied the Soldier quickly.

Singh noticed that he looked pretty relieved about the position. The Captain almost asked, and Collins almost said, 'less likely that they'll attack the middle' out loud.

"Zoms getting close Sir," called out Frankline from the rear.

Liberty slung her sniper rifle behind her; though it was a little hard with her Dora the Explorer backpack. Then she drew her silenced Glock 22.

Silently urging Collins on, Singh made sure the bus door was closed. He wished they had time to board up the broken windows. Instead, he power-walked back to the tank and saw Bath standing close to it.

"We'll be back soon," she was saying softly, and patted the armored skirt of the tank, carefully above the gore. But then her nose wrinkled in distaste. She glanced down at all the zom-bits in the tracks. "*And* we're going to need to give you a great big bubble bath, sweetie."

"Sergeant," said the Captain softly, but she did respond at first.

Suddenly, she looked up.

"Oh! That's me," she said with a smile. "Sorry sir."

"It's okay. We need to go," he said.

"I know," she nodded.

"Why don't you take the middle," suggested the Captain.

Bath smiled at Singh. "My mama would be so proud that I got to be Sergeant."

"And well earned," nodded the Captain. "*But* we really need to go."

"Right! Sorry sir," said Bath, and she was about to go. But then she stilled. She looked down at her M4 carbine and then back up at him. "Sir, I'm a Sergeant now."

The Captain waited, curiously.

Sergeant Bath continued. "I shouldn't hide in the middle of the pack."

With a proud nod, Singh said. "I'm already planning on me, Ruiz, and Washington at the front, and I got Collins in the middle. You could help cover the rear though just in case we need Liberty elsewhere."

"Yes sir," replied Bath with a sharp salute.

"But please, please be careful," said Singh.

The mechanic looked at him with suspicious eyes. "Did you tell that to Frankline or Collins?"

Singh continued quickly because he knew danger when he saw it. "No, but they can't drive the tank." Then he

190

smiled warmly. "And I'd hate to lose a new sergeant so soon. It's unprofessional."

"Oh!" nodded Bath, understanding. "Okay, I'll be careful, I promise."

Singh let out a mock bark. "Then get to your position Sergeant!"

With a chipper 'Yes Sir', Bath moved to the rear.

Satisfied that the bus was empty, Singh closed the door and called out.

"Okay, everyone! Form a thin line! Follow me!" said Singh. "Walk at the pace I do."

"And don't forget where we parked!" called out Bath from the back. That got a tiny chuckle throughout the group, that lifted spirits as it went.

In the middle, Collins tried to look as small as possible. He was walking beside Uncle Danny, who had put Tessy between them.

"What're we doing out here," hissed Collins. "This is crazy!"

"Doesn't look like we have much of a choice," said Uncle Danny.

Tessy held his left hand with the hurt shoulder. Now, he hoisted his shotgun one-handed with the other. Not something he had even really done, so he hoped that he could do it. And he really hoped that he didn't need to find out. He needed to start practicing, just in case.

"We should've stayed in the bus!" hissed Collins more forcefully.

"And do what?" asked Uncle Danny. "Just wait for…"

191

"Someone could've gone for more gas," insisted Collins.

*"Neta,"* muttered Danny.

"Are we going to be okay?" asked Tessy worriedly, who was looking between the soldier and her uncle.

Danny replied to the little girl quickly. "Yes! We should be fine. We got *Tia* Liberty at our back, so we're already doing better off than most."

"You're perfectly safe," said Giselle from in front of them.

"Well....I wouldn't go that far," countered Uncle Danny wearily.

Giselle, who was holding the hand of a child, shot him a Disapproving Look.

But, he had grown up with his *Abuela*. Utterly unruffled, he said. "The Coast is not safe. *But...with care,* it can be managed."

"Is that why we're walking kinda slow?" asked Tessy.

"*¡Orale!* If we move too fast, the alien-birds will see us," said Uncle Danny. "Right now, us moving a little faster than those zoms back there, is the best that we can do."

"She's just a child," said Giselle disapprovingly. "And you're scaring her."

Uncle Danny looked up. "Sugarcoating isn't going to keep her safe. She needs to know where the danger lies, and how to avoid it."

"Like not letting the zoms box you in," said Tessy. "Make sure you have an exit."

"Because last stands are for...?" prompted Uncle Danny.

"Dead people," chirped Tessy brightly.

"You remembered," grinned Uncle Danny.

"You make me repeat it *allllllll* the time," moaned Tessy with an eye roll.

"Unbelievable," huffed Giselle.

"So, THAT'S IT!" cried a voice behind him. "We're just going to head to the marina like it was a Sunday stroll?"

Danny glanced back at Ted, a thin man with face red with frustration.

"I know it's frustrating…," began Uncle Danny.

"Don't talk to me like a child!" snapped Ted.

Uncle Danny started in surprise. "I...I wasn't…"

"Yeah man!" said Collins nervously. "You really don't want the attention of these freaking birds."

"You shut up soldier-boy!" snapped Ted, and then he glared at Danny. "Don't tell me I didn't hear what I heard."

Ted moved a little quicker. With reedy legs, he stepped out of the line. For a second, Uncle Danny thought he was going to get too close to a zom, but the man managed to dodge it. Then Ted was moving outside the line.

Uncle Danny looked at Giselle.

"Was I talking to him like a child?" he asked in concern.

"I don't think so," said Giselle with a shake of her head. "Some people handle the stress better than others."

"But usually, people are past that point by now," said Danny. "Unless he's been locked in since Day 1."

The street they were on would soon reach a large 'T'

intersection up ahead. Then beyond that was the parking lot of the marina. However, in the street ahead, the right lane had two solid lines of cars, forever stuck in a traffic jam.

Seeing Ted move quickly towards the marina, Renoir became concerned. However, he first looked past Giselle to Danny.

"*Le* Uncle Danny! Should we be going any quicker?" asked Renoir.

"No!" said the Big Mexican quickly. He wished that they could go faster too. But instead, he spoke earnestly to all the people around him. "*¡Por favor!* This is a good pace. We'll get there soon! I promise."

"Too fast is bad," squeaked Collins, who was sweating up a storm.

Renoir looked once more from Ted to his love, Dr. Milton, and she gave a beneficent smile.

"Mr. Danny is our Subject Matter Expert," she said.

"A what?" asked Tessy.

Dr. Milton looked back at the little girl. "He knows what he's talking about."

"Oh! That's true," nodded Tessy. "He's my Uncle."

"You're so lucky," smiled Dr. Milton.

"Oh No!" hissed Uncle Danny breathlessly, but not about the little girl. He was looking far ahead.

Ted had jumped past Singh, Ruiz, and Washington. And the moment that he was clear, the man had torn off, sprinting for the traffic jam of cars.

194

"Fuck this!" cried Ted. "I don't have to listen to this!"

The Staff Sergeant and the Medic started to move forward, but their Captain called out.

"Ruiz! Washington!" ordered Singh. "Do. Not. Follow!"

The Staff Sergeant turned to look at him.

"But...," started Ruiz, but then she shook her head in frustration.

"I know," said Singh quickly. "It..."

"Sucks," finished the Medic, Washington.

"Totally!" replied Staff Sergeant.

Watching Ted, the Captain said with curiosity. "Huh! Maybe he'll make it."

Ted dodged around the zoms and shot out into the 'T' Intersection.

Angling like a hawk, the alien-bird with the Magenta tuft flew into view from behind the corner, . At the last moment, Magenta's wings unfurled to slow her momentum. Ted had only just started to turn his head when the bird kicked out.

From where he was, Singh could almost hear Ted's femur shatter. He winced as Ted hit the ground and skidded painfully to a stop.

The alien-bird with the Magenta tuft went a little past, unable to completely stop her own momentum.

However, the bird cried out. "*Hie Tah! Hie Tah!*"

"Oh God! Oh God! Oh God!" cried out Ted. "Help! Help me...Oh No!"

Down the street another alien-bird appeared with a grey

195

tuft. It trotted to the spot where the action had been.

"Get away!" shouted Ted and he started waving his hand wildly at it.

Grey Tuft saw the movement and snapped at the waving hand, taking off a couple of fingers. Ted started to scream more.

As Magenta skidded to a halt, she turned. The cuts around her face, from when Uncle Danny had sent a shower of glass at her, looked bad. The device in the back of her head was buzzing hard. She saw the other bird pecking at Ted.

"YI!" screeched Magenta. She ran back over and snapped at Gray Tuft, who waved his wings menacingly.

All the while, Ted was still hollering.

"We have to do something," hissed Washington.

And Singh instantly made the calculations in his head before nodding in agreement.

"Staff Sergeant!" said the Captain. "I need you to take these people around that traffic jam of cars and get them to safety."

"Yes sir," said Ruiz, who waved to the people behind slowly. "Come on! Follow me. This way!"

As Ruiz was getting everyone moving again, Liberty came up to the middle and turned to the soldier there.

"Hey Collins?" asked Liberty. "Can you help Frankline and Bath cover the back?"

Collins looked immediately towards the marina, but then he reluctantly nodded. "I guess."

"Thanks," said Liberty. She moved out of line and dodged around a few zoms. She reached a car parked halfway onto the sidewalk and climbed up. Dropping to one knee, she raised her sniper rifle to look over the heads of the zoms.

"Can you hold your shot?" asked Singh over the earpiece.

Liberty looked up and over at him.

"We don't know how many more there are," continued Singh. "Let me scout ahead and make sure there isn't any more."

Without waiting for a reply, Singh stepped forward. Moving a little faster than he should have, he headed for the corner.

"Sir?" hissed Ruiz.

"You have your orders," said the Captain over his shoulder.

The line of people was moving again, but Liberty waited on top of her car. Uncle Danny turned to Tessy, and the girl gave a tremendous sigh and replied to the unspoken question with an aggrieved voice. "Yes! You can go help *Tia* Liberty."

"If anything happened to her...," started Uncle Danny.

"I know," nodded Tessy.

"And if something goes wrong, head for the marina," said Uncle Danny. "We'll be right behind." He looked up at Giselle. "Could you take her?" But the woman was still trying not to look at the birds fighting over a blubbering Ted, so he tried again. "Hey!"

197

Tessy however, let go of him and took Giselle's free hand. That shook the older woman out of her own horror.

"What?" blinked Giselle.

As Uncle Danny fell back, he heard Tessy say to the older woman. "He did something he shouldn't have done."

"I...guess that's true," admitted Giselle.

Up ahead, Singh called out.

"Okay everyone," he said. "Keep going. Be careful. Call out if you see anything with feathers." And he gave a quick chuckle about that.

As the procession wound around the traffic jam of cars, Sergeant Bath called out. "Keep watch between those cars."

"Yes Sergeant," replied Frankline professionally.

"I hope it's not chicken for dinner tonight," muttered Collins nervously.

Bath and Frankline chuckled as they kept moving.

Behind, Uncle Danny moved out of line. He hated to leave his niece out here, but those birds were too close. Tessy was in the middle of a group of people—relatively safe—while Liberty was out there, exposed.

The Big Mexican moved over to Liberty, who looked really cheesed-off.

"What the hell?" she swore under her breath as he got close.

Uncle Danny looked under the car, but there were no ankle-biters. He moved around and onto the sidewalk, hoping to get the best vantage point.

Danny sighed, a little guiltily. "I told him not to go."

"No, not him," said Liberty, a little sharply. "Why didn't Singh want me to take the shot?" She looked back through her scope. "I can take them easily."

"I think he's worried that more of the birds are around," said Uncle Danny. "And there's a lot more than the half dozen that we first met."

"There're getting reinforcements," said Liberty with a heavy voice.

"*¡Ya te cargó el payaso!*" muttered Uncle Danny in a dour voice.

Ted was still calling for help, but his cries were getting weaker. Liberty looked away and saw the sad look on Danny's face.

"At the very beginning of all this, when the President was still trying to downplay it, there was this...well, I was trying to warn a group of people, but they said I was a girl and thus being hysterical," said Liberty.

Uncle Danny looked with fire in his eyes. "That *tonto del culo.*"

"That's what I said," chuckled Liberty sadly. "But...you can't save people, who don't want saving."

"*¡Orale!*" nodded Danny. "So, what happened?"

"The guy in charge marched right up—yelling about 'lazy millennials'—and tried to pull the zombie makeup off this poor zom," said Liberty.

Danny laughed. "I bet that didn't go well."

"Worse yet," said Liberty. "When he got bitten, the rest ran to help him."

"*No Pos Wow,*" hissed Danny with a shake of his head.

As the line moved around the corner, Liberty looked around. It reassured her to have Uncle Danny with her.

Shortly, Singh called over the earpieces. "Street looks clear other than our two birds. Liberty, take the shots!" said Singh.

"What?" asked Library.

"We're clear for the moment," said Singh. "Hurry! And everyone else! Watch for trouble!"

Liberty hesitated for a second more, but then she remembered that this was what she had wanted. Just as Singh was going to tell her again, she raised her rifle.

Gray Tuft's head jerked to the side, and the bird dropped on top of Ted.

Moving her rifle just a little bit, Liberty tried to get a bead on the other alien-bird. But Magenta was already bolting off. The Librarian compensated and she had the bird, dead to rights. She began to squeeze the trigger.

There was a loud bang behind the tank/bus.

Liberty hesitated for a second, but then saw that Uncle Danny was covering behind. Focusing through her scope, she aimed, but Magenta had already disappeared behind a building. Nothing in front, she twisted to look back, but there were only garden-variety zoms behind.

Turning back, Singh was firing after Magenta as he moved towards Ted.

"Damn, those things are fast," snarled Liberty.

Uncle Danny was going to protest calling the birds 'things', but he let it go.

"Come on *Mija*," he said instead.

200

Sliding off the car, Liberty tried to power-walk, but she soon growled. "Ugh! I want to run."

"We'll get there soon enough," said Uncle Danny soothingly.

"I know," hissed Liberty. "I'm...I'm just mad that I missed that second bird." She glanced back for a moment.

"I didn't see what made that noise. And really, isn't hitting a moving target kinda hard?" asked Danny.

The Librarian turned and squinted at him.

"Don't be so hard on yourself *Mija*," said Uncle Danny. "At least one is down."

"True," admitted Liberty, a little grudgingly.

As *dos amigos* walked towards the end of the block, an alien-bird looked out from behind the bus. Red Tuft was relieved that the other bird had gotten away. However, Rakduson focused back on Danny. She spread her wings and swiftly flew up to a nearby roof, following.

Liberty and Uncle Danny soon reached the Captain.

"Can you give me some cover?" asked Singh when *dos amigos* had arrived.

Without a word, Liberty moved to one side of Ted, who still had a bird heaped on top of him. Uncle Danny stayed to cover the other side. The Librarian was sure that she had heard a voice under all those feathers.

But Singh did not reach out to the fallen at first. He circled with his M4 Carbine to look at the alien-bird's face. It was really dead. Nevertheless, the Captain shot it twice more in the head, just in case. Letting his M4 Carbine hang by the strap, he pulled on the bird.

201

"Ugh, this guy is heavy," said Singh. "Danny?"

Uncle Danny looked at Liberty. *"Mija?"*

"I got you guys," nodded Librarian, but then she glanced back at her friend. "Go slowly. And be careful with your shoulder."

The Big Mexican smiled indulgently. *"Si,* I will."

Watching the streets, Liberty kept guard as the two levered the bird off. For a second, she thought she saw something up on the rooftops, but then it was gone.

"Ueergh," grunted Uncle Danny. "Almost put my back out on that one."

"But you're okay, right?" asked Liberty worriedly, without looking back.

"Yeah, I'm good *Mija,"* replied the Big Mexican kindly, and she could hear the grin in his voice.

Ted was laying on his stomach. Singh knelt down next to the man and touched his neck. The Captain wasn't sure whether he wanted to find a pulse or not.

The man jerked upward.

"What the hell?" cried Ted. "What took you so long? Get me out of here! Now! But find my fingers first. Hurry. You know I pay your wages right, and..."

As Ted kept blabbering, the Captain stood and touched his earpiece. "Listen up, I saw one of those emergency stretchers by the marina office. Collins, Frankline, bring it here!"

Ted screeched from the asphalt. "Hey! Don't ignore me!"

But Singh did.

"Captain...?" asked Washington through the earpieces.

"I got this," replied Singh as he crouched down.

"Roger Sir," said Washington.

Pulling out a small med kit, the Captain opened it. There was only a little bit of everything, and he muttered to himself. "Well, it's a start."

"What do you need?" asked Liberty.

"Find my fingers and put 'em on ice," whined Ted, insistently.

Ignoring Ted, the Captain replied to her as he stood. "I got it," "Thank you."

Singh stepped over the shattered leg, which was laying at an unnatural angle. Ted kept nattering on, but the Captain stopped by the good leg.

"Hey! Wait!! What're you doing?" asked Ted. Still on his stomach, the man tried to roll over and screamed in pain. But, then he tried again.

Absently, Singh dropped a knee on Ted's butt to hold him down and drew his knife.

"Wait! What?" babbled the man.

The Captain plucked at the fabric of the pants.

"Hey! Wait! These are the only pants that've really fit well since this all began!" wailed Ted.

Singh went to work, and he sliced two quick strips out of Ted's pants.

"Captain?" called out Frankline as he and Collins arrived.

"Good," said Singh. "The rest of the people?"

Collins was holding his end of the stretcher with one hand, and his rifle ready with the other. His eyes darted around.

"Staff Sergeant is getting everyone onto the boats Sir," reported Frankline.

"Good," nodded Singh.

Going back to the hand with the missing fingers, the Captain grabbed it and held it tight. He swiftly wrapped the sterile gauze over the stumps and tied it loosely with one strip of pants. Ted cried out, but the Captain ignored it.

"Get my fingers and put 'em on ice," ordered Ted loudly.

The Captain looked at the dead bird, who had the fingers still somewhere inside him.

"¡Hijole! Now, where does he think we're going to get ice from around here?" asked Uncle Danny incredulously.

Singh stood up, glancing at the dead bird. "And he thinks we're going to do Alien Autopsy, next on Fox."

"And out here no less," continued Liberty.

The Captain looked down at Ted. "We're not going to be able to do that. We're risking a lot, just getting you to safety."

Collins stared down at Ted, who was still whining.

Singh looked quickly up at the two soldiers and pointed down.

"Get 'em on the stretcher and onto the boats," ordered Singh. "We'll cover you."

"Yessir," said Frankline quickly, but before he could

kneel down, the other soldier spoke up.

"No," said Collins simply, and he let go of the stretcher as one end clattered to the ground. He took a few steps back, in the direction of the marina.

Singh blinked.

"What?" he asked in confusion.

"We shouldn't be here!" said Collins urgently, shaking his head. "We need to go back. To the boats." He took another step back.

"Yes," said Singh. "And we will. With this man on a stretcher."

"He was stupid," snapped Collins. "And we're out here, exposed for him. With those *Things* out here!"

Frankline hissed to Collins. "So! That's why we need to go quickly."

Below them, Ted started to complain about being left behind, as well as his lost fingers, but everyone just ignored him.

"No!" said Collins. "We should leave his sorry ass and get back to the boats, as fast as we dare."

Liberty glanced and saw Collins looking nervously about.

Singh's eyes narrowed, dangerously. "You're serious?"

"Does it look like I'm joking?" huffed Collins with disbelief.

The Captain put up a hand. "Can we talk about this later? Let's just get this done now."

"No," said Collins, and his voice quavered hard. His

eyes became moist. "I think this is the best time to talk about this. We were *safe* on the carrier. Then you had to take us back out here. I vote that we head back to the boats and leave his sorry ass here."

"We can't do that," said Singh simply.

"The hell we can't," said Collins. "I mean, getting everyone on the bus is one thing, but this is putting us at risk for no good reason." He turned to Frankline, pleading. "You said this was crazy when we were walking up here."

As Singh turned to him, Frankline looked like he was a deer caught in headlights.

"Private?" asked the Captain.

Frankline dropped to one knee beside Ted. "Um....Private Frankline is going to help the idiot on a stretcher, Sir...if that's okay. Um, I'll probably need some help though. Sorry Sir."

"I'll help," offered Uncle Danny.

Liberty almost said something about the Big Mexican's shoulder but bit her tongue.

However, Danny said to the Librarian. "I'll be careful of my shoulder."

"I didn't say anything," she replied, a little defensively.

"I know," said Uncle Danny with a little smile.

Singh looked at Frankline, who sweated a little. Then the Captain said. "Carry on." The Private nodded, ducking down his head.

"What the heck Frankline!" snapped Collins.

The Private twisted and spoke softly. "Dude, he's right.

We can't leave anyone out here."

Glaring at Frankline, Collins looked like he was about to froth at the mouth in fury.

However, the Captain abruptly closed the space between them. While Collins was taller, Singh was made of sheer force of will.

"If you want, you can go back to the boat right now...," started Singh. "...just leave your dog-tags and your rifle. When you get to the boat, give the Staff Sergeant your handgun."

Collins took a step back, as if he had been struck. "But..."

"I need your decision!" said Singh, and his voice dropped to a dangerous place. "Now!"

"Sir...," started Collins.

"Now!" said Singh.

"I...," began Collins, but then he deflated. "I...just can't. Not for this."

Singh just held out his hand. After a moment, Collins handed over his rifle. The Captain took it with one hand but gestured with the other. Stiffening, the private pulled off his dog-tags.

"Please get to the boat," said the Captain. "Safely."

Collins turned, hesitated, but then he started to power-walk away as Frankline and Uncle Danny lifted up Ted, who unfortunately could still talk.

"I got birds! Or, contacts, shit! Trouble!!!" called out Liberty.

Singh turned just as two alien-birds dropped right next to them. Without thinking, the Captain fired Collin's rifle with one hand sending a wild spray of bullets. It didn't hit, but it did make the creatures stumble.

A rifle shot dropped one of them.

Uncle Danny cried out. *"Mija!* BACK!"

Liberty didn't hesitate. She jumped back just as a Purple Tufted bird dropped down. Shooting her rifle, her bullet streaked across the alien-bird's back, but it did not kill him.

Whipping around, Purple Tuft was about to leap on her when Singh pressed his own rifle at the creature's back. The alien-bird shuddered as the bullets tore through him. Purple tried to turn around, but staggered and then collapsed.

Liberty and Singh were already moving away.

"This way!" cried the Captain. He pointed with Collin's M4 Carbine and used his to cover their rear.

The Librarian power-walked along the double row of cars past Uncle Danny.

At the end of the row, she stopped at the far car and hopped up onto the trunk. She was close to the marina entrance, with another car between her and it. Kneeling, she aimed her rifle back the way she had come.

"I got more!" called out Liberty. Farther down the street, there were at least a dozen alien-birds, forming up to charge. "A bunch more!"

The flock of birds suddenly shot towards them. Liberty could almost hear the devices in their heads, buzzing madly.

Singh fired single shots, more as a warning than anything else.

Aiming, Liberty fired at one of the furthest-most birds. The alien screeched and went down, but she didn't think she had killed it. However, that had not been the point. She fired again towards the back and dropped one.

The entire back of the group began to lose cohesion. Some tried to run to the front, which caused chaos. The birds suddenly began to scramble away in all directions.

Uncle Danny hoisted his end of the stretcher, but he winced a little as his shoulder flared up.

Liberty forced herself to not fuss over him, and then her eyes darted right.

"Bitch please!" snapped the Librarian as she let go of her rifle with one hand and smoothly pulled her sidearm. She fired two shots between her car and the next. A bird, who had been trying to sneak up, scrambled away.

Liberty called out after it. "You thought I wasn't looking for that!!"

Holstering her Glock, she gripped her rifle, but then noticed Danny looking at her with amusement.

"Such language," said Uncle Danny with mock affront.

"Oh, ah...," began Liberty, face burning with embarrassment. But then she stopped indignantly. *"Hey!* The kids aren't around. And that jerk was trying to eat me."

Uncle Danny just grinned as he and Frankline took Complaining Ted around the cars and through the marina entrance.

209

Surprisingly, Collins was standing there, looking towards the water.

As they got close, Frankline asked. "Hey Collins, can you take this end of the stretcher? I think they may need help back there."

Whipping his head towards the Private, Collins glared at him, hard.

Frankline looked away. "Oh-kay then." He and Uncle Danny did not stop walking, and Collins did not utter a word.

In no time, Danny and Frankline were halfway across the parking lot.

"Hey!" called a voice close to the water. The medic, Washington, was power-walking towards them.

Before the medic reached them, Uncle Danny asked. "Is everyone on the boats?"

"Yes, yes," reassured Washington. "I put your niece onto a boat myself."

Uncle Danny deflated a little. *"Gracias."*

*"Da nada,"* replied Washington smoothly, and he continued in Spanish. "Wait! Why're *you* carrying someone with a wounded shoulder?"

Danny also replied in Spanish. "Someone had to do it."

Switching to English, Washington said. "Give that to me." The man, who was even bigger than Danny, pushed in and took his end of the stretcher.

Uncle Danny was almost insulted, but then he remembered that Tessy was safe, however Liberty was not. He nodded to the medic. "Then I'll go back."

As the Big Mexican walked quickly back towards the fray, Washington called out. "Hey!"

But Uncle Danny did not even slow for a second.

Washington huffed. "I was trying to get him somewhere safe." He shook his head with a grumble. "Patients never do what they're told."

However, Frankline had missed what the medic was saying, because he was watching Uncle Danny.

The Big Mexican slowed to a stop, just before he reached Collins, who had moved deeper into the parking lot.

Uncle Danny looked at the Soldier.

"WHAT?" snapped Collins. "You're gonna tell me that I made a mistake?"

"Nope," replied Uncle Danny calmly. "But it ain't too late to...."

"RETREAT!" called out Singh from the street. He was backing up as Liberty jumped off the car that she was on. Moving next to the Captain, she brought up her rifle.

Singh grunted. "Not good."

The birds were advancing again, more swiftly this time. They moved towards them in a zig-zag pattern. He tried to get a bead on them.

Suddenly and silently, two more birds dropped down behind Liberty and Singh, almost on top of them. Their retreat to the marina cut off.

Instantly, Uncle Danny sprinted away from Collins.

*"Ya te cargó el payaso,"* hissed the Big Mexican in fear. But no matter how fast he ran, he knew he would not make

it there in time.

"Damn!" said Liberty softly as she reached for her handgun, but they were almost on top of her this time.

The Librarian fired her rifle one handed and managed to hit one, making it stumble to a halt. But the other one, with a Dark Blue Tuft, kept coming. Her hand had only touched her sidearm when it loomed over her.

A shadow descended upon the bird. Something hit the alien like a snowplow and both parties went tumbling to the side. Dark Blue Tuft hit the ground really hard. The bird tried to right himself, but then he saw who had hit him. A foot smacked Dark Blue's head, making it rap against the asphalt. It hadn't been hard, a warning, so Dark Blue decided to lay right where he was.

"Liberty!" called out Singh.

No time to process who had hit Dark Blue, Liberty turned to the oncoming horde and fired her Glock, since it was already drawn.

But the horde of birds were only 20 feet away.

Jumping up from Dark Blue Tuft, an alien-bird ran in a wide arc around Singh and planted herself right in front of the charge.

The Captain nearly shot the bird in the back.

The new alien waved its wings, but there was a pattern to it.

"*Klas du ren, Rit!*" cried the new alien with the Red Tuft.

The bird's charge immediately slowed, confused. But one of them, with a Yellow Tuft, tried to sprint past.

The Red Tufted bird kicked out and knocked it to the

ground. That made the rest stopped dead in their tracks. As Yellow Tuft tried to get up, Red Tuft lunged at his neck, but stopped, just in time. Yellow Tuft went limp on the ground.

"Rakduson?" whispered Uncle Danny next to them in shock.

Liberty and Singh jumped a bit, not realizing that he was back. They looked up at him in surprise.

"That's...?" started Liberty.

Singh whispered urgently. "Later. Back up slowly and reload. Just in case." And then he remembered to add. "Please."

So, they started to back up, and reloaded.

"Sure, we shouldn't just run?" asked Liberty.

"Never run from predators, *Mija*," said Uncle Danny.

One of the alien-birds pointed their beak towards the retreating humans. Rakduson hopped left and kicked a hunk of broken bumper on the ground. It biffed the other bird right in the chest.

"*Hojot Teal!*" snapped Rak, adding a literal snap of her beak. And she continued to talk quickly.

The bird that Liberty had shot was trying, unsuccessfully, to get up. Liberty trained her handgun on it.

"Let's not shoot anyone else," suggested Singh. "Unless they attack."

"Jus' a friendly warning," replied Liberty, without any heat, and the bird settled back down.

Singh nodded and finished reloading his M4 Carbine. He let it hang from its strap as he turned to Collins' rifle. The Captain patted his pockets. "Darn, I'm out." Checking, he found a handful of bullets in Collin's rifle and touched his earpiece. "Staff Sergeant...?"

"Captain?" called out Ruiz. "We can back you up, right now!"

"Are all the people on the boats?" asked Singh instead.

"Just got the idiot on the stretcher on board. Boy, he complains a lot," said Ruiz. "And Frankline said Collins was coming back, but he hasn't arrived yet."

"We'll look for him. Okay, I want you to head back to the Fleet," said Singh. "We can hitch a ride on Liberty and Danny's boat...um, I don't know the name of it…"

"We don't have one," said Liberty, embarrassed.

"We really nee….," started Uncle Danny, but he stopped. "No. Wait! I already said that."

Liberty gave him a soft smile. "Yeah, we really do need a name."

"It's okay…," began Uncle Danny, but he glanced at the birds and then did a double take.

"What is it?" asked Liberty, seeing the look.

"I think…" And Uncle Danny squinted. "Yes! Yesterd… ¡Hijole!...that was today! This morning felt like a long time ago.

"I know what you mean," nodded Singh with a tired smile.

Uncle Danny continued. "Anyhow, I shot at one of the birds through my passenger window. And I think it's that

214

one in front with the...is that Purple-ish?"

"Oh, that's Magenta," said Singh. Uncle Danny looked at him with surprise for a moment, but then turned away quickly, thinking it rude. But the Captain did not take it badly.

Singh softly explained. "My little girl was *very* into fashion for a while...until she discovered Transformers. Shortly thereafter, she wanted to clothe the robots, because she declared, 'In real life, people can't go around with their ding-a-lings hanging out'."

Liberty wanted to say more, but she stopped herself.

Singh continued. "But...that Magenta Tuft is also the one that killed Private Sondes this morning."

Backing up steadily, they had reached the marina parking lot, and the talk between the alien-birds had erupted into a full blown argument. Rakduson and the Magenta Tuft bird were doing most of the talking. But the others were slowly closing in ranks behind Magenta Tuft. The devices in the backs of the other bird's heads was now a steady, rising shrill buzz.

"I'm sorry Mr. Danny. Your bird friend is not going to stop them," said Singh and he called out over his earpiece. "Staff Sergeant! Cast off now!"

"I take that as an order," said Ruiz, half-asking.

"Yes Staff Sergeant," said the Captain softly. "I order you to get everyone to safety."

"Yes sir," said Ruiz. "I'll...see you soon."

Singh smiled, even though she could not see it. "See you soon."

215

Behind them, they heard the boats give a throaty roar as they started to leave.

Magenta whipped her head in that direction and gave a rending scream.

Suddenly, Magenta leapt towards Rakduson, and two other birds followed. Rak just managed to dodge Magenta, but not the one with the sickly-green tuft. That one kicked out. Rakduson twisted to avoid getting her chest caved in. But the blow still hit her hard and she went down.

"No!" cried Danny.

Rak bounced against the asphalt and did not get up.

Magenta Ruft jumped onto a car.

"*KLAS DU REN!*" screeched the alien, and the other birds jumped up onto the cars to face them.

"Get ready," said Singh with a calm voice. "Back up towards the edge of the pier to our right. Jump in the water, if necessary." He leveled Collins' M4 Carbine.

Behind the cars, Rakduson tried to get up. But then she collapsed.

"Rak!" said Uncle Danny. "I think Rak's alive."

"One thing at a time," said Singh, with a calm voice.

The alien-birds, almost flocking as one, jumped towards the marina entrance.

"Back up and fire!" called out Singh.

Liberty tried to get Magenta, but her shot missed. Though she did get the Sickly-Green Tuft bird behind her. The Librarian fired as quickly as she could. While the main group of alien-birds were still in one bunch, however two others peeled off to flank them.

Singh fired into the mass as they moved steadily backwards. But not fast enough. Collin's M4 went empty, and Singh began to throw it aside as he raised his own rifle.

Someone grabbed it. "Thank you!" said a voice.

Singh just managed not to shoot the man.

Collins lobbed something forward before slapping in a fresh magazine.

"IS that...?" started the Captain.

In the midst of the birds, a grenade went off. It scattered the aliens.

For a second, Singh gave Collins an incendiary glare and the soldier looked down.

"It was my last grenade," whined Collins.

The mass of birds fell into a chaotic mess, but it would only last for a moment more.

The Captain turned towards the mass of birds and cried. "On me!"

Plunging back towards them, Singh started firing single shots with his rifle, as fast as he could.

Liberty and Danny leapt after him.

Collins though had not moved, still talking to the ground. "I jus' couldn't give up my last grenade, just in case..." He blinked and suddenly realized that they were all gone. "Aw Beans." He sprinted after them.

The two birds that had been trying to flank them stumbled to a halt and then turned to run back towards the fray.

217

As Singh got close to the horde of birds, he switched to full auto and let loose, tearing into them.

Though rattled, a bird tried to lunge towards the Captain. His M4 clicked empty. Flipping the rifle, he slammed its butt into the bird's face. As the alien went down, the captain drew his sidearm, firing.

On his right, Liberty was not as subtle. She fired her rifle in one hand and her handgun in the other, because it was hard to miss at this range. This further upended the bird's advance.

"*Yieta! Roe ta...,*" began Magenta, who looked like she was pulling a group of birds off to the side to flank. But she glanced forward and saw Uncle Danny, almost upon her.

With a leonine roar, the Big Mexican slammed the stock of his shotgun into Magenta's head. The bird stumbled but kicked out a leg. However, Danny was already past her firing into the group.

To the other side, Collins shot at the two birds who had been trying to flank them.

One of the birds dove behind a car, and then stuck his head up long enough to give a shout.

"*Guk Fen!*" cried the bird.

Collins' next bullet shattered the car window near the bird's head.

Sprinting off at a low angle, the bird screamed. "*GUK FEN! GUK FEN!*"

Suddenly, the other birds began to scramble off in every direction. Some took to the air, but others ran between cars.

Singh backed carefully to Liberty. He was joined by

Collins, who aimed at a bird that was trying to hobble away. The Captain saw the bird tense up; tensing like a dog that knew that they were about to get punched.

"Private STOP!" ordered Singh.

Collins froze, confused. "What?"

"That's enough," said Singh in a normal voice.

"But...but, they would've killed us," started Collins, who began to aim, but the bird had already made it behind an SUV.

Singh put his hand on Collins' rifle.

"That's enough," said the Captain, and he pushed down the rifle. "Just...make sure that none of them try to circle back. We've gotten so fuc..." And in his mind's eye, his father was about to raise an eyebrow, over the use of That Word. "...*freaking* lucky out here. Let's not push that luck any further. We're getting outta here."

Collins looked Singh square in the eye, as if to argue. But then he dropped his gaze and nodded. Turning around, the Soldier made sure that nothing would sneak up on them.

"And Collins," said Singh. "Thanks for the help."

"I...," started the Soldier.

"Let's talk later," said Singh quickly. "Once we're..." The Captain noticed Liberty looking around wildly. But then she pointed.

"There he is!" she cried.

Turning back to the entrance to the marina, Singh saw Uncle Danny.

219

And the Big Mexican was half-carrying someone.

At the same time, Collins glanced back and growled. "Are you shitting me?" He twisted and began to bring up his rifle.

Without a word, Captain Singh just reached out and pushed the barrel of Collin's rifle down with one solitary finger.

## Chapter Sixteen

One bird started screaming and suddenly the rest scattered. At that moment, Danny realized that the devices in the back of each bird's head were not buzzing anymore. The devices that drove them crazy had gone quiet.

Liberty, Singh, and that other guy stopped fighting and fell back into a defensive stance.

They were safe. His *amiga* was safe.

Staying low, Uncle Danny immediately power-walked out of the marina and towards the traffic jam of cars. Fear piercing straight through him, Danny feared what he would find, but he couldn't leave her a second time.

"*Gand dakdu*," cried a bird up ahead.

Near the cars, Uncle Danny saw two alien-birds, who looked like they were ready to pounce on someone.

Without realizing it, the Big Mexican was tearing through the air towards the birds. Because of his injured shoulder, he shifted to hold the shotgun one-handed.

Rak was still there, partly down.

"Get away from her!" snarled Uncle Danny. He aimed the shotgun right at them.

Their eyes went wide with fright, and the two scrabbled to get away, almost comically.

"And don't come back!" spat Danny.

The sun was starting to set, and as he looked down, he saw Rakduson trying to get up.

Joyfully, Uncle Danny leapt forward, but the alien with the Red Tuft snapped her beak at him.

Screeching to a halt, Danny held up his hands. Realizing that one handheld a shotgun, he gently—ever so carefully—put the weapon on the trunk of a car.

Rak's eyes tried to focus on him.

Does she recognize me? he wondered fearfully.

Pointing to himself, he said. "Danny."

The alien-bird's head dipped. She rocked a little. Rak was propped up on one wing and the knee of her good leg. A soft noise came out of her.

Danny could see the broken device in the back of her head. Glancing up, he noticed that those two birds were at a healthy distance—for them—but they were still lurking.

The Big Mexican almost looked up to his *Abuela*, but his decision was easy.

"Come on," he said gently. Moving forward, Rak froze

as he got close. But then he carefully helped her stand up. All that time, taking care of his brother with his bad back, meant that he knew how to care for someone in terrible pain.

The Red Tufted bird tried to put her foot down, but immediately winced in pain.

"I got you," assured Uncle Danny, and he ducked under her left wing, hoping that this would work. Carefully straightening, he managed to support her.

"*Kulong?*" she muttered.

"Let's go," said Danny, and he slowly started to move forward. It took a few tries, but soon they found an easy rhythm. Passing by the car, he grabbed his shotgun.

Even with her propped on his right shoulder, the strain of carrying her was hurting his left one. But he bore it quietly, and happily. It was good pain.

They entered the marina and there were all the birds, injured and dead. Rak made a sad noise but said nothing more.

Still, Uncle Danny felt he needed to defend himself.

"They attacked," he whispered, regretfully. "We tried to back up, but they came right for us."

Rak did not reply. Her head drooped more.

Nonetheless, Uncle Danny steered her around some cars towards a path that had no casualties. It would be further from Liberty, but he wondered if the smell of that much blood would trigger a panic. Not unreasonably, he thought.

However, Liberty was moving towards them.

The soldier that had run was trying to say something,

but Singh shut him down. The Captain was moving towards them too.

Between helping Rak, the pain in his left shoulder, and the sheer exhaustion of a long, hard day, Uncle Danny just wanted to get Rak somewhere safe where she can recover. Get Tessy. Then he could...

ZOMS, he realized with a jolt. He needed to watch the cars underneath ; in case any were around. There was almost too much to keep track of.

A terrible, rending screech tore through the air.

Rak stiffened against him.

Suddenly, the Big Mexican saw the Magenta Tufted bird stand up. The alien stumbled a bit but stayed upright.

Liberty started to raise her rifle.

Without warning, Magenta shot forward, moving so fast. She leapt over the fallen birds and then hopped onto a car, almost on top of Danny and the bird.

A minivan was in Liberty's line of sight.

The alien was about to leap when Singh was there between Magenta Tuft and Danny with Rak.

"Don't even think it!!" said Singh.

The Captain did not shout. He did not need to. His M4 Carbine was pointed directly at Magenta. And it did not waver for a second.

With a blistering fury in her eyes, Magenta took a step forward, up to the edge of the car.

Singh took a step towards her. "Back off! I don't want to kill you."

Magenta hesitated and Singh shot forward and his rifle barrel almost touched the feathers on her belly.

"Go. Now!" said Singh through gritted teeth and he nodded towards the Marina entrance.

The Captain's mind raced for a split second. They had killed his people-- like Sondes-- but admittedly, he had killed theirs too. And if they were enslaved by that device...

Singh continued with a weary voice. "There's been enough death today. Don 'cha think?"

The fury in her eyes banked down and Magenta took a step back.

Singh mirrored her step away, lowering his rifle, just a bit.

"Go on Uncle Danny," said the Captain with a low voice. "Hurry."

"Not sure how fast I can go," mumbled Danny, slightly slurring.

Magenta took another step back and glanced at the birds, some dead, but others just injured.

Singh started to move towards the Marina. "Liberty, Collins, move slowly towards the boats. If she sees that we're not going to attack, maybe we can get out of this in one piece."

Liberty, rifle ready to support, hesitated for a moment. She had almost taken the shot. She had had Magenta's left eye, dead to rights. But, if they were not animals, then they were victims.

The Librarian lowered her rifle. She stepped away towards the wooden stairs and down a little towards the dock. Collins too looked like he was going to argue, but he went as well. But neither went too far.

Uncle Danny kept going. His whole world was a deep fog of pain and exhaustion. And yet, he felt better than he had in days. In fact, the best since he had had to aim his shotgun at Rak. His heart sang—which he always thought was just some made-up, flowery stuff—but it did.

To Magenta, Singh said. "We just want to go home."

Stepping back subtly, he moved to keep himself between Danny and Magenta. While still holding his M4 Carbine steady at the alien, the Captain pointed to himself. Then he pointed towards the docks. Magenta's eyes followed his hand. Next, he pointed at the alien-bird, and then in the opposite direction, towards the entrance to the Marina.

Pointing last to his rifle, Singh dropped it, ever so slightly. Without turning his back on the bird, the Captain kept moving.

Magenta looked from Rak being carried away, and then to the birds. Some of the fallen were not beyond help.

Uncle Danny heard Singh whisper. "Yes, please take care of your people, and let us go."

In the distance, the Captain heard the throaty roar of boats coming in fast.

Magenta squinted out at the water and took a step towards her people. The device in the back of her head suddenly went off again. The injured birds in the middle of the parking lot instantly began to flail about and get up.

Magenta did not make a noise as she leapt down to the ground, straight at Singh.

Uncle Danny felt Rak slide away from him, dropping to the ground.

With madness in her eyes, Magenta kicked high. "*Klas du ren!*"

Singh did not shoot but brought his rifle up like a barrier. The bird's foot, instead of collapsing his chest, slid off the rifle and glanced off the Captain's arm.

As Singh fell back and knew that his right arm was broken. Smacking the ground hard sent shock waves through him.

But the damn bird was already above him. One foot ready to stomp his head in. Even as he brought his good arm up—futilely—he thought of his wife and daughter, gone even before this happened.

Uncle Danny was already twisting, ignoring the fire in his shoulder. His shotgun fired.

Magenta staggered back, as if hit by a sledgehammer. However, one leg still rose, ready to curb stomp the Captain.

Rakduson shot into view. She came in low and fast, but without a noise. Suddenly kicking out at the last moment, she knocked Magenta away, who slammed hard into a car. Magenta tried to straighten up and looked up in surprise at Rak.

"*Hun kion?*" asked Magenta softly. Slowly, she slumped to a sitting position, head lolling.

Diving forward, Rakduson went to the bird's side. Magenta's beak opened and closed, as if she were trying to make words, or even sounds. Rak leaned forward, and she rubbed the side of her beak against Magenta's neck.

A last breath fell out of Magenta, and the bird seemed to collapse in upon herself, falling away from Rak's nuzzling beak.

Singh tried to move. Despite a bit of pain, he found that his upper arm was not floppy, so not shattered. That's something, he thought. He wondered if he had gotten even lucky with only a hairline break. Actually, he was alive, so he amended that he was already very lucky.

Uncle Danny was soon there, and he helped the Captain to his feet.

Rakduson lifted her head up to the sky. *"Roat Du forta mot!"*

Several wounded birds took up the cry for a moment.

Singh straightened his turban and then held his rifle ready with one hand.

The Red Tufted bird stood back and tried to walk, but she immediately collapsed herself.

Sure, that the Captain was okay, Uncle Danny moved a little closer to Rak. She glanced at him with a look of pure sorrow.

Moving slowly, the Big Mexican stopped just shy of her.

*"Ay, pobrecita,* I'm sorry," he whispered. "So sorry."

Danny gestured that he was ready to help her.

After a moment, Rak lifted her left wing, and he helped her up. Her head was lolling, and she was getting heavier.

Suddenly, Liberty was there, just in front. She fixed Danny with a hard look.

"You ran off again."

"Only after the action was done. And I didn't go that very far," said Uncle Danny quickly, defensively. "An' I was planning on coming right back...Did come right back! Wasn't running off wildly this time."

Collins had come up behind the Librarian, and he blinked in confusion.

Liberty nodded. "That's true. But you still scared me a little."

"Sorry *Mija*," said Uncle Danny softly. "I just..."

A small smile came across the Librarian's face. She stepped to Rak's right side, opposite Uncle Danny. Carefully climbing under Rak's wing, she gently helped support the alien-bird.

"Come on," she said to both of them. And they started moving Rak to the docks. The alien looked muzzily back and forth.

When the bird caught Liberty's eye, the Liberian said. "Hi. I'm Liberty. Glad to finally meet you."

Rak blinked, a little confused.

Collins ran past them in confusion as well.

"Captain?" asked Collins.

"Let's switch weapons," said Singh.

Without thinking, Collins changed rifles with the Captain.

A little awkwardly, Singh checked the clip. Satisfied to see bullets in there, the Captain put it back in. Rifle in one hand, he moved out in a wide arc to cover Uncle Danny, Rak and Liberty as they moved towards the steps.

229

Collins followed along. "Um, why did you give me your rifle?"

"Because mine's out of bullets," said Singh, not taking his eye off the wounded birds. Despite their injuries, the buzzing was making them try to move.

The Soldier blinked. "Wait. Did you just go up against that bird, without any bullets? Were you bluffing?"

Instead of answering, Singh said. "My squad's going to be traveling back and forth to the Coast for the next…" He paused. "Well, I don't know how long. Days, weeks, years. To begin with, we're coming back tomorrow to find a safe place for the tank and get our dead."

"Oh," started Collins softly.

"You came back and helped, *but only* after you left," said Singh without heat. "And you held back a grenade, after I asked for all of them."

"But it…," started Collins.

Singh just gave the Soldier a flinty look.

Collins ducked his head. "When that bird stuck his head in our car—you know, when they killed Sondes—I've never been so scared than in my entire life. Even when the zoms first appeared."

"I understand," said Singh.

"I just..," started Collins.

"I'm going to talk to the Rear Admiral though," cut in the Captain. "Maybe find a better place for you on the carrier."

Collins looked up with a mixture of surprise and disappointment. But then he nodded.

"Everyone has a right place in life. The right seat to sit in," said Singh, and he gave a little smile. "I'll help you find yours."

"We're heading down the stairs," called out Liberty. Then they heard the Librarian say to both Danny and Rak. "Carefully you two. One step at a time. Not too many."

"Come on," said Singh to Collins. "Let's follow."

The dock stretched out ahead, past a two story building and then it took a hard right turn. Soon, they saw Lieutenant Washington by two Bowrider boats.

"What the...?" exclaimed Washington as he trained his rifle on the bird.

"It's okay," said Liberty quickly. "Don't shoot!"

"We come in peace," giggled Uncle Danny, almost drunk with fatigue.

The Captain moved swiftly around them, skirting the very edge of the dock.

With a calm voice, Singh said to the Medic. "Stand down."

Washington looked at his commanding officer and grinned. "Captain!" But then his brow furrowed. "Wait? Is there something wrong with your arm?"

"Had a minor scuffle," replied Singh offhandedly.

Collins piped up. "He took on a bird with no bullets. And won!"

The Medic glared at Singh. "Are you trying to get yourself killed?"

"All in a day's work," said Singh with a lop-sided smile.

"And I thought I ordered you all to take everyone back to the refugee ship?"

Standing even straighter, the smile disappeared, and Washington said. "We followed that order to the letter. Sir." And he let it lie there.

After a second, Singh made an aggravated noise. "Damn! But, I didn't say that you weren't to come back."

"Sir, No Sir," said the Medic, trying to keep the smile off his face.

Singh chuckled. "Good job."

"Now, let's get you guys in...," started Washington. However, he looked at Rak, who was almost to them. "Um..."

But Uncle Danny cut in. "Is Tessy safe?"

"Tessy?" asked Washington. "Oh yeah! The little girl that was with you? Yeah, she's good." However, he looked pointedly at the alien-bird. "But are you going to be alright?"

Liberty spoke with a flat voice. "We're going to take our second boat, and go back to our ship,"

"Okay, but...," said Washington.

Thrilled that he, and so many of his people, were still alive, Singh found himself completely amused.

Cheerily, the Captain explained. "They're not asking us."

The Medic looked at the Captain in surprise.

"*Disculpe,*" said Uncle Danny as they neared them.

Singh spoke up. "Washington, Collins. Why don't you

get in our boat."

"Okay," nodded the Medic. Washington climbed into the boat, and—after letting Collins onboard—reached out to help the Captain.

"I'm not broken," grumbled Singh, disagreeably.

Washington looked him dead in the eye. "Sir, you're a little broken. Let me help you! The rest of the team's worried enough as is."

Grudgingly, Singh let the Medic help him onboard.

"If you got hurt more," continued Washington with humor. "Staff Sergeant Ruiz is going to throw me overboard and make me swim back home."

"We wouldn't want that," chuckled Singh.

"No, we don't," agreed Washington.

Soon the Captain had sunken into a comfy pleather seat and a small smile flitted across his face. He wanted to sleep for a hundred years. However, he heard voices, and he could not help himself.

Softly, Uncle Danny said to Liberty. "I almost want you to go in the other boat."

However, the Librarian scoffed jovially. "Like that was going to happen."

"Rak might come outta her daze—confused!—and might be a bit...angry. *Estar que ladra*," explained Danny urgently.

"Then we'll set her away from us," said Liberty with a flat voice.

"But...," started Danny.

Amused, Singh interjected. "She's not asking."

233

This made the Big Mexican gave a little laugh.

"I assume we're taking her back to our nameless ship?" asked Liberty.

Uncle Danny paused. *"Si.* That is what I was hoping."

"Okay. Let me get into the boat first," said Liberty.

"WAIT," called out Washington as he climbed out of his boat. Captain Singh was about to say something but stopped himself from being a 'Mother Hen'.

Liberty, who was the most awake, watched the medic as he ran up with his medical supplies.

Washington said to her. "Let me help you get them inside."

It took a few tries, but they managed to get everyone in. Rak was set towards the back, not that it was that big a boat.

Washington checked Liberty first, but it was just scrapes and bruises.

Next, the medic double-gloved and checked Uncle Danny, redressing his wounds. But then Washington turned to Rakduson. He stood before her, and she eyed him wearily.

"How intelligent is it?" asked the Medic of Danny.

"It?" growled the Big Mexican.

To Danny, Liberty said urgently. "We didn't know that 'she' was a 'she' at first. We thought that they were just..." Glancing at Rak, she didn't finish her sentence.

"True," sighed Uncle Danny, and he looked at the Medic. "I think...wait, no, I'm sure that she has human level intelligence."

Washington looked at him in surprise, and then down at Rakduson.

"I want to help," said the Medic. He knelt before the bird, so that they were on the same level.

Rak looked from him to Uncle Danny, and the Big Mexican pulled open his coat to show his bandages. Then he smiled warmly.

"Where does it hurt?" asked Washington. His voice calm and soothing.

The bird looked at the Big Mexican again. Danny poked his own wound and went 'Ow'. Then he pointed at the medic and gave a relieved smile.

Washington said to him. "I should've bandaged your wound in front of her, that way she knows I'm just trying to help."

Uncle Danny furrowed his brow and then lurched to his feet. In the small boat, he climbed around Washington and sat a little heavily beside Rakduson. Then he reached into his coat and tore one of his bandages off.

"Ow," muttered Danny.

Washington was about to chastise him, but Danny bared the wound for Rak to see. The medic rolled his eyes.

"I guess that works," grumbled the Medic without heat. Rak watched with surprise as Washington bandaged the wound again.

Uncle Danny saw Liberty's disapproval.

"Toxic masculinity can be fatal," sniffed the Librarian.

"*¡Orale!* So, I've heard," smiled Danny.

235

Liberty rolled her eyes and turned to guard the boats. Only then did she allow herself to smile.

After Danny, Rakduson allowed Washington to examine her. As best as he could manage it, he bandaged the few wounds that he could.

Standing up, the medic smiled at Danny and Rak. "You two need to rest, at least a couple of days."

Rak looked at him, not understanding.

Washington saw it and mimed sleeping.

"Huk," said Rakduson, which Washington took to mean 'yes'.

To the Librarian, he said. "Well Ms. Liberty, your people are all going to make it."

"Glad to hear," she smiled. "Thank you!"

After Washington returned to his boat, the Liberty took the controls of their boat but froze.

Suddenly, she turned to Singh in the other boat. "Call me crazy. But it was..." She stilled and then looked at the Red Tufted bird. She couldn't remember the alien's name! "Crap! I'm sorry...long day! I can't remem..."

"Rakduson," supplied Uncle Danny helpfully.

"Yes!" cried Liberty.

Rak opened an eye for a moment, but then closed it again.

The Librarian looked back towards the Captain. "Call me crazy, but it was Rakduson who jumped between us and those other birds. *And* she tried to get them to back off."

"Put her life on the line!" cried out Uncle Danny loudly,

because he couldn't get himself to stand.

Singh nodded solemnly. "I'll note it in my report."

"Thank you!" cried out Uncle Danny.

Liberty started the boat and soon took them away from the Coast.

# Epilogue

Not long after, Uncle Danny was softly snoring when he awoke in a panic. "Tessy! Where's Tessy?"

Calmly, Liberty said. "She's safe. On the new refugee boat."

"We gotta get her. Right away!" said Uncle Danny.

The Librarian looked back. "I already got a plan. We're going to our ship first though."

"No!" said Danny as he tried to move. "We gotta get Tessy."

Whipping around, the look on Liberty's face made him freeze. She dropped into her You-Cheesed-Off-The-Librarian voice. "You are going back to the ship. I'll get Tessy."

Uncle Danny was going to argue but decided that it was

safer not to.

Shortly, the Librarian was pulling up behind their ship. She heard the Navy Engineer before he appeared.

"You're alive! Oh, Thank God!" called out Smalls and then he ran into view. "I was..." He glanced down and almost did a comedic doubletake. "Sweet Baby Jesus!"

"Don't swear like that," said Danny urgently, though a little muzzily. "*Mi Abuela* will hit you with her shoe. An' it'd hurt."

"But...but...," started Smalls.

"It's a long story," said Liberty. She glanced back at Uncle Danny, and then at Smalls. "I'm actually just dropping these two off. Then..."

"You sure you don't want me to go with?" asked Uncle Danny.

Liberty gave him a stern look. "You're going to lay down." Then she turned to Rak, who was watching her as well. "You too!" To Danny, she said. "I'll collect Tessy."

Uncle Danny looked down. "I don't want her to think, that I don't love her. That she isn't important enough for me to pick up myself."

The Librarian was going to say that that was nonsense, but she stopped herself. Then she turned to Smalls. "Are the guys here?"

Smalls shook his head. "Tagg and Colin planned to stay late tonight on the *Salk.*"

"Okay," said Liberty. "I'm going to collect everyone." She turned to Danny. "But You! You're staying in the boat."

239

"Okay *Mija*," nodded Uncle Danny, barely keeping his eyes open.

*

A voice called out from the ship ahead. "Over here!"

In a blur, Tessy ran to the side of the boat and hopped up onto the rail. Captain Singh was right behind her with the older lady, Giselle, who was cradling the baby they had rescued.

Waving one arm wildly, Tessy called out. "Is that you? *Tio* Danny???"

However, Liberty could not hear her yet. She did wave back. Soon, she pulled up alongside the old freighter. It was close enough that Tessy could see Uncle Danny practically laying in the back of the boat, next to Rakduson.

"Oh no oh no oh no oh no," began Tessy with a near panic.

As the boat drew close, Liberty saw the panic in the little girl. Her stomach dropped, wondering what was so wrong. She immediately glanced back into their boat.

Whipping back to the girl, the Librarian called out.

"He's okay! He's okay!" she cried. "He wanted to come with, but he's just tired. Really, really super tired."

Uncle Danny jerked awake and gave a little wave with his right arm. "Hey! Sorry, I fell asleep. I'm an old man, you know."

"No, you're not!" snapped Tessy with concern.

Liberty turned back to Uncle Danny and said. "You! Stay Here."

"*¿Neta?*" asked Danny.

"Yes, really '*neta*'," said Liberty, and then she paused for half a second. "Whatever '*neta*' means."

Which made Danny chuckle. "*¡Orale!*"

Liberty just rolled her eyes with mock annoyance. But satisfied, she turned to Rakduson with a small smile. "You! Stay here as well." And she pointed at Rak and then in the boat with mock insistence.

Immediately, the Librarian feared that she might have gone too far. That the alien might not understand that it was a joke.

However, making a show of being greatly amused, the alien laid back, relaxing, even puffing out her feathers a little.

Liberty turned to concentrate on safely reaching the temporary dock beside the freighter. She hadn't been driving boats that long.

Dr. Washington and Private Frankline headed over to help secure Liberty's Bowrider boat. But Frankline skidded to a halt when he saw the bird.

"Oh shit! They really did bring a bird," said Frankline in surprise.

"She's with them," said Washington without a beat.

"She?" asked Frankline tentatively.

"She," nodded Washington decisively.

"OOOOH-kay," said Frankline with a high-pitched voice. That settled, he moved quickly to help lash Liberty's boat to the temporary dock.

Before it was exactly safe, Liberty jumped out and ran up a temporary gangway to Tessy. The second she got to the little girl, Tessy leapt forward and clenched her arms around the Librarian's middle. For someone so small, she nearly squeezed the life out of Liberty.

The Librarian, for her part, wrapped her arms tightly around the little girl.

"I'm so glad you're okay. And he's okay too! Thankfully," said Liberty soothingly. "The big galoot."

Tessy looked up, wide-eyed. "*¿Neta?*"

Liberty smiled and nodded quickly. "Really. We'll go down in a minute but first, I just need to talk with Captain Singh..." She glanced up and saw Giselle with a bittersweet smile. The Librarian said. "Thank You. *Really!* Thank you for taking care of her."

"It was a pleasure," said Giselle. "If you ever need a babysitter..."

"Hey! I'm not a baby," exclaimed Tessy.

Singh smiled. "You are a little bit 'baby'."

"What?" cried Tessy and she turned to scowl at him.

Liberty gave the girl a little squeeze. "Okay. We'll argue about that later." Looking at Giselle, the Librarian said. "Thank you, I'll keep that in mind." Then she nodded at baby Francis in the older woman's arms. "Though it looks like you already have your hands full."

A bright, warm smile went across Gisele's face, and she looked down at the baby in her arms. "It's only one. I can handle that easy."

Liberty turned to the Captain, who had a splint on his

upper arm and his forearm in a sling. She began. "Are you...?"

"*Liberté!*" cried a voice from across the ship.

The Librarian's hand automatically went to her sidearm. She could not detach Tessy in time as she turned.

Suddenly, he was there.

Renoir, the HairArtiste, appeared next to her and dropped to his knees. "You! Who have given us *liberté* from our refuge to this fine, fine sea air. Which is as fresh as..." He gave an exaggerated shrug. "Well, sea air." But then he added earnestly. "No! I refuse to complain!"

"Get up. Get Up!" She reached out and pulled him to his feet. "It wasn't that big a deal."

"Ah! But it was!" countered Renoir. "For without you and The Uncle Danny, this whole venture would have fallen."

"Captain Singh and his people had a lot to do with it, really...," said Liberty and she glanced at Singh.

The Captain cut in. "Actually, you and Uncle Dann...Great! Now I'm calling him 'Uncle' too."

"It's like a disease," nodded Liberty sympathetically.

"Anyhow," said Singh, shaking his head. "You two made sure that I came home with more people than I probably would have. And we might not have been able to save everyone too. No, you and Danny made a difference. Thank you."

More people were arriving to thank Liberty. But quickly, it was a crush of people, and her heart sped up exponentially as they came closing in on her from all sides.

Walling her in.

Pressed against the Librarian's chest, Tessy immediately heard her heart begin to pound. Looking up, she saw that Liberty was just barely holding back her panic. It was too many people for the Librarian.

"I Want To See *Tio* Danny!" demanded Tessy loudly.

Liberty blinked and looked down at the girl.

Tessy's eyes sharpened, but the Librarian could see that the girl was pretending to be petulant. That the little girl was trying to help.

"We need to go! *Now!*" demanded Tessy loudly, and she nodded towards Liberty's boat.

At first, Renoir had turned to reproach the little girl, but then he saw the sheen of sweat which had broken out on Liberty's forehead.

The HairArtiste swiftly turned back to the crowd and started to create a space. "*Oui! Oui!* The *Liberté* has had a hard day. We should probably let her go home for a long nap and some food." As Renoir began to move them back towards the boat, he fixed the Librarian with a paternal look. "Better! Eat, and then sleep. You need nutrients!"

"I will," smiled Liberty indulgently. She was so grateful when they had left that suffocating crowd.

Tessy was still attached to her side, but the little girl reached out as they passed and quickly squeezed Gisele's hand.

"Don't grip old people's hands too hard," admonished the older lady sternly. "Some people have arthritis."

And then they were back on the boat. Washington and

Frankline were waiting to help them in, but Liberty gently waved them off. She stopped on the temporary gangway and turned to Renoir.

"Thank you," she said, and Liberty looked at Tessy as well. "You too. Thank you."

Renoir gave a flourishing bow. "Always at your service." Straightening, he began to reach for her head, but then he stopped himself. "May I lift up your beret, to plan for your *magnifique* hair style."

"Sure," said Liberty and she bent a little forward. "Just know it's been a long day.

Delicately, without touching her at all, Renoir lifted her beret. His eyes widened with horror for a nanosecond, but then, with an easy, professional smile, he returned her beret. "Ah! Now I can plan to make you look *étonnante*. Or more *étonnante* than usual."

Not knowing what he was talking about, Liberty just smiled.

After the HairArtiste had inspected Tessy's hair, Liberty loaded Tessy into the boat and hopped in herself. The little girl immediately jumped into Uncle Danny's lap. He gave a little 'whoof' of surprise but held her close.

"*Au revoir!*" called out Renoir as the little boat pulled away from the freighter and towards the boys on the *Jonas Salk* medical ship.

Nestled against Danny's chest, Tessy opened an eye and then froze. She had been so excited to see her uncle that she had not looked carefully at the rest of the boat.

"Um, is that one of the birds?" she asked, hesitantly.

The little girl felt Uncle Danny's chest shake with laughter. "Let me introduce you to a new *amiga* of ours."

Halfway through their ride, Liberty remembered.

"Aw beans," she muttered, and immediately turned back towards the refugee ship.

When they were close once more, Singh came over her earpieces.

"Liberty? You guys okay?" he asked worriedly.

Killing the engine—now that they were in range—Liberty said. "I was going to ask you about your arm? And I still have my earpiece. Do you need it back? Oh, and Danny still has his. We'll have to…"

The moment she took a breath, Singh quickly said. "It's okay." He kept going. "My arm is probably only a hair fracture—so that's good—and keep the earpieces. I will undoubtedly need your help once everyone is better."

## Epilogue One

Behind the Big Mexican, he heard the Librarian call out. "There he is."

A few days had passed now, and Liberty and Tessy walked up to stop beside Uncle Danny.

The little girl gave him a hard look. "Shouldn't you be resting?"

In his deck chair, Uncle Danny beamed at her. "It is *so wonderful*, once again, to see you every morning *Mi Mariposa Unicornio!* Except, now I don't have to worry about keeping us alive." Delighted, he reached out and gave her hand a hard squeeze.

Tessy yanked her hand away and grumbled testily. "Ms. Giselle says not to squeeze people's hands so tight, because they may be old and have arthritis."

Unruffled by his niece's acerbic tone, Uncle Danny sighed happily. "You're finally here."

"She is right though," said Liberty. While she was behind Tessy, she had her hands protectively on the girl's shoulders.

"I'm just keeping an eye on her, " he replied soothingly.

Uncle Danny was on one end of the helicopter pad, and at the other end was Rakduson. She was eating a big fish and making happy noises. Her bandaged leg was out, so she was sitting a little awkwardly.

Rak's eyes though were watching the newcomers wearily.

"Where'd you get the fish?" asked Liberty.

"Ah!" replied Uncle Danny happily. "That's why Smalls called me during breakfast." He looked at Tessy. "After you went to bed last night, I made some calls. We have some decent wine to trade with—not great, but decent— and food helps people heal."

Tessy glanced uncertainly at Rak. Then, she said thoughtfully, but without judgement. "And she is people."

The alien-bird paused. She looked down at her food, took another delicate bite and carefully stood up. Favoring her good leg, she moved away from her half-eaten fish and walked towards them. Her movements were careful and deliberate.

Rakduson's wings slowly unfurled, showing all the colors beneath.

Liberty had to force herself not to grip Tessy's shoulder any more tightly. She compensated for this by reaching over and grabbing Uncle Danny's good shoulder. His eyes instantly widened with agony.

Silently, the Big Mexican looked up at her, but she was watching to see what Rak would do next.

Figuring he had earned a little pain for worrying her— Twice!— Uncle Danny ignored the intense pressure on his right shoulder and watched.

At first, the alien-bird moved her wings in simple sweeping motions. Before Uncle Danny knew it, the movements grew faster and more complicated though. It was going really well until Rak took a step sideways on her injured leg.

"*Ee-kp*," squeaked Rakduson.

As she stumbled, Uncle Danny jumped up. She was trying to regain her footing when he got close.

Rak, sensing something closing in on her, snapped her beak at the intruder, mostly in irritation.

"Uncle!!" cried out Tessy immediately.

As the Big Mexican immediately froze, the alien-bird stilled, realized who it was.

Slowly but surely, Danny backed away.

Rakduson's eyes grew wide.

And Uncle Danny wondered if he really was seeing shock and fear in her eyes. He did not know if he was— well, he couldn't think of the word in English—but he knew when someone assigned human characteristics to an animal, it was '*antropomorfismo*'.

Had he been doing that? Danny wondered. Was he wrong to think she was…

"*Ka-bal,*" said Rak suddenly.

Uncle Danny stopped and looked more closely.

Rakduson dipped her head. "*Ka-bal. Eata et.*"

"Did...did you just say you were 'sorry'?" asked Uncle Danny.

Rak's eyes lit up and she stomped her foot.

"Um, wow!" grinned Uncle Danny. "Apology accepted." He glanced back at Liberty and Tessy for a second before turning back to Rak. "*¡Hijole!* Can...can I introduce you to my best friend and my niece..." He paused and chastised himself. "I should have put my niece first. Anyhow..." Stepping to one side, he gestured for her to join him.

The alien-bird looked a little perplexed— obviously not getting all of that—but she still hobbled beside Danny.

Uncle Danny introduced them all briefly.

"That was a pretty dance," said Tessy, and Uncle Danny was proud of her for being so diplomatic.

Rakduson cocked her head to one side, not understanding.

Tessy put her arms out slowly and moved them like Rak had.

The alien straightened. "*Mas Ren Kah.*" However , she saw the blank looks and she clicked her beak, growing mildly frustrated.

"It's okay," said Liberty kindly.

Rak looked up at her in surprise.

"Yeah," continued Uncle Danny. "I need to learn your language too." He blinked and looked at Liberty. His eyes wide with delight at the idea. "What we need are picture books. Maybe next time we're on the Coast."

Liberty's brow furrowed and then her eyes lit up like the sun. She was going to sprint off, but she remembered that there was a predator here. She steered Tessy.

"What?" asked Tessy.

"Help me check the library," said Liberty.

Uncle Danny smiled. "She can stay."

Liberty looked at him. "You good?"

The Big Mexican smiled. "We're all good." He held out his hand to Tessy and she took it. The little girl moved tightly to his side, but—despite her nervousness—not behind him. Danny thought that was so brave of her.

As Liberty left, Tessy took a closer look at Rak, and the little girl's eyes widened.

"Wow. Your feathers are really pretty," she said in wonder.

Rak's head cocked to one side.

Uncle Danny held up one finger and gently reached out. He touched one of her feathers. "Feather."

Rakduson's eyes lit up. *"Casta."*

Danny repeated the word as he pointed to her feathers again.

Soon, he, Tessy and Rak were trying to name different things. They were well into it when Liberty ran back. However, she did slow down when she got close to Rak.

"Sorry, sorry," said Liberty. "Took me a second." She held open up a large brochure for their boat, which was almost a book. Taking out a Sharpie, the Librarian labelled a picture of the boat. But then she flipped through the pages to a flamingo, which she labelled as 'bird'.

Rak leaned forward when she saw the flamingo. *"Uut."*

Uncle Danny grinned. "It's a start."

***

*"Criss-Nas?"* asked Rak tentatively.

"Christmas, yeah," said Uncle Danny. "It's...it's like…"

Tessy suddenly looked to the end of the dinner table, where Rak was sitting with her nightly fish.

*"Loos Du Ren Kah,"* said the little girl quickly.

"Whaaaa….?" whined Uncle Danny.

Tessy turned to him. "I tol' her that it's like Du's Celebration of his Molt."

But Rak was responding enthusiastically, and Tessy immediately turned back to her.

Suddenly, the two were speaking rapidly back and forth.

Uncle Danny blinked. He'd understand a word here and there. 'Du' was their God, he knew that.

Suddenly, he noticed that Liberty was smirking at him.

"What?" he said, a little testily.

"Kids learn faster than ollllllld men," smirked Liberty.

*"¡Aquas!* I resemble that remark," replied Uncle Danny with mock indignation. But then he paused. "Hey! When is Colin getting back?"

252

Liberty glanced at her watch. "He and Tagg are running a little late." She made an unhappy noise. "And we do need to get away from the Fleet, sooner rather than later."

"Colin isn't as good at talking to Ms. Rak as I am," sniffed Tessy.

Uncle Danny leaned towards her. "It's not a competition."

Tessy glanced at her uncle suspiciously.

"And" added Liberty. "It's not very nice to say it that way."

"What way?" demanded Tessy.

Danny interjected. "Don't speak to *Tia* Liberty that way."

"What way?" asked Tessy in exasperation.

"Acting better than someone else," said Uncle Danny. "Your great grandmother would say that everyone is equal in the eyes of the Lord."

Tessy rolled her eyes. "I *didn't* say that I was better than him."

"You implied it sweetie," said Liberty.

The little girl huffed. "Everybody's always picking on me, except for Ms. Rak."

"We're not picking on you," replied Uncle Danny. "We just want you to grow to be the wonderful woman that we know you can be."

"It's not fair," grumbled Tessy.

"We love you," tried Uncle Danny.

However, Tessy did not reply. She just sullenly ate her

food.

***

The next morning, Liberty knocked on Uncle Danny's door for the second time.

"I GOT IT," cried a little voice from the other side.

The door swung open and Tessy, using one of Danny's t-shirts as a nightgown, grinned up at the Librarian.

"Hi Aunt Liberty," said the little girl breathlessly. "How're you doing? What're you doing here so early? Are you going somewhere?"

Liberty pulled Tessy into a quick hug.

"Good morning sweetie," said the Librarian. "Yes, I am here to pick up your degenerate uncle so he will go to the gym."

That elicited a moan of woeful despair from the blanket on the floor.

"Ah! The beast awakens," grinned Liberty.

"What's 'de-generate'?" asked Tessy.

"Someone who's definitely on Santa's Naughty List. Like someone who needs to work out, but is still sleeping in," replied Liberty with mock iciness.

"Oh, okay," said Tessy. A yawn rolled across her face.

"You," said Liberty to the little girl. "You can go right back to your nice warm bed and sleep."

"'K" muttered Tessy. Her eyes had already fallen to half-mast, so she went to climb back into bed.

Liberty stepped into the room. Sticking out of the blanket on the floor was a single foot. She gave it a gentle boot.

"Come on sleepyhead," chided Liberty.

"It's tooooo early," grumbled Uncle Danny.

Liberty sang, a little off-key. "You made me promise to get you up."

"*¡Neta, no manches!*" said Uncle Danny. "That doesn't sound like something I'd do."

Tessy chimed in sleepily. "Yes. You did."

"Ughh-ergg," replied Uncle Danny. "That was a mistake."

"And you need to start doing pull-ups too," said Liberty.

"Who says?" growled Danny.

"You did," replied Liberty swiftly.

"When?"

"Right after we got Tagg from Dyson and we were heading towards the Fleet."

"*Pollas en vinagre,*" grumbled Uncle Danny. "I don't recall."

"I do," sniffed Liberty.

"What if I say 'No'," asked Danny, and even he could hear the whine in it.

"I'll get a bucket of water," said Liberty. "Or...maybe just start playing Barry Manilow."

Uncle Danny pulled the blanket off his head to glare at

her. "You wouldn't."

Liberty did not reply, she just gave him a Look that said, 'Watch me buddy' in any language.

"¡Vete a freír espárragos!" cried Danny in despair. "You would, wouldn't you. You are foul. *Evil!*" But he did get up.

Putting their play aside, he stopped by the bed and rubbed the girl's arm gently. "You okay, *Mi Mariposa Unicornio?*"

Tessy nodded. "...sleepy."

"Okay," said Uncle Danny. "But, if you need us, we'll be in the gym. You know where that is, right?"

"Yes, yes," growled Tessy with sleep-induced irritability.

Uncle Danny smiled as he left with Liberty.

Not far off, Dr. Miles McTaggert was waiting outside Colin's room. He straightened as Uncle Danny eyeballed him.

With a dark and dangerous tone, Uncle Danny commented to him. "*Ay, hombre*, you've been spending several nights here,"

"Ah, well...," started Tagg.

With a loud thwack, Liberty smacked Danny in the arm, and he looked at her with surprise.

"¡*Huy!* Bony knuckles hurt," said Uncle Danny.

"You said that before," replied Liberty without any sympathy.

"It bears repeating," shrugged Danny.

"I'm a big girl," she replied with a hard look. "And

you've had your fun!"

For a moment, it looked like Uncle Danny was going to argue, but then he gave a little chuckle.

"*Si. Tú eres una mujer.* Okay *Mija*," said the Big Mexican. He turned back to Tagg, who watched him wearily. "Just...just take good care of her." However, the dark look came back. "Or, you'll have to answer to me!" Then, with *grande* eyebrows raised, he looked quizzically at the Librarian.

Liberty shrugged. "I guess I'm okay with that." Turning to Tagg, she asked. "Is Colin coming with you again today?"

"Yeah," replied the doctor. "If that's okay. He's actually been pretty helpful around the lab. Almost..." He paused, but then shook his head. "Nothing.

Liberty stepped in a little closer and touched his muscular arm gently. "Please."

"It's...just that he seems almost too helpful, if that makes any sense," said Tagg with a low voice.

"What do you mean?" asked Danny with concern, and he moved closer too.

"It's just that...he seems almost too eager," said Tagg and he sighed. "I guess I'm not making any sense."

"Like...he really wants to be there," said Liberty. "I know he really liked it when you autopsied that bird."

"Oh Yeah! That was fun," smiled Tagg, but then his mirth immediately faded. "But this..."

Colin's door opened and the 11 year old boy looked out. His eyes instantly suspicious.

"What's going on?" asked Colin.

"Well, ah...we were just talking...," stammered Tagg.

"Were you talking about me?" asked the boy.

Tagg opened his mouth to lie.

"Yes," interjected Liberty. Colin looked at her with surprise as did Tagg and Uncle Danny. She regarded the men. "We do ask the kids not to lie to us..."

Tagg's eyebrows went up and Danny nodded slowly in agreement.

"Why're you talkin' about me then?" asked Colin quickly, defenses up.

Liberty gave a gentle smile. "I guess we were trying to make sure that you're all right."

"I'm fine," replied Colin instantly. He dove through the narrow space between Tagg and Liberty. Then he started down the hallway at a fast clip.

The men looked at Liberty.

"I guess I started this," sighed the Librarian. She took off after the boy. By the time she had almost reached him, she realized that the guys were right behind her. She pulled a little ahead to walk next to the boy.

"What?" snapped Colin.

"What?" asked Liberty with comical surprise. "I'm allowed to walk here."

"You want to 'talk' don't you?" asked Colin.

Liberty thought for a second. "I mean if you want to. But, if you don't..." She took another moment. "What do you mean by 'talk'? Is something worrying you."

258

Colin's head went a little forward as he poured on more speed.

Liberty did not try to pace him. She tried to remember what she knew about the boy. He hadn't had the best of parents. But something itched at her.

"I love you," she said impulsively.

Colin screeched to a halt and whipped his head around.

The Librarian hit the brakes and immediately stopped.

With bared teeth, Colin demanded. "What do you want from me?"

Liberty paused a moment, before answering. A swift glance behind showed that Uncle Danny had stopped Tagg about 10 feet behind.

"What do I want?" asked Liberty of herself. Then she looked up at him. "Um, I want you to be healthy, and happy. *In* that order."

"I'm healthy. I'm happy," spat Colin.

"Could've fooled me," called out Uncle Danny.

"Like he would notice?" muttered Colin under his breath.

Liberty's eyes widened and she looked at the boy in surprise.

"I...," started Colin. But then he turned on his heel and nearly ran away.

Liberty was about to follow, but Tagg was suddenly there. He put a hand on her shoulder, and he looked up at him.

"Maybe...we should give him some more time,"

suggested Tagg, but then he added nervously. "If that's okay."

"Actually, a little more time might help," sighed Liberty sadly. "I mean, there *have* been a lot of changes around here."

"What changes?" asked Uncle Danny defensively, and he declared. "He's still ours. Just like before."

Tagg made a noise. "But-- um-- he also gained a little sister, *and* an Aunt Rakduson, *and* I've been staying over a lot more."

Uncle Danny's mouth made a little 'o'.

"But at least he didn't run off to join the circus," suggested Tagg.

Liberty snorted in laughter, and then immediately said. "Sorry, I snorted."

Uncle Danny's mind was swirling about, trying to work the problem. But even through that maelstrom, he noticed the complete and devoted affection with which Tagg looked at Liberty. And he was really glad that his friend had found a good man. Not that he was going to admit it out-loud, though.

"So," said Danny instead. "What do we do?"

"I'll take him with me today...if that's okay," suggested Tagg. "If he wants to talk, I'll...well, I'll do my best." His face was pinched with worry and anxiety. "Hopefully, it'll be good enough."

Liberty put her hand on his arm again. "You'll do fine." As Tagg smiled at her, the Librarian's hand slipped into his.

"OKAY," said Uncle Danny loudly. "I didn't get up at

this Godforsaken hour to watch this syrupy stuff. Reminds me of *Mi Abuela*. She loved sappy movies...and big, hunky *La Luchadores* beating the snot out of each other. She was complicated like that."

The Librarian chuckled. "We better hit the gym."

Reluctantly, Liberty let go of Tagg and they said their goodbyes.

Tagg moved swiftly through the yacht to where the smaller boat was tied up. The boy stood there with his arms folded, looking sullen and sad. Unsure of what to do, he decided to try to start by lighting up the mood.

"Arrr," he called out. "Into the boat with ya matey. We cast off at once."

Colin gave him a withering look, as only a pre-teen can. *"What...was* that?"

"Pirate talk," replied Tagg, with a mock defensive stance. And then he added. "Arrr!"

The Scientist moved past the boy and got into the boat. After a moment, Colin climbed in himself, undoing the ropes.

"We're not pirates," grumbled Colin.

Tagg took them away from the unnamed ship and towards the Jonas Salk Medical Ship.

"If they can be pirates," said the doctor thoughtfully. "And you live on their ship. And I...well, I'm here more and more these days. Well, why can't we be pirates too? If we live on a pirate ship."

"But...we don't go to the Coast," said Colin.

"Not every pirate probably boarded other ships," said

261

Tagg. "We're their support."

"We're no help."

"*Au contraire..*," started Tagg.

"What?"

"It means 'I disagree' in French. I keep all of you healthy, and you...are a great help in that."

"I just fetch stuff for you," spat Colin. "Like a dog."

"*Pfft!* As if," scoffed the doctor. "Every day, you're learning more and more. And if you kept at it, one day, you could even be my partner in the lab. *But!* That's only if you want to. No pressure."

Colin looked out to the water and did not reply.

Tagg decided not to push his luck any further.

So, he let the boy stew while he reviewed their conversation—a little obsessively—to see if he could have said something better. Maybe said something that fixed everything right up, just like in the movies.

***

Liberty counted off her pull-ups.

"So, I assume you are sleeping with the good doctor?" asked Uncle Danny.

The Liberian immediately lost her count and dropped to her feet. "What?"

But the Big Mexican was looking the other way, counting off reps.

"None of your beeswax," huffed Liberty indignantly.

"Just be careful. If we need to go to the Coast for...supplies, we can," said Uncle Danny. "I just don't want to become an uncle again so soon."

"You just be careful of that shoulder, old man," replied Liberty, only half-joking with a growl. "I hear that wounds heal more slowly in old people."

"Ouch," grinned Uncle Danny.

Liberty hopped up again and finished her pull-ups. On the Coast, they never knew when they might need to climb something, real quick-like.

"I'm worried," said Danny after a moment.

"About me leaving you stranded on the Coast?" asked Liberty with mock frost in her voice.

Uncle Danny chuckled. "No. I would probably deserve that." But he paused, more soberly. "I want to make sure that you're okay."

"I'm a big girl," said Liberty.

"I can worry about my friends," shrugged Uncle Danny. "It's in the Rulebook."

The Librarian was about to argue but stopped.

"Fair enough," said Liberty. And she went to the treadmill in case she needed to outrun anything. After a minute of jogging, she spoke. "We're taking things slow. I mean, there's no rush."

Uncle Danny nodded. "As long as you're good." Then he looked over at her, waiting.

Liberty rolled her eyes and answered his unspoken

263

question. "I'm good."

"Okay then," nodded Uncle Danny.

"Okay then," replied Liberty and, despite herself, a smile crept across her face.

Uncle Danny paused. "And I hope Tagg has some luck with Colin."

"Me too," agreed Liberty. "Or we'll just all sit down with him tonight."

"Sounds good," nodded Uncle Danny, but then he stopped. "But we gotta make sure it doesn't look like we're ganging up on him."

"Oh! That's true," agreed Liberty fervently.

Tessy staggered in. She had her blanket draped around her like a giant shawl.

Liberty and Uncle Danny looked at each other in surprise.

Going to a weight bench near her uncle, Tessy immediately curled up upon it and closed her eyes.

With her eyes still shut, the little girl murmured. "This boat is too big."

Soon, it appeared as if she had fallen off into a deep sleep.

Liberty immediately started to slow her pace because the treadmill suddenly sounded really loud. Reaching a brisk walking pace, she kept moving. After a moment, Uncle Danny moved to her side, still working with his dumbbells.

The Big Mexican spoke in a subdued tone. "She goes to sleep in her own room just fine, but then, she always comes in, an hour or so later."

"We need to get you something to sleep on," said Liberty.

Uncle Danny shrugged. "*¡Neta!* I'm used to sleeping in uncomfortable places."

"Still," insisted Liberty with finality. "It's not good for your back, especially long term."

"Maybe a small one," allowed Danny, realizing he didn't need to be macho and stupid; not beside a friend like her.

"And, as for Tess," murmured Liberty.

"I don't know," said Uncle Danny worriedly. "It might be that...what do you call it when you can't be apart from someone without getting panicked. I know it's '*ansiedad de separación*', but I'm not sure what it is in English."

"Separation anxiety?" asked Liberty.

"Sounds like it," shrugged Uncle Danny.

"Well, that's something we need to work on," said Liberty. "You and me, *mi amiga.*"

Uncle Danny grinned at that.

"And we need to put together a shopping list," said Liberty. Her voice returned to a more normal level but not too loud. She glanced at him. "We'll look today, but if we can't find something on board, you need a mattress. And I need to hit a drug store for...well, stuff."

Uncle Danny didn't even want to ask. "Whatever you need *Mija.*"

A little voice rose up. "I'm worried."

Liberty and Uncle Danny looked at each other, and then

265

over at Tessy.

"What's wrong?" asked the Big Mexican.

"That you're going to go back," said Tessy. Her eyes were half-open. "That you're going to go back to the Coast."

Liberty stopped on the treadmill and she and Uncle Danny went over the little girl.

The Big Mexican took the weight bench next to Tessy, and Liberty just sat on the floor.

"We have a job to do," said the Big Mexican. "Obligations."

"I know," moaned Tessy.

"And the people in the Fleet need what we get," added Liberty.

"*Don't* want you to go," said Tessy and she began to cry.

Immediately putting down his weights, Danny knelt beside her. He rubbed her shoulder and got close.

"We are very careful," said Danny.

"Still…," moaned Tessy.

"And we need both of us," said Uncle Danny.

"To keep an eye on the other one sweetie," added Liberty.

"Promise me that you'll never get hurt," cried Tessy suddenly, eyes packed with tears.

Liberty and Uncle Danny looked at each other and then at her.

"We…we can't promise that" said Danny gently.

"We'll try and be as careful as possible," added Liberty.

Tessy leaned forward into Uncle Danny, and he pulled her into his big arms. Liberty reached out and rubbed her back as she cried for a while.

Finally, one little hand reached out towards Danny's chest. Above the collar of his Hard Rock shirt was the top of his chest tattoo; a woman in a sombrero.

The little girl sniffed and said with a disappointed tone. "You have too many tattoos."

Uncle Danny looked down in surprise, but then he just chuckled. "I guess I do." His brow knitted. "But, you know who gave me all these?"

Tessy just shook her head, disapprovingly.

"Your Uncle Pepe," said Danny, and he saw Liberty's curious look, so he said to her. "Not her real uncle, but Pepe is family."

"Fake Uncle," murmured Tessy as she touched the tattoo of roses on his right forearm. "But why did he give you all these tattoos. Was he mad at you?"

Uncle Danny laughed. "No *Mi Mariposa Unicornio*. When we were young, he wanted to be a tattoo artist. The Greatest In All Mexico! But he needed to practice."

"He practiced a lot," said Tessy softly.

"And I might have let him practice too much on me," admitted Uncle Danny. "But that's what friends do."

Tessy thought for a moment. "Like you and *Tia* Liberty?"

"Exactly," chimed in the Librarian.

267

"Do you guys really keep an eye out for each other?" asked Tessy, slowly

"Absolutely," said Liberty with utter conviction. "And, if we're taking the tank....."

Suddenly curious, Uncle Danny looked at the Librarian. "So, they did secure it?"

"Oh!" said Liberty quickly. "Captain Singh called to check up on us the other day. Sorry, I keep forgetting to tell you."

"It's cool. I've been running around a lot," said Uncle Danny.

Liberty smiled. "They got the tank and the bus into a safe place—he wouldn't say where over the radio."

Uncle Danny nodded. "Makes sense."

"And they have a little...what did he call it? Um, 'beachhead'?" muttered Liberty. "Something like that. But everyone's safe. And Frankline's even working his darndest, for some reason, to get promoted. I mean, Frankline didn't say that, but..."

"Our Frankline?" asked Danny. "Private I-Lost-My-Rifle?"

"The same," nodded Liberty with a smile, but it faded as she looked down. "So, Tessy, we have good friends out there as well."

Tessy turned in Uncle Danny's arms so that she could look up at both of them with sudden excitement.

"You guys should take Rak!" said the little girl. A giant smile appeared behind her tear-streaked face.

"Really?" asked Danny. "You think she would go with

us?"

"Maybe," shrugged Tessy.

"And maybe we can figure out what that device thing is, that's in the back of their heads," said Uncle Danny.

"Possible we could block it," suggested Liberty with interest.

"We gotta talk to Mr. Smalls," said Tessy. "He'll help." Her face turned serious. "I can ask him."

Jumping up, the little girl swiftly rearranged her blanket like a shawl and ran towards the door. She stopped to look back.

"Come on!" ordered Tessy.

Liberty and Uncle Danny looked at each other and shrugged.

"HURR---E!" demanded Tessy.

"Let's not keep the *senorita* waiting," grinned Uncle Danny.

"Never," agreed Liberty with mock seriousness.

And fervently the Librarian hoped that they would have a similar breakthrough with Colin. He was the first person to give her hope out here. Her mentor, Mr. Jamie had only taught her how to stay alive. It wasn't that Colin may have a vaccine, but just because he had been him, with his bright smile and cheery attitude.

\*\*\*

It was late afternoon that day on the Salk Medical Ship and

Colin had just finished washing the dishes in the lab. Putting away his step-stool, he stomped over to the doctor.

"What's your game?" demanded the boy; his voice a snarl.

Jumping in surprise, Tagg blinked in confusion. "Um, what? Did you say 'Game'?"

"I had this big fight with Liberty and Uncle Danny this morning," growled Colin. "An' you haven't mentioned it. ONCE!"

"Um…was I supposed to…no, no, that's not right. What did you expect me to do today?" asked Tagg, anxiously.

"Spend *the whole day* telling me I was wrong," said Colin. "In *Every! Single! Little! Detail!*"

Tagg thought furiously, floundering. Panic was setting in because he didn't know what to do. In that haze of anxiety, he saw the raw pain in the boy's face.

And he remembered Rule #1.

Dr. Tagg blurted out. "I don't know what I'm doing."

This time, it was Colin's turn to blink. "What?"

"I…I want you to be an awesome person, when you grow up, because I think you're pretty awesome," said Tagg. "But I've never done this before. I was an only child, and I only babysat a little when I was a teenager."

Colin squinted. "What's your point?"

"I jus' wanted to let you know that—despite all that!—I'm going to help you every day. However, I can!" said Tagg. "Forever! If you want of course. I'll always be there…at least as long as I'm still alive. 'Cause I'm pretty positive that I can't come back as a ghost. Sorry about that."

The boy's jaw dropped.

The Scientist plunged on. "An', I don't know why you're hurting...well, not quite. But...I'm here to talk about it. And...and *definitely* not to criticize. Or belittle you..."

"Belittle?"

"Um, that's when you make someone feel stupid," explained Tagg, breathlessly. "At least, I'm pretty sure that's what it means. *Anyhow,* I wanted to give you your space. Maybe, to give *you* time to figure out-- yourself-- why you're so upset."

Colin looked down at the floor. "Um..." But the boy stopped. Tagg did not move, though still anxious, he forced himself to sit patiently. "What... what if I don't know?"

"Oh!" said Tagg with a manic laugh. "That just means you're human."

"What?"

"Well, we don't always know why we hurt."

"That doesn't make sense," said Colin coldly.

"You're right, it doesn't. But...I'll listen to you while you don't know. Though, I have a feeling that the answer is there. If you want, we can go up on deck. We have been working hard since 8 o'clock, with only a quick break to get food."

The boy nodded.

Tagg patted him on the back as they went out and onto the deck.

Once outside, the Scientist started in surprise, looking around.

"It's a really nice day," he said  "We should do this more often.  I mean, why aren't we eating up here every day."  Then he scrunched up his face.  "Arrr, we could take this ship, an' sail the high seas.  Just you an' me matey."

Despite himself, a little laugh escaped from Colin.  "I thought I said, 'no pirates'."

"Arrr, if you don't want to be a pirate, that's all right, but I intend to be one," said Tagg, still in his bad pirate accent.

"Can scientists be pirates?" asked Colin, now a little fascinated.

Tagg became thoughtful for a moment, but then he nodded enthusiastically in his normal voice.  "Oh yeah!  Sure.  I'm pretty sure that there's a kid's book about pirates and scientists, but I just saw it in a store.  I never read it.  BUT I do know that some scientists have stolen data from other scientists, and others whole labs, and even departments."

"Really?" asked Colin.

"Absolutely, though stealing data is the worst," said Tagg.  "For that, you should walk the plank in shark infested waters."  Suddenly, he pointed.  "Dude! Watch out for bird poop."

They veered around a particularly bad patch.

"Would you ever do that?" asked Colin.  "You know, steal data."

"Never!" said Tagg with conviction.  "It...it would be terrible."  The doctor blinked.  "Though really...scientists are sort of pirates."

Colin looked questioningly as they plopped down on a

clean portion of the deck. They faced the Theodore Roosevelt carrier, a little ways off.

"Science is about building on the work of others," said Tagg, getting excited as he talked out the idea. "My vaccine research is built on those who came before me. So, really I'm sailing in a ship that someone else built."

"So, we really are pirates," sighed Colin dejectedly.

Tagg leaned over and bumped his massive shoulder against the boy's.

"*I am.* Be you're going to be whoever you want to be," said Tagg.

Colin sighed. "I...I don't know what I want to be."

"Again, human!" said Tagg. "People often don't. So, try everything, like a buffet." The doctor blinked. "Shi...I mean, shoot. Now, I want Chinese food." He raised his fists to the heavens. "IT'S NOT FAIR!!! I haven't gotten good kung pao shrimp in, like, FOR-ever!!!" He made a plaintive howl before laying back onto the deck and wailing. "Don't even get me started on crab Rangoon."

Colin let out a hearty chuckle.

"Are you laughing at my pain?" asked Tagg with mock affront.

"No," said Colin automatically.

Tagg just gave the boy a beady-eyed glare. "Rule Number 1."

Colin rolled his eyes. "Okay, maybe I was...just a little."

The doctor patted him on the back, but he stayed lying on the deck, because it was comfortable.

273

"Now, as punishment, name off all the bones in the human hand," said Tagg and he lifted up his hand.

"Ugh, really?" asked Colin. But as much as he tried to be angry, he couldn't quite manage it.

***

At 6:04pm, the Bowrider boat that Tagg had been loaned was leaving the Salk. It moved away from the Fleet towards the unnamed yacht.

"Uncle Danny lied to me," said Colin. He said it so softly that Tagg almost didn't hear.

Tagg's brow furrowed. "When?"

"He swore on his *Abuela* that I was family, and now...," began the boy, but he stopped. "I don't think Uncle Danny likes me anymore."

The Scientist looked over. "Wait? What?"

"And Liberty, she...," started Colin. However, he stopped once again and looked out at the water. He said something more, but the doctor could not hear it.

Tagg slowed the boat and they started to putter along.

Colin looked at him with surprise. "Wha...What's the matter?"

"We have time," said Tagg, and he turned in his chair.

"But Liberty wants us back right away for dinner," said Colin. "She was very insistent."

"I'll take the heat on that one," replied Tagg, and then he repeated softly with utter assurance. "We. Have. Time."

***

Not too long after, Colin and Tagg stepped through the unnamed ship.

The hallway soon grew pitch dark because they hadn't found replacement bulbs last week. But they soon stepped into the bright dining room.

When Tessy saw them, she bounded over. "Oh good, you're alive!" She looked them up and down critically. "Okay, you look okay."

"Of course," grumbled Colin.

"It's just a short ride," said Dr. Tagg gently to Tessy.

"And yet," said a new voice. "You're late!"

Liberty, with fists on her hips, looked at him with a mock scowl.

"See, we're in trouble," hissed Colin. He suddenly slid away from Tessy, who was trying to take his hand.

Tagg glanced around until he found the boy in a new place, by the dark hallway. He quickly assured Colin. "It's all good." Then he turned back to the Librarian. "It's all my fault. Really! Throw me overboard, but not the lad."

Liberty chuckled. "We'd never throw Colin overboard, but *you...You* better be careful, Mr. Doctor-Man."

"Ooooh," called out Uncle Danny from another part of the room. "She's dropped the 'Mr. Doctor-Man' on you. You're in trouble now!"

"I'm sorry we're late," said Tagg to everyone. "It

couldn't be avoided." He sniffed the air. "And something smells great." He looked at Liberty, but she pointed to Uncle Danny.

"I've been slaving over a hot stove all day," announced the Big Mexican with an aggrieved voice. "So, you better like it."

"But..," said Tessy. "...we were in the galley for only an hour."

With an exaggerated movement, Uncle Danny put his fingers to his lips . "Shhhh. We don't need them to know that."

Tagg looked over at Liberty, who wore one of her three scrounged dresses. He waved a little shyly, but then looked back at everyone.

"We probably shouldn't keep dinner any longer," said the Scientist.

"WHAT?" asked Uncle Danny of Tagg with a dark voice, and he did not sound like he was joking. "You're just going to go to the table."

Tagg froze, heart-pounding. "Um, if that's all right."

"¡Neta! You've been gone all day, and yet you have not given Liberty a hug, much less a kiss, to show that you missed her," said the Big Mexican. "Tsk!"

"Oh, um...," started Tagg and he began to blush. But he went right over to Liberty, who was trying not to laugh. She squeezed him tightly.

In her ear, the Scientist whispered. "I...I...I...really did miss you, but I thought that we weren't allowed to...um..."

"Shhhh," she said softly, gently. "Don't argue with the

nice man." With her wrapped around him, he relaxed, and the world seemed to shrink away.

"Okay! Enough already! Come on," cried out Uncle Danny. "We're hungry. Are you just going to canoodle all day long?"

Before Tagg could stammer, Liberty turned to her best friend.

"Cram a sock in it," she replied with a mock snarl.

And Uncle Danny let out a joyful bark of laughter.

Liberty turned back to Tagg. "We better kiss too, just so we don't get in any more trouble."

"Oh...okay," he said. And they exchanged a sweet little kiss.

Colin tried to look away, but he immediately found Tessy standing right next to him, so he turned the other way.

And there was something big in the darkened hallway. It was coming swiftly towards him and Tessy.

"Wha...? Liberty! Uncle Danny!" cried out Colin with alarm. The boy immediately jumped forward to face the hallway.

The dark shadow stopped in surprise, and then cautiously moved back until they were under a working light.

"It's Rak!" said Uncle Danny with relief as he walked over. But he also noticed where Colin had moved when he thought there had been danger.

The boy, for his part, went wide-eyed and his stomach dropped.

Back in the hallway, the alien-bird started speaking quickly.

"She said that she didn't mean to surprise you, but she didn't want to interrupt," translated Tessy behind Colin. "Well, more or less."

Uncle Danny waved to the bird. "Come on." He turned to Colin, but the boy had already disappeared. Concerned, he looked around swiftly and saw that Colin was already at the table, hunched over his empty plate. Glancing over to Liberty, he saw that she and Tagg were looking with concern at the boy.

Rakduson appeared at his side, looking uncertain. He smiled at the bird and gestured to the table.

"*Hu-kong*," tried Uncle Danny.

Rak looked at him in surprise.

As Tessy took the Big Mexican's hand, she let out a bright little laugh. She said to her uncle. "It's '*hu-chong*'."

Danny started to look at her, but it was Liberty who spoke up.

"Now Tessy," said the Librarian as she walked over. Her voice was gentle, but correcting. "It's not nice to laugh at others. Especially about learning languages."

"Why not?" asked Tessy defiantly. "It's not that hard."

"Ah!" said Uncle Danny kindly. "But what is not hard for one person, can be *very* hard for another." He put his arm around her shoulders. "Come on, *Mi Mariposa Unicornio*, can you help an old man bring out dinner."

Tessy rolled her eyes, aggrieved. "I guessssss….."

Wandering away from that discussion, Tagg stopped just

behind Colin. "See," whispered the Scientist. "They just want both of you to grow up to be great people. We all do."

The boy continued to look down, not answering.

Giving the boy a quick pat on the shoulder, Tagg walked around the table. The Scientist sat at his regular place, across from the boy.

Colin swiftly glanced up at him, but Tagg was looking towards Liberty with big cow eyes.

With a little bounce in her step, the Librarian plopped into the chair next to Tagg, bumping shoulders.

"Oh! You're in for a treat tonight!" called out Uncle Danny as he returned from the galley with multiple plates. He was favoring his right side since the left was still a little tender.

Colin saw Tessy come out a moment later with more dishes, looking severely put-upon.

"This reminds me," said Uncle Danny wistfully. "Of working in my friend Pepe's restaurant."

The Big Mexican put plates before each person, except for Rak. He had even put one at the empty chair next to Colin. But then Danny swiftly disappeared back into the galley. Liberty noticed the alien-bird looking a little jealously at her plate.

"Do not despair," cried out Uncle Danny from the galley. The door banged open and out came the Big Mexican with a huge serving tray. Actually, he was having a little trouble.

Liberty started to stand. "Do you need...?"

"I got it," croaked Danny. He just managed to set the tray down in front of Rak, and then he pronounced. *"Buen provecho!"*

Rakduson's eyes lit up. There was everything the rest had gotten, plus a huge slab of tuna. She said softly, in awe. *"Unghot!"*

"Delicious," translated Tessy, off-handedly.

Liberty looked at the little girl. "You know. It really is true about languages."

Tessy looked at her wearily.

The Librarian continued. "Young people have an easier time learning new languages than us old-folk."

"Old-folk?" asked Tagg with mock indignation. "Speak for yourself."

Without taking her eyes off Tessy, Liberty leaned her head against his shoulder for a moment. A soft, gentle touch.

Tessy straightened with interest. "Is it **really** true about young people and languages?"

"Really truly," nodded Liberty. "That's why you've gone farther than any of us with Rak's language."

"And she did grow up in a bi-lingual household," interjected Uncle Danny.

"A what?" asked Tessy.

"At home, with your Papa, we spoke both English and Spanish," explained the Big Mexican.

"Oh, that's true," nodded the little girl.

"And Tessy might just have a gift for languages too," suggested Dr. Tagg warmly. Then, he guessed that that conversation was over, so he jumped in quickly. "**Well!** I would also like to talk about **my** star pupil today."

"Oh! I wanna be a star pupil too," wailed Tessy with complete and utter despair.

"You already are," insisted Uncle Danny. "With languages."

"Oh!....Yeah," said Tessy. She gave a toothy, embarrassed smile and then ducked down. "Never mind."

"It's okay," said Dr. Tagg with warmth and honesty. Then he turned to the boy. "Did you know that Colin can now name all the bones in the human hand, and the arm too?"

Liberty looked at the boy in surprise. "I'm impressed! I hated anatomy class. Too much memorizing. So, Nice job."

"He got an 'A' for sure," said Tagg.

"Good job Colin!" added the little girl.

Uncle Danny made a scoffing noise. "You sound surprised! But not me! He's a smart guy, our *Cobayo* is!"

In spite of himself, Colin gave a small smile.

The Big Mexican looked around for the Navy Engineer, who piloted the boat. "Well, since Smalls is running late, I say we dig in."

"Thank you!" wailed Tagg ravenously. "I nearly ate Colin's arm off on the way back. It was a near thing."

Liberty glared with mock sternness. "Now Dr. McTaggert, we talked about this. No eating our children."

Colin looked up at that in surprise.

However, Tagg was focused on Liberty.

"What about other people's children," he asked in mock

281

seriousness.

"Harrumph," replied Liberty. "We'll see."

"¡Neta! Enough," grumbled Uncle Danny, good naturedly. "I'm trying to eat here."

As Smalls came into the room, laughter rolled across the table like waves across a shore. The Navy Engineer was carrying a grey box as tall as Danny's hand.

"Sorry! Sorry! Sorry," moaned Smalls. He sat beside Colin and put the box down on the far side of the boy. "I just needed to get something ready." He looked at the food. "Oh! This looks delicious, I love spaghetti."

"One of my favorites," nodded Colin happily.

As Smalls began to eat, Liberty went around asking each person about their day. Rak spoke a little haltingly, and with some help from Tessy. But the alien recounted how the Navy Engineer had managed to stabilize the device in the back of her head, which got a big cheer from the rest of the table.

For his part, Colin gave a cursory review of his day, and Tagg helped with the bits that were grad-school-level science.

Finally, Liberty called out a person's name.

However, there was no response.

She cleared her throat. "Mr. Smalls?"

But the Navy Engineer was completely focused on the electronic box next to him.

Colin elbowed Smalls gently.

"What?" asked the Navy Engineer, concerned. "What's

wrong?"

Liberty was about to be stern, but then her look softened. "No video games at the table."

Smalls blinked in confusion. "Games?"

Colin subtly gestured to the grey box and said softly. "Dude!"

"OH! That's not a game, it's our radar!" replied Smalls excitedly.

"Our...what?" asked Liberty.

"Like, a monitor for our radar?" asked Tagg.

"Exactly!" said Smalls. He turned the gray box towards the rest. It was just a dark screen with green circles. "That's why I was late for dinner, because I've been having so much trouble enjoying my meals."

"Because of the radar?" asked Liberty.

"You were worried that some *los villanos* would sneak up on us?" asked Uncle Danny.

Smalls shrugged. "I do feel better, once we're away from the fleet at night. AND, the Rear Admiral said it was my job to keep you safe, so..." His voice fell away.

Liberty smiled warmly. "And it is greatly appreciated. So, you built that thing to keep an eye out while we're eating."

"How does it work?" asked Colin as he leaned closer. "That must take some BIG batteries."

"Actually, I worked out a rechargeable battery for it. But I have to plug it in often," said Smalls thoughtfully. He looked up at Liberty. "We should see about getting some solar panels from the Coast."

Inwardly, Liberty had a flash of concern. But she decided not to say anything in front of kids, so as not to worry them.

"Is there an issue," asked Tagg worriedly, and Liberty groaned to herself.

"No, no," said Smalls quickly. "But it'd ultimately save on fuel consumption."

"Good to know," said Liberty with relief.

"But wait!" said Colin curiously. "So, this is, like, hooked up to the real radar?"

Smalls began to explain, and Colin kept asking more and more questions.

Of everyone, Tagg was able to follow the longest. He had taken two engineering courses in college, before realizing that it was not the profession for him. After a bit though, even the Scientist leaned over to whisper in Liberty's ear.

"They could be speaking Rak's language at this point, for all I can make out," said Tagg.

The alien-bird herself had stretched her long neck out, to listen better. Slowly, her head tilted in confusion.

Leaning towards her, Uncle Danny whispered. "It's okay. I don't think anyone else understands either."

Rak looked at him with relief and said. "*Tut.*" Which, he was **pretty** sure meant 'good'.

Glancing around, Smalls suddenly did a double take when he noticed all the glazed eyes around the table. Despite not being used to teaching, he did try to explain things. Soon, the rest of the table began to glean more.

Uncle Danny spoke at last. "So, basically, we can now watch the radar from anywhere in the boat."

"Yeah, basically," said Smalls. "Welllll, this is more of a prototype. But I could set up fixed-ones around the ship. Which is why solar panels would help, to get more electricity."

Liberty grinned. "Brilliant. Thank you!"

Uncle Danny leaned back happily. "Well, I can't eat anymore. But I need a moment before I even *think* of tackling the dishes."

"But you cooked," said Liberty thoughtfully. "So, we should clean." And she looked at Colin and Tagg. "And by 'we', I mean me, and the two of you."

The boy made a disgusted sound and grumbled. "Uncle Danny already said that he was going to do it. Why're you volunteering me?"

"I volunteered *us*. And we just got fed a great meal," said Liberty with a tone that she thought brooked no argument. "It's the least we can do."

"What if I want to go back to my room?" asked Colin in a dark voice, and he slowly stood.

"You can," said Liberty. "After the dishes."

"Why is this so important?" huffed Colin, and his voice showed more frustration than anger.

"Um...," started Tagg, and it looked like Uncle Danny was ready to speak as well. But Liberty gave both of them a quelling glance, and they wisely backed down.

The Librarian turned back to the boy.

"Because family has to pitch in and take care of each other," she said, with more patience than she felt. "*And*, if Uncle Danny cooked, then we should clean. If we cook, then he can clean. It's only fair."

"Why do I have to do what you say?" demanded Colin, raising his voice.

"Because you're my son," replied Liberty without hesitation. Hearing herself, she had a moment of panic and wondered, 'Did I just say that?'.

Colin's eyes widened. Without a word, he dropped back down into his chair.

Liberty saw the rock hard truth of it and a warm, happy smile came over her face. Her eyes felt watery.

"Because...," she continued slowly. "Because I want you to grow up to become a man, who is even greater than your Uncle Danny. Even greater than your Da...". She stopped suddenly and looked at Dr. Tagg. Her stomach lurched sideways; scared that she had overstepped her bounds. Said too much, presumed too much, way, way, way too soon.

However, Tagg smiled at her and then turned to Colin.

"I'm good with Dad."

Colin's jaw dropped. "Real...Really?"

"If you want," said Tagg quickly, nervously. "I mean... I'm not as cool as Uncle Danny..."

"It's okay," said the boy, just as swiftly, but then he hesitated. He tried to think of what to say. Finally, he just said. "It's...*Yes*. That would be good."

Liberty turned to the boy. "But-- just so you

understand-- we're not here to be your friend. This is about raising you right. We need to make sure that you are safe, healthy, a good citizen and happy. In that order."

"I...I don't know what to say," said Colin.

"I love you too," smiled Liberty.

"But...," started a small voice.

Everyone looked at Tessy, who seemed to shrink down into herself.

Colin immediately asked. "What's wrong?"

"It...it's just...," began Tessy.

Liberty's eyes widened. She swiftly looked at Uncle Danny. Whether it was all the fighting they'd done together, or their friendship, the two could communicate with very little words.

"Is it...," she asked breathlessly.

Uncle Danny nodded earnestly. *"Si, Mija.* Of course!"

Tagg was looking between the two, and finally settled on Liberty. She looked for his permission, but he looked confused. Leaning over, she brought her lips to his ear and swiftly explained.

After a moment, Tagg said. "Oh! Oh Yeah! Of course! We should."

Liberty pulled back to look him in the eye. "Really? It's...about us."

Slowly, Tagg shrugged. "We can still play everything else slow. Just like we talked about."

Suddenly, the Librarian grinned and kissed Tagg so hard that his front teeth hurt for a moment; not that he was complaining.

"Ewwwwww," exclaimed Colin in disgust.

This made Tessy giggle, even with tears in her eyes.

Liberty turned first to the boy with a look of mock annoyance. "You keep quiet."

And Colin replied with a huge unrepentant smile.

The Librarian started to turn to Tessy when she froze. She wasn't done. Her stomach clenched. But she didn't want to put *him* on the spot, not in front of everyone.

Turning to Tagg, she whispered. "We, or at least, I need to talk to him, but not in front of everyone."

"Why would you...," began Tagg, but then he understood. "Oh yeah! Yeah, that wouldn't be cool."

"What wouldn't be cool?" asked Colin wearily.

"Why are they whispering?" asked Tessy with concern. The little girl looked at Uncle Danny, but he just smiled reassuringly.

Liberty looked at Colin.

"Can we talk?" asked the Librarian, and she nodded away from the table. "Just...over there. Quiet-like. Nothing bad. I don't think..."

Tessy looked at the boy with rising panic. "Wait? Why do they need to talk to you?"

Colin replied to her. "I'm not sure..." But then he stopped and looked at Liberty. "Unless...wait! Is this about Tessy?"

Now alarmed, the little girl asked. "What about me?" Her chest started to rise and fall rapidly. "Am...am I going somewhere?"

"No!" said Liberty and Uncle Danny as one.

The Librarian looked at the little girl. "No! It's okay! We're *not* going to send you away. *Ever!*"

"We worked hard to get you here," added Uncle Danny.

Liberty grinned at him. "Worth it." Then she turned back to the little girl. "Totally worth it."

"But...I just figured that if you had adopted Colin," said Tessy with despair. "That he's going to want me gone."

Colin whipped his head towards her, and she flinched a little.

"What're you talking about?" he demanded loudly.

Tessy shrunk even more upon herself.

"Colin?" murmured Liberty with a warning tone.

The boy's head snapped towards her. "What?"

Liberty's face softened, and she nodded at the little girl. "Your voice was kinda loud, sweetie."

"No, it wasn't," replied Colin defensively.

"Dude," continued Tagg, and he made a small gesture towards the little girl. "And I think she's worried enough already, don't you think?"

Colin threw up hands in annoyance, but then he saw Tessy flinch and lean a little away from him. His brow furrowed in confusion, and he froze. Slowly, the boy put down his hands and reigned in his voice to say to her. "I don't know why you're so worried. They just want to talk to me about adopting you as well."

Tessy stiffened and slowly looked from the boy to

Liberty and Tagg. And then to her Uncle.

"I think I'm best suited to being an uncle," said Uncle Danny. "If that's all right?"

"Well, um…," started Tessy. She stopped and looked at Liberty and Tagg again.

The little girl couldn't see that, under the table, they were holding hands. In fact, Liberty had a death grip on Tagg's hand, practically mashing it. But he barely noticed the pain because he was suddenly really worried.

Tessy turned to Colin. "But, what about you?"

The boy blinked and asked. "What about me?"

"I figured you'd want to send me away," said Tessy.

"Why would I want to send you away?" asked Colin in confusion, trying to keep his voice in check.

"Because…you don't like me," she said quietly.

"Where'd you get a stupid idea like that?" demanded Colin.

Tagg was first to react, clearing his throat loudly. Colin looked at him in exasperation. Squinting at his son, Dr. Tagg then nodded towards the girl.

"Dude," whispered the Scientist.

"It's okay," said Tessy and she looked down. "He doesn't have to like me."

Colin made an aggrieved noise, but he kept his voice level. He looked at the girl. "I would never, ever ask that you be sent away. Besides, I agree with Liberty, I mean Mom…" He looked at the Librarian. "Sorry."

"It's okay," said Liberty quickly. "We're still figuring this all out." She gave a bright, toothy smile and he gave one of his own.

"So…," began Tessy hesitantly. "You…". She looked up at Colin. "You wouldn't mind if they adopted me too?"

"Of course not," shrugged the boy.

"I thought you hated me," said Tessy.

Freezing, Colin said. "What? I don't hate you!"

Tessy looked down at her plate and said softly. "Well, you never want to talk to me."

The boy opened his mouth, but then closed it, unsure of what to say.

Jumping in, Tagg said. "After my Grandmother passed, we inherited her dog, Honey. And I guess that me and my best friend, Harry, weren't being as friendly as we could. We weren't mean or anything, but…my Mom said that we were all part of the same pack. So, Mom asked us to make an extra effort to let Honey know that she was part of *our* pack."

"I'm not a dog," said Tessy with more amusement than annoyance.

"You aren't," replied the Scientist swiftly. "You are an *adorable* little girl." And Tessy beamed at that. "But we've all ended up in the same boat in a *very* short amount of time. And ultimately, we're all in this together."

Tagg looked at each person, including Rak. He finished at Liberty, who was gaping at him. Suddenly, he became unsure of himself

"Um, if that's okay," said Tagg.

"*Yes!*" cried Liberty with a jovial tone. "That's…well,

that's what me and Uncle Danny have been trying to do." She looked at Colin. "But...maybe we haven't been doing as good a job as we could."

Without taking his eyes off the radar, Smalls piped up. "It's not an easy task Liberty. When my Mom got remarried, we had to move into this new house with her new husband's three daughters. And the first couple of months..." He looked up and grinned. "I'm still surprised that the neighborhood was standing afterwards. There was soooooo much fighting."

"But it got better, right?" asked Tagg.

"It did," said Smalls. "At least, it was getting better. Then I graduated high school and joined the Navy. But coming back for Christmas was better. Maybe, if we'd had a few more years." The Navy Engineer gave a small, sad smile.

Colin reached out and patted Smalls shoulder.

"So, what you had was a blended family, right?" asked Liberty quickly. And then she looked around at everyone without a word.

"So, basically what I'm saying," said Smalls. "This is at least going better than my experience." He looked at Colin and Tessy. "It's going to be okay."

And everything seemed better, so the Librarian decided not to push her luck.

"Okay," said Liberty. "Now, we should probably wash up the galley." And she looked expectantly at Colin and Tagg.

The boy's eyes darted over to the doctor.

"Think we can run?" asked Colin.

Tagg grinned. "Hah! We wouldn't get 10 paces."

"That's enough outta you two boys," said the Librarian with mock sternness.

\*\*\*

Colin was drying the last of the dishes when Uncle Danny stuck his head in the galley.

"Hey Liberty?" called out the Big Mexican.

The Librarian looked over swiftly "Everything okay?"

"We're fine, we're fine *Mija*," said Uncle Danny with a gentle smile. "No...um, I was wondering if I could borrow the boys."

Both of the aforementioned 'boys' looked with equal measure of suspicion and curiosity.

Liberty said. "Um, oh yeah, sure."

Tagg looked at her. "Is there much more to be done?" He looked at Colin. "It's not cool to leave someone stuck with *all* the rest of the work." Then he turned back to Liberty.

The Librarian grinned, appreciatively, showing all her teeth. "We're pretty much done. I'm good."

Colin followed Tagg out, but the boy did not escape Liberty without a quick hug. After much protesting, she let him free.

Walking through the ship, Uncle Danny moved beside Colin.

293

"You know *Cobayo*," said Danny to the boy. "I wasn't trying to ignore you, and I'm sorry."

"I know," said Colin quickly.

Tagg cleared his throat behind them.

The boy glared back at the Scientist

"Rule number ONE," mouthed Tagg in response to the boy's Withering Look.

Colin sighed—with preteen melodrama—but then he turned to Uncle Danny.

"It's just...we haven't had a chance to do anything. since Tessy and Rak showed up," said Colin to the floor. "I'm mean, I know you've been busy, an' they seem nice enough..."

"You're not wrong," nodded Uncle Danny. "It's been *loco* around here, *but*..." He opened the door to the movie room, which was empty of everyone, but Smalls.

The Navy Engineer, who was looking through the DVDs, called out. "Ooooh, they got 'Bad Boys'."

"The first one?" asked Uncle Danny wearily.

Almost insulted, Smalls replied. "Of course!"

"Then that's a possibility," nodded Danny.

"What?" asked Colin as he and the Big Mexican stopped just inside the room.

Tagg came to stand on the other side of the boy.

Colin looked up at Uncle Danny with delight. "Boy's night?"

"Only the best *Cobayo*," nodded Uncle Danny. "And speaking of Action, Mr. Smalls missed some this evening."

Everyone looked at the Big Mexican in confusion.

"Action?" asked Colin.

"Big Action," nodded Uncle Danny and he glanced at Smalls. "You know the hallway without the lights."

"Oh yeah," said the Navy Engineer quickly. "I looked all over the ship trying to find replacements..."

"It's okay," said the Big Mexican sincerely. "You're fine. It's just that before dinner, Colin saw a large shape down there, in the darkness."

"Oh no," moaned Colin. ""I'm really, really, sorry."

Uncle Danny looked at the boy. "Why are you 'sorry'? I'm proud of you."

Colin blinked. "What?"

The Big Mexican looked at the other guys. "So, Colin sees this big Shape in the dark an' what does he do? He jumped between the hallway and Tessy."

"I did?" asked the boy.

"Oh, I saw something," said Tagg. "But I didn't know he moved." He beamed down at Colin. "Good job."

"But...I didn't mean to be rude," said Colin, a little confused.

"Had you said something mean afterward, that would have been bad," said Uncle Danny. "But you got startled."

"I just...," started Colin.

"...Jumped! Like a tiger," said Uncle Danny, and he caught the boy's eye. "I'm proud of you."

"Um, I didn't realize...," started Colin.

"You just 'did'," said Uncle Danny. "Sometimes out there on the Coast, you don't have time to think. And it's at that point that you show who you truly are. In your case, brave."

"But I insulted Rakduson, didn't I," asked Colin.

"Your Aunt Rak was not hurt. I promise. I checked."

A great breath of relief came out of the boy.

"That's my dude," grinned Tagg, patting Colin on the back.

"Now," said Uncle Danny. "Now, let's see what we got."

***

Later that evening, Liberty stole up to the door and peeked inside. There was some cowboy movie with Clint Eastwood on. Colin, enraptured, sat on the edge of the wide couch while the others lounged back. Tagg's head lolled towards her, showing that he had fallen asleep, drooling adorably.

Moving away, like a ghost, she left with a warm smile on her face.

***

A strident French voice demanded. "Did you even wash your hair?"

"You asked me to," came back Uncle Danny with annoyance.

"*I did ask!* But that does not answer the question of what happened before this moment.!"

Uncle Danny huffed. "I did wash my hair."

Renoir clicked his tongue. "As Mama would say, '*Hai voluto la bicicletta? E adesso pedala!*'"

"What?" asked Danny.

"Nothing. It really is just this bad," said the HairArtiste, Renoir, as he inspected Uncle Danny's long mane of jet black hair. "But do not worry *mon ami!* I shall save you."

"You know what he needs...a bouffant?" grinned Liberty. "Or maybe a perm"

"*¡Aquas!*" said Uncle Danny warningly to her. "Just...gimme a haircut. 'Kay."

"A Haircut?" replied Renoir with loud distaste. "JUST a haircut? Renoir does not *traffic* in such peasantry."

"*Vete a freír espárragos,*" grumbled Uncle Danny.

With a mock 'Mom' tone, Liberty said to Danny. "Be nice," said "Or no lollipop after."

Uncle Danny just scowled at her, but she just smiled back sweetly.

"No more talk," declared Renoir. "Only Action!"

While the HairArtiste began to work, Liberty looked at her disheveled hair in a hand mirror.

"You do realize that we might not let you leave," she said, only half-joking.

"Alas, the Rear Admiral has me and my fiancé on the carrier for now," said Renoir. "So, he has her hostage at the moment...though mostly because she was feeling a little

297

under the weather, my poor sweet doctor."

"That fiendish admiral! Well, we can't take you without her," declared Liberty playfully. "So, we'll have to let you go for now."

"Believe me," said Renoir. "I would love to travel in such opulence."

"*¡Hijole!* Let's just get this over with," grumbled Uncle Danny.

"*Oui*, back to work," smiled Renoir.

\*\*\*

On Christmas morning, Rak was talking so quickly that not even the kids could keep up. Gently using her beak, she picked up her present. Towing it, she swiveled her head 180 degrees to lay it across her back.

Everyone's eyes went wide.

The Alien-bird quickly arranged it to her satisfaction and then turned back to the rest. She was still talking fast, but now the kids could keep up.

Tessy translated first. "She really, really likes her woolly blanket. She likes to sleep out on the deck, but sometimes it gets too cold. And…" She furrowed her brow.

"I think she's saying that they were not allowed to bring any possessions," added Colin.

"Oh! You're right," said Tessy. "That's definitely 'possessions'."

"It's not about being 'right'," shrugged Colin. "I didn't

298

get that first part. When Aunt Rak gets going really fast, we really do need both of us."

Tessy grinned at him with all her teeth, and then turned to watch Rak settle in.

The little girl said to her. "We call that a 'woolly blanket'."

"Wool-E blane-ket," said Rak and delight came to her eyes. "Love woolly blanket."

Uncle Danny just grinned, which warmed Liberty.

Tessy wrapped her arms around herself. "Actually, that sounds like a good idea." She turned to her parental figures. "Actually, would it be okay if I went back to my room for a blanket? Just real quick. It's kinda cold this morning."

"Of course," said Liberty immediately.

"It is unseasonably cold," added Smalls, and he glanced briefly at his portable radar, but it was clear.

Tessy started to stand when the alien-bird piped up.

"*Utu*," said Rak and she lifted up a wing.

"Really?" asked Tessy with delight.

Rak nodded.

The little girl gave a happy little squeak and scrambled under the wing.

There was a little bit of rearranging when Rak made a pained noise.

"Ooops, didn't mean to kneel on your feathers," said Tessy.

But soon enough, she was totally encased under Rak's

299

left wing.

"Oooooooh, this is much better than a blanket," moaned the little girl happily. "Oh! And look at the feathers underneath the wing. So many colors!" She gingerly petted them.

"Um," started Colin.

The bird looked at him but then understood. She lifted up her other wing and the boy smiled with delight. But he did stop by Tessy's pile of presents and grabbed her Nintendo Switch.

"Don't forget this," he told her. After handing it to her, he snuggled in with his own Switch. The kids took a moment to get comfy. Both had their games in hand.

"Um. Let's wait 'til all the presents are unwrapped," said Liberty.

"Okay," sighed Colin. He did put his down, but it was right where he could easily grab it. "Okay, this is really warm," he admitted. After a pause, he looked up at Rak. "Um...*Hootah*."

"You are welcome," replied Rak.

Tessy looked at Colin. "You do know more than you were letting on!"

Colin shrugged. "Well, not as much as you."

"I could teach you more," said Tessy earnestly.

"Maybe...," said Colin, but there was a spark of interest in that idea.

Library tried to smile surreptitiously to Danny and Tagg.

Colin whipped her head around, glaring at the adults.

"What?"

"Hmmm?" asked Liberty noncommittally. She knew she looked guilty because she had never been good at lying.

"You were all looking at each other," declared Colin suspiciously.

"I think Liberty was just having a great Christmas morning," said Uncle Danny. "I know I am *Cobayo*."

The boy was going to say more, but Tessy started talking to him and they disappeared into their own little world.

Once everyone was snuggled in, Uncle Danny reached behind him.

"Well, then we've got to give Liberty a gift, which I've been holding onto since we left the Coast with Tessy and Rak," he said.

Liberty looked at him in surprise. "What're you up to?"

Uncle Danny handed her a wrapped present.

"You snuck by me and got a gift?" she said with amused annoyance.

The Librarian took the package, which was soft. At first, she thought that it might be clothes. Unable to restrain herself, she tore open the wrapping paper, and her eyes grew so wide.

"Oh. My!"

Liberty jumped up. She held the flag open for everyone to see and squealed. "We got a Jolly Roger flag!!!! Oh My God! Oh My God! Oh My God!"

Turning it this way and that, Liberty showed everyone.

"On no," moaned Smalls with mock horror. "The U.S.

Navy is supposed to fight pirates, not fly under their flag."

"Oh! But it's really more of a...," started Liberty.

However, Smalls raised his hands in supplication, and she stopped.

"I was kidding, mostly," said Smalls. "Just...getting adjusted to my new situation."

Uncle Danny nodded. "I know what you mean."

"Then again, I guess being a pirate is kinda cool," admitted Smalls. "As long as we're not taking ships."

"Only if they've been bad," said Liberty.

"'Been bad'?" teased Uncle Danny. "Those naughty ships."

Liberty let out a huff. "You know what I mean."

"I know what you mean," assured Smalls, and Liberty smiled at him.

Then she turned and squinted hard at Uncle Danny. "You!"

The Big Mexican suddenly looked nervous. "¿Que?"

"Ooooh, Uncle Danny's in trooooouble," grinned Colin.

"He's been naughty," added Tessy with mock seriousness. The two kids looked at each other and started giggling.

Uncle Danny looked at them with mock disapproval, but Liberty was suddenly there with a wrapped present.

Danny's eyes opened wide. "For me?"

"Open it!" said Liberty with a little bounce. "Hurry!"

"Wait!" said Uncle Danny. He felt through the package.

It was a book. "Were you…?"

"I was probably grabbing it while you were getting the sail," smirked Liberty. "And I *had* to get it!"

Uncle Danny made quick work of the wrapping, and then held up his present with a big smile.

"More pirates," moaned Smalls with a mock roll of his eyes.

"The Big Book of Pirate History'," read Uncle Danny.

"We never named the boat," said Liberty excitedly. She sat back down, and leaned back against Tagg, as if he were a welcoming tree.

"If we're going to be pirates," said the Navy Engineer with mock seriousness. "We should do this right." They all looked at him. "We should name it after a great pira…well, not that pirates were great. But an important pirate."

"Like Blackbeard!" said Uncle Danny excitedly.

"Him, or Henry Morgan," nodded Smalls.

"We'll have to see what their ships were called, *but* only after presents," said Liberty.

"Aww, I wanna play with my present," whined Uncle Danny with mock despair, and the kids laughed at that.

\*\*\*

The wrapping paper was now picked up, but bodies were still strewn across the floor.

No longer under Aunt Rak, Tessy and Colin were playing their Switch's in one corner.

303

And taking up a huge chunk of carpet, Uncle Danny lay on his stomach, pouring over his new pirate book.

"This...this can't be right," muttered Danny with deep concern.

Snuggled against Tagg on a couch, Liberty looked up from the book that she was re-reading. "What's wrong?"

"I was looking at ships that pirates sailed on...," started Uncle Danny.

Everyone, including Smalls, looked up with interest.

"Blackbeard sailed on a boat called...the *Queen Anne's Revenge*," explained Danny with a hollow voice.

"You're kidding," said Liberty.

"Oh, that's....," started Smalls. "I don't think that that's what you're looking for." But then he added. "Unless I'm wrong. I could be wrong."

"No," said Danny quickly. "I was looking for something a little more..."

"Piratey?" suggested Liberty.

"Yeah," said Uncle Danny, but then he admitted. "And maybe a little more *macho*."

"Well, there were more than a few pirates," said Smalls. "Another one *must* have a suitable name."

"Let me see," said Uncle Danny. He scanned the pages quickly. "Black Bart had the *Royal Fortune*...and Sir Francis Drake had the *Golden Hind*."

Colin suddenly sniggered. "The *Golden Hind*?" He caught Tagg's eye.

"The *Golden Hind* End?" finished the Scientist with a

growing smile.

Liberty fixed them both with a disapproving Look. "Hey."

"But...they're not wrong *Mija*," said Uncle Danny without looking up. "One pirate had the *Bachelor's Delight*."

"Okay! That's a definite 'No' to that one," declared Liberty flatly, which made Danny chuckle.

As he read out the names, the joy in the room plummeted. Finally, Uncle Danny closed the book.

"Sorry," said Liberty.

Uncle Danny blinked. "What? Why're you sorry?"

"I just thought it would be fun to have a cool pirate name," said Liberty.

"¡Neta, no manches! It's NOT your fault that some of these ships had...," began Uncle Danny, but he was not sure how to finish.

"Silly names" said the Navy Engineer with distaste. "I mean, '*the Squirrel*' or '*the Rose Pink*'?"

"Or even something like '*the Revenge*'," added Tagg thoughtfully. "Which... really doesn't sound like you two."

Uncle Danny looked at the Librarian.

"They're right *Mija*," he said. "It was a wonderful thought. And I'm still going to read the whole book."

"*And...I* might ask to borrow it after he's done," said Smalls meekly.

Uncle Danny grinned at the engineer. "Of course!"

"Maybe...," suggested Tagg slowly. "You should name the ship after another type. Like the carrier, the '*Roosevelt*'."

Smalls quickly rattled off the names of several Navy ships, but then he looked down. "No, that doesn't seem right. And the only other ship I can think of is 'The Flying Dutchman', or the 'Mary Celeste'. And neither of those are a good choice."

"What about fake ships?" suggested Tessy.

"There's Jack Sparrow's ship, the 'Black Pearl'," suggested Tagg. Liberty and Danny straightened for a moment, but then the Librarian shook her head.

"I'm pretty sure that the 'Pearl' was a slave ship, at least originally," said Liberty.

Uncle Danny scrunched up his face.

"Yeah, that's not...," he started, and it turned into a big sigh. However, he quickly gave a great, big smile. "That's okay, we'll think of a name. We don't have to do it today."

"True," said Liberty. "Between all of us, we're sure to find something that fits."

Colin sat bolt upright glancing at Tagg. "Between all..." He made an excited noise, and everyone looked over at him. "You had that dog, after your grandma passed."

"...Honey...," supplied Tagg, unsure.

"That's it!" cried the boy.

*\*\**

Under the Jolly Roger flag, the yacht sailed towards the remains of the Santa Monica pier.

"Does everyone have their water bottles?" asked Tessy.

Like a drill sergeant on inspection, the little girl walked around Liberty, Uncle Danny and Rak. Indulgently, Danny just pulled his coat aside to show his canteen.

"You already asked that," called out Colin, who was sitting nearby.

Tessy whipped around. "It's important to stay hydrated!"

"We got our water bottles," assured Liberty gently.

Uncle Danny smiled. "Thank you for making sandwiches too."

Rak made a happy noise. "Tu-nah fish!"

Eyes narrowing, Tessy continued, searching for issues. "And Uncle Danny's shoulder and Rak's leg are fully healed. And you got your ammo."

Uncle Danny stepped forward. "We're going to be as careful as we can."

"And we're working with Captain Singh today," added Liberty. "So, that will help."

"It's just...," said Tessy sadly.

"If we can...," started Liberty.

Tessy cut in. "I know, I know, I know. If you can get the equipment for Dad, he'll be able to work here on the boat and not have to go to that medical ship all day. I just get..."

Uncle Danny enveloped her in a gigantic hug. She squeezed him back really hard. Liberty came in and then Rak. They all gave the little girl a big hug.

After a moment, Tessy pulled away and they all parted. Despite watery eyes, she defiantly stuck out her chest and regarded them.

"I hope you all have a good and safe day," said the little girl.

When Tessy looked away to check over Uncle Danny once more, Liberty caught Colin's eye. The Librarian nodded towards the little girl with a silent plea.

Reared back a little, Colin looked skeptical.

"Please," asked Liberty without sound.

The boy rolled his eyes and walked towards Tessy.

As he passed her, Liberty whispered. "I love you. You're the best."

Stopping, Colin looked down, embarrassed, but then he whispered urgently. "Be careful. All of you."

Swift as a snake, Liberty snagged the boy and pulled him into a hug.

"Hey!" grumbled Colin. "What's with the hugging?" But he didn't step away.

After Liberty reluctantly let him go, Colin walked over to Tessy.

The boy gave a little tug on her shirt sleeve. "Come on."

Tessy turned to him. "I'm...I'm just making sure that Uncle Danny has his water bottle."

"He does," said Colin softly. "You've got them better prepared than they've ever been. Believe me!"

"That's true," admitted Uncle Danny.

"Totally," said Liberty. "We never remembered water."

Tessy looked at them, and then she turned back to Colin.

He stood a little ways away and gestured towards himself. The little girl looked back and forth a few more times, but then she nodded slowly in acquiescence.

Stepping over to the boy, Tessy stopped beside Colin.

"They're going to be as careful as they can," whispered the little girl to herself, over and over.

Her hand reached out and took Colin's. For a moment, the boy looked like he was going to bolt. But then, his hand closed around hers with a reassuring grip. Tessy's little chest relaxed.

"We'll be back as soon as we can, *Cobayo*," said the Big Mexican.

"You know I looked that word up in the Spanish dictionary," replied Colin with a hard tone.

"And...?" asked Uncle Danny. If the boy asked not to use it anymore, he would. He would miss calling him that, but he would stop for him.

Colin gave a smile and a little shrug.

"Just...," he started. But then, he faltered.

"We will," said Liberty. "We promise." She blew him a kiss. "I gotta come home to my kids."

Colin looked both elated and embarrassed at once. Instead of responding, he led Tessy away.

"Come on," he said to her. "Let's get breakfast."

Tessy blinked. "Oh. I am actually really hungry."

A garbled voice came in. "Is.........berty?" Liberty and Uncle Danny automatically touched their earpieces.

"Captain Singh?" asked Liberty.

"Ca...you..ear me?" asked Singh.

"You're coming in better," said Liberty, and she looked over to see the Captain on the beach. He waved.

"It's about time you showed up," grumbled Singh good-naturedly.

"Had to make sure that the kids were alright," said Uncle Danny.

"And I'll assume they are," chuckled Singh. "By the way...we saw the pirate flag. *Tres chic.* So, did you ever name that damn thing?"

"Yes sir," grinned Liberty and she gave a little salute. "The pirate ship S.S. *Wolf Pack*, reporting for duty!"


*Fin*


*Liberty and Uncle Danny return next year for "Liberty " 3.*
*Be there or be octagonal.*

# About the Author

## Walter G. Esselman

*Apparently, I'm supposed to write this bio to humanize me.*

*It is bold of them to assume that I am a carbon-based lifeform from Earth, but regardless...*

I grew up in Michigan, practically on the campus of MSU. Not that I follow sports, humorously enough. I've been writing forever but never really sent anything out. So, I pushed myself to get short stories out there and became a regular contributor at World of Myth and Dark Dossier. I recently started turning my eye towards novels, which is the first step in that process.

My wife Amy and I still live in Michigan because it's the

most beautiful state.  Not that I like to go outdoors, humorously enough.  I mean, seriously, there are bears out there, Sharks!  I even saw a Bearshark once.  A chilling sight.

After tooling around the Commonwealth with Cait for many years in Fallout 4, I'm back in the land of Skyrim once again.

*Khajit will shoot arrows if you have the coin.  Or, it's a dungeon with a lot of loot.*

I hope you have a wonderful day!

## Author's Notes & the History of Liberty's Run:

This record, regarding the history of "Liberty's Run", is *partly for me.*

*When my first book, "SuperhorrorMax", sold, the initial writing had been yeeeeeeaaaaars before. I suddenly had to wrack my brain to remember what went into the book's creation. So, I decided to write up this history to help me remember, 10, 20 years down the road.*

*~W*

*"I don't know, I'm making this up as I go."*

~Dr. Henry Jones, Jr.

Actually, the creation of *Liberty's Run* (Books 1 and 2) was a complete, utter, and total fluke.

Long story short, I had stopped writing screenplays and instead started concentrating on putting those ideas into short stories. Mainly because I had fallen out of touch with the only person that I knew in Hollywood: Eric Payne. A pity because he was a nice fellow.

First, it's important to note that an idea cannot be copywritten. But, if you put that idea into a story, it's protected by copyright. Then if you get it published, I figure it's double-copyrighted. *(Not that that is a thing.)*

So, I wrote down this little germ of an idea about aliens creating a zombie virus.

To be even more accurate, I had started writing it, but I had not finished, for reasons lost to me. *(This is why it's important to write these things down while you can still remember them.)*

Regardless, I was telling my Cousin-In-Law, Dave Russell, about this story, and he encouraged me to finish it. In fact, I'm pretty positive I finished it the *very* same night we talked in Portland, OR. *We were there for my Cousin Andrew's wedding.* Here's my note from that short story:

*"Thanks to Dave Russell for giving me the impetus to get this story done."*

Admittedly, the short story did just end with Liberty saving the boy from the aliens and running off. That was it. I was deep in the weeds on other projects, possibly my not-yet published Punk Rock novel/fable, *Sorry I Banged Your*

*Mom.*

Anyhoo, I sent *Liberty* into the magazine, "The The World of Myth" *TWoM*, hoping that they'd like it well enough to publish it.

What I didn't expect was for my now-buddy, David Montoya, to ask for the rest.

*

*Tue, Dec 4, 2018, 8:48 PM - SubMythion: Liberty's Run*

*to JayZoMon/Dark*

*Hi Dave!*

*…*

*A librarian named Liberty rescues a little girl from Zombies. Liberty and the others are safe for the moment. But then she sees an Unidentified Object over L.A. Deciding to investigate, Liberty goes to investigate and finds an alien species who have come to save the planet. However, she soon realizes that the aliens are saving the planet from humankind by means of a zombie virus.*

*Thanks for all your support!*

*Walter*

*

*Tue, Dec 4, 2018, 10:17 PM*

*JayZoMon/Dark Myth Company*

*Walt,*

*Oh my Gosh! I was on the edge of my seat! I hope that this is something that turns into a serial! I was completely invested and really wanna know if Liberty and Colin make it out and back to the other building! And, what happens to the Aliens who started*

315

*the plague!!!*

*Dave*

*

I stilled.

But.....*There Was No More!*

I admit that, for a hot second, I toyed with just saying—truthfully!—that there was no more.

But...what a challenge!   What an opportunity to test myself.

*

*Tue, Dec 4, 2018, 10:18 PM*

*Walter Esselman*

*I will have to look towards more then!*

*Thank you!*

*~W*

*

*Tue, Dec 4, 2018, 10:48 PM*

*JayZoMon/Dark Myth Company*

*Yes, please! The ghost of George A. Romero is going, "Dooooo iiiit!" LOL!*

*

*Wed, Dec 5, 2018, 2:16 PM*

*Walter Esselman*

*What???  You're lucky.*

*When George talks to me, he's always whining about the lack of great Rom-Coms these days.*

316

*It's always Hugh Grant this, and Sandra Bullock that.*

*Sigh.*

*I'm working out a framework for a serial that is kick butt, but doesn't tread on territory, like 'Z Nation'. Maybe that Colin can actually help reverse the disease all together and cure the zombies! Hmmmmm!*

*Anyways, have a great day!*

*~W*

*

I fleshed out "Liberty" to four chapters and found a solid ending.

Actually, what is now chapter 2 was originally titled: "Liberty's Call ~ Part 2 of the Liberty Schonhauer series". Each chapter was going to be "Liberty's *Something*". But TWoM titled chapter 3 as "Liberty's Run", and I didn't fuss.

Uncle Danny, who was not supposed to survive past the very first story, got a second lease on life *Cue heavenly music*. But, when I voiced my intention to end the story at the fourth episode, commentors on The World of Myth, Rebecca Lynch, and an Anonymous person, said not to stop. Later, TWoM editor, Stephanie Bardy, would echo that very same sentiment.

*

*Tue, Jul 16, 2019, 12:49 PM*

*Stephanie Bardy*

*Honestly, I will be sad when this series ends....LOL!! ...*

*Stephanie*

*

317

The crowd had spoken, and they wanted more "Liberty".

So, I decided to keep going, though as a bi-monthly serial. The bi-monthly was so that I didn't have to rush the final product. *However,* the story still had to be interesting and thrilling to me. In addition, I wanted there to *always* be a solid and organic reason for why someone would leave a safe environment and go into a deadly one, which the Coast definitely is.

Going forward, the The World of Myth steadily published Volumes 1 and 2, plus the Interludes.

After I finished the Interludes, (late 2019 or early 2020?), I decided that writing one episode/chapter at a time was pulling me away from other work.

More important work? Maybe so. *(Oh No He Didn't!).*

Thus, I decided to write a bigger story, but it needed a solid catalyst.

Again, why would they leave safety, and an opulent yacht at that. Of course, Tessy was still on the Coast, but she was still safe in the Old Armory. Though while I was editing, I did beef up the discussions of 'Could we get Tessy out safely?', but I thought it reasonable to say 'No'. Cars break down, and walking is dangerous.

Plus, I wanted to bring back the hairdresser Renoir, whom I loved as a character. So, having his girlfriend, Dr. Milton, get pregnant was a good catalyst. They wanted a safer place to raise a child. Reasonable. And the story quickly evolved to the idea of the tank/bus.

Putting aside every other project, I dove into writing all of Volume 3 at once. Then Covid-19 hit. I was fortunate to be able to work from home during the Lockdown in Michigan.

No more drive to-and-from Royal Oak anymore.

In the past, I had always used part of my lunch hour at work to write, but now I had all this time in the morning as well!! I started getting up earlier and earlier. Currently, since we're still working from home, I'm up at 5:30am. *I've gone back to the office since writing this, but still getting up Too Bloody Early. Grin! ~W*

Ferociously, I dug into Vol. 3, and finished the 1st draft by August 2020. The Plan was to edit one episode bi-monthly until it was all edited. That would give me *plenty of time!*

Humorously, in October 2020, on a Monday afternoon, I learned that I had won the Open Contract Challenge. My other book, *SuperhorrorMax*, would be published!!!!!

The moment Dave Montoya texted me, I immediately messaged my supervisor /awesome friend, Alana.

\*

*14:27 Walter Esselman: Dave just sent me a text. Maybe about the Book Contest?* Dave *included a smiley face. If it's all right, I'm going to take a fifteen* minute break *to call him back.*

*14:27 Alana DeMorris: go for it!*

*14:27 Alana DeMorris: have fun!*

\*\*\*

*14:52 Walter Esselman: I won. I will have "SuperhorrorMax" printed on real paper.*

\*

319

Here is a contemporaneous note:

*"Found out on October 5th, just now at 2:31pm EST, in the Year of Our Lord 2020, that I have won the Grand Prize for the Open Contract Challenge. Print edition and a plane ticket* to a convention.

There were two people in the final round, including me, and the other person did not submit their manuscript. Didn't sound like they had even told Dave M. why. Maybe they hadn't finished their novel, I speculated. Dave countered that they could just slap on an ending. But, I suggested, not if they were 100 pages away. However, this is just speculation. I don't know why the other person did not send theirs in. The long and short of it was, that I won by default. Honestly, that's okay. And the third place person was moved to 2nd place, so her novel will get an eBook. Awesome."

While Dave M. and I were talking about winning the contest, he said that they also wanted to publish whatever I had of *Liberty's Run!*

This is actually kind of funny.

I hadn't told Dave M. or Stephanie Bardy much about working on Volume 3. Maybe I had mentioned it to Steph, but not how much of it there was.

And there was a lot.

While we talked, I jumped on my computer to figure out that *Liberty's Run* now clocked in at roughly 120,000 words. I think Dave was a little stunned at first.

\*

Fast forward momentarily to March of 2021.

Steph did an interview for *SuperhorrorMax* on her podcast, "Lupa's Bits", and Dave M. joined in. It was Steph's first interview and she killed it.

During it, I tried to be humble. I said that I had won a chance to publish *SuperhorrorMax*, but that I was lucky enough to get a book deal for *Liberty's Run* as well.

Dave leaned towards his camera, and in this serious tone, he said, 'You won the contest, But *You* earned the book deal for *Liberty*'.

*I'm not crying, you're crying!*

\*

Back to Fall of 2020.

Contracts were signed and *Liberty* would be published in September 2021.

After I had finished everything for *SuperhorrorMax*, I dove into editing *Liberty* around November 2020.

It is super crucial to note that the book was…...weeeeeell, a bit of a mess.

A Hot Mess, but a mess, nonetheless.

For one thing, it was not supposed to be a book.

So now, I had to create a continuity to hide that fact. The large, monstrous thing had to all make sense. Not a small task. But, when faced with such a big, complex task, I always start by breaking it down into smaller, bite-sized chunks.

Thus, I went back to Chapter 1. At least now, I knew where the story was going.

It is also critical to mention that the The World of Myth magazine has a 3,000 word maximum. Thus, every Liberty chapter was a little below that. But now, I was going to be able to go back through and fatten it up. I probably did not need to add that much more, but it gave me room to flesh out characters and dialogue. Grin!

\*

In the very first Liberty story, Uncle Danny is dropping his niece off at the Old Armory because he'd been bitten.

Uncle Danny is unapologetically, and reverentially, based upon the great actor Danny Trejo, whom I had first seen in Robert Rodriguez's *Desperado*. Why use actor Danny Trejo for this? Because I'm such a big fan, and it was a one-and-done story, just to get the idea down. So, this was really like a cameo.

As I had said earlier, when I had taken on the challenge to create chapters 2, 3, and 4, I had kept Uncle Danny around. *BestBestBest Decision Ever!* But what was really interesting - without any interference from me - Liberty and Uncle Danny quickly formed this amazing friendship. Like, Best Friends Forever. *I would be surprised if someone in the future didn't Ship them together, but in my mind, they're just friends. Sorry, not sorry.*

When chapter 3 was originally published, there was this note at the end: *To be concluded in the next issue of The World of Myth! Be there or be octahedron!*.

The series was supposed to end after chapter 4.

In fact, Uncle Danny was going to succumb to zombism. No Fooling! Here, I'll prove it. This is the original ending of Chapter 4. I have only added in *"and Tagg"* to clarify.

# *Liberty's* ᶤRUП 2: TANKS FOR THE MEMORIES

*Uncle Danny succumbed to the zombie virus two days later. The moment they were on board the medical ship, he had voluntarily put himself into quarantine. But he talked with Colin for as long as he could.*

***

*Liberty and Tagg would have twin girls who believed— even from a young age— that it was their mission in life was to run Colin's life. A development he oddly enjoyed. Besides, since he had been adopted by Liberty and Tagg, these were his little sisters.*

*

*But,* people wanted more "Liberty", and so Uncle Danny got a reprieve!! *Cue heavenly music Remix!*

And I believe that I was going to insinuate that Danny did eventually get cured of the virus.

Let me state for the record though -  going forward - there will be no more Liberty without Uncle Danny, and vice versa.

*

When editing the book, One aspect that was CRUCIAL for me was the fact that Uncle Danny's character was Mexican. He was not Mexican-American, but had spent most of his life in Mexico, so—of course—his primary language was Mexican-Spanish.

This led to one SLIIIIIIIIIGHT problem.

I didn't speak a lick of Mexican-Spanish.

Okay, it turned out that I knew more words than I thought. But it was absolutely crucial that Danny was Not going up to other characters saying, "Heeeeeey! **Esse!**

323

Wha's happenin'!" with a bad Mexican accent. A caricature, in other words.

*No.* I needed to learn some Mexican-Spanish. At least I knew enough that Mexican-Spanish was different from other forms.

Thus, I started researching, and I even went through the first Unit in 'Rosetta Stone - Spanish (Latin America)'. So now I can say, *Una mujer no maneja un carro. No, un perro roja maneja un carro. The woman does not drive the car. No, the red dog drives the car. Grin!*

\*

In Chapter 4, I introduced Uncle Danny's cleaver. Please know that I will argue—vociferously!—that a dull machete is the best weapon during a zombie apocalypse. But since The Real Danny IS Machete, so I went in a different direction.

As some may know, Mr. Trejo spent some time in prison when he was younger, and then later in life became a Great Actor.

On playing bad guys, he told Las Cruces Sun News that:

*"Bad guys die,"* Mr. Trejo said. *"If they ever try to offer me a part where I'm the...killer, and then ride off into the sunset...No! I can't do that, man. It's completely the wrong message."*.

For a fleeting moment, I considered giving Uncle Danny a villainous past, but there was another very important consideration. Over the past decade, Mexicans, and people of Latin and South America, are being Unjustly Demonized by some losers in the United States. Not wanting to add to that deplorable chorus, I needed to go in a different direction.

Thus, the only thing that Uncle Danny ever did wrong — outside of exceeding the speed limit — was to overstay his Visa. *But* he only did that, to keep his brother's garage open. *I think I picked an auto garage because it would show why Danny was so good with getting cars to run. (See this is why I'm doing this history now.).* And truthfully, if he hadn't been with his niece when everything went bad, she wouldn't have made it.

*

Uncle Danny and his brother grew up with very little money. His parents died in a car accident when the boys were not-quite teenagers. The parents were — Ahem! — fooling around while driving. Just a bit of adult mischief that sadly had terrible repercussions.

In fact, his parents had a decent amount of money, *but* it was all invested in a big venture that would've REALLY paid off Big. However, without the two of them at the helm, the venture quickly fell apart.

Which is the reason why, despite the fact that Uncle Danny is so darn smart, he was unable to afford to go to college.

*

For some characters, if I don't use an archetype like Senior Trejo, I may not have a clear image of what they look like. Sometimes it's just bits that describe them. It took me forever to settle on the coloring for my dragon character, Pavataro *black and electric blue* in the Dragonson series. Like seriously, probably over a decade.

However, when Liberty popped into my head, I knew exactly what she looked like, top to bottom; including the

325

beret and full-sleeve tattoos. By the end of Volume 1, she had completely gelled as a librarian-turned-sniper. Not sure why she's a librarian (The ThisIsWhyIWriteThisHistory remix). Later, while writing her, I reasoned that a sniper could be useful to protect people who were trying to get to the Old Armory. But really, I retconned that. I wanted her to be a sniper, so I had to work backwards to make it work.

The idea of her having a mentor like Mr. Jamie made sense, since prior to the initial outbreak, I knew that Liberty had never fired a gun. Mr. Jamie saved her outside her library, but as things were falling apart quickly, he couldn't just leave her. And the library had too many ground-floor windows to be safe for long.

The more Liberty proved herself, the more Mr. Jamie taught her.

Mr. Jamie was inspired by Jamie Hyneman of MythBusters, who always wore a beret.

In the backstory to the first book, Liberty had bugged Mr. Jamie for a long time to try on the beret. She was like a bouncy little kid. Finally, he relented. But then she started imitating his big, walrus mustache and gruff, even voice. So, she didn't get to wear the beret again.

Why is Mr. Jamie not still around? Well, it wasn't because he got bit.

Mr. Jamie had a heart condition that was getting worse by the day; because of all the stress that he was putting on his body. He knew that one day, he was just going to keel over dead, and maybe in the middle of something important.

He, Liberty, and a bunch of others were trapped in a building, which was surrounded by zoms. *You know, a normal Tuesday.* Mr. Jamie knew that an improvised explosive device (IED) could open a path, but with IEDs, people are just as likely to blow themselves up at the same time.

While Liberty was getting some well-earned sleep, Mr. Jamie - *Quietly!* - set down his beret and his Steyr SSG 69 sniper rifle beside Liberty. Then he went out front. He had found a way to climb over the zoms blocking the door. Heart racing, Mr. Jamie climbed up, and then scooted out onto some metal scaffolding to drop the IED on the zoms below.

In position, Mr. Jamie gave a loud shout to everyone inside. "Get ready dammit!".

Waking swiftly, Liberty immediately saw the beret and rifle and her heart dropped. Grabbing the hat and weapon, she scrambled out with the rest. She was pretty sure that Mr. Jamie smiled when he saw her. He started moving forward again.

Just as Mr. Jamie was over zombies, the scaffolding gave. Upon impact, the explosive went off bending the front door inward. Liberty wanted to break down and cry, but she realized what had just happened. What Mr. Jamie had done.

Rallying the rest, she ran to the front door and tried to open it. But when the explosion had hit, it had jammed the metal doors. Running to the side, she found a window, but it was boarded shut.

One of her hands was full of beret, and the other full of sniper rifle. Not having time to think, she slapped the beret on her head and slung the rifle across her back. She and others yanked off the boards and crawled out the window before more zoms could refill the space.

They were free.

However, by the time Liberty got to the Old Armory, where we meet her in chapter 1, it was just her.

One night at the Armory, she saw Simon giving Sergeant Wu a tattoo and she straightened in her chair. Not long after, she and Simon began her full sleeve tattoos.

Liberty did have to sneak out to get more tattoo ink, which Wu was livid about. But she needed to do this. Interwoven into the tattoos are the names of those who had fallen beside her, especially Mr. Jamie. So, she'd never forget.

*

Regarding the cover of "Liberty's Run" Book 1. It was at the end of 2020 when Dave M. sent me the photo that now graces the cover. I was pretty excited. The model could definitely be Liberty.

However,…the model didn't have Liberty's signature beret, rifle, and tattoos. So, I wrote Dave back about that. I assumed that we were getting a model session. But, it was just the picture, as is. Dave and I talked about it back and forth, well…texted.

Ultimately, Dave asked the Great Jenna Sparks to put Japanese-style tattoos on Liberty's arms. And I had to tell Dave that yes (Sorry, not sorry), the tattoos covered both arms. Please recall, since Day 1, Liberty has appeared on the page looking just like that.

Now the cover looks pretty darn good. Hats off to Dave

for finding that pic on the website, Photodeposit. I greatly appreciate it. And to Ms. Jenna for putting on those tattoos. Also, thank you to the model, photographer, and the people who created the picture. I don't know who they are, but thank you, nonetheless.

*

In case anyone wonders why Liberty carries a Glock 22, there is actually a specific, though somber, reason. The sad fact is that in the early days of a zombie outbreak, it is first responders who will be in the greatest danger. They are the people most likely to get bitten. So, my research found that a large percentage of police officers carry a Glock.

Thus, in the early days of the zombie apocalypse, Liberty took a Glock off a fallen police officer to defend herself. And as time wore on, she kept it because it was easy to find ammo for it. Now she's just used to it.

*

I had to research more heavily on this book than I normally like to. Actually, I'm not a big research guy. But it was, and is, hugely important to give these stories an air of authenticity. In an *X-Files* episode, Deep Throat says that "A lie is best told between two truths". And that applies to Writing. Having just enough facts grounds the audience and makes the story more real.

*

I had completed the main story for Volume 3 and got the survivors, including Tessy, off the Coast. But much to my surprise, the characters had a lot more to say. I swear, *Liberty* has more epilogues than Peter Jackson's *Return of the King*. The novel just had a ton of loose ends, which needed

329

to be tied together, even if it was just for my sake.

One loose end was that the yacht was now full of people, and one of them was not human.  How was that going to work out?  Was it going to work out?  *Bites nails furiously!* Following the characters, there was a slim possibility that not everything was going to work out, all hunky-dory. *Thank God it did!*

The same thing happened when Liberty and Uncle Danny were showing the Rear Admiral the yacht at the end of Volume 2.  I wasn't exactly sure how the Rear Admiral would react until I wrote it.

\*

One of the most important scenes in Liberty's Run books 1, 2, and 3 *which should be released 2023*, is in Book 2 during the Epilogues.  It is the scene at the dinner table with the whole dang family.  It took a few tries before I got it right. There were soooooooo many balls in the air, starting with both kids being worried.  And in some ways, they were both worried about the same thing: Not being part of a family.

That's why it's so important when Liberty-- without any forethought-- tells Colin that he is her son.  And she freezes for a second, wondering if she really messed up.  But then she realizes swiftly that she is speaking Her Truth.  Taking Tessy under her fold as well made perfect sense, especially since Liberty is terribly fond of Tessy.

\*

*Liberty's Run* was a tale that came out of taking a chance; Of challenging myself.  To create something because I needed to, and not because of some 'divine inspiration'.

Now I'm more confident as a writer. And I know that if an opportunity comes along to write something different, I can jump at it, with a good margin of Success.

When creating *Liberty*, I set a pretty high bar for myself. After Volume 1, I was going to create more stories, but they also had to be interesting to me as well. And to make matters worse, I insisted that they be logical as well. *Oy Vey!* Because who's gonna go back to the Coast unless they got a Really Good Freaking Reason. Kind of like James Cameron's Aliens, Ridley only went back to LV-426 because there was a colony of families in trouble.

I guided *Liberty's Run*, but—Shockingly—it came out Cotton Candy and Pollyanna all on its very own. And I'm okay with that.

Grin!